Everything you always wanted to know about

CRIME

THE MOST PROLIFIC U.S. SERIAL KILLER
was Donald Harvey, a hospital orderly in
Kentucky and Ohio who murdered more
than 67 patients in his care.

THE FIRST TRAIN ROBBERY
took place on October 6, 1866, perpetrated
by the notorious Reno brothers
near Seymour, Indiana.

THE LONGEST PRISON TERM
was given to crooked Bangkok businessman
Chamoy Thipyaso, who was sentenced to
141,078 years for swindling the public.

THE POSTHUMOUS TRIAL
of Thomas Becket was held three centuries
after his death—when his skeleton was
hauled before King Henry VIII's notorious
Star Chamber and convicted of treason.

THE LAW IN OKLAHOMA
states that it is illegal to intoxicate a fish.

THE MAN WHO SHORTED OUT THE ELECTRIC CHAIR

MITCHELL SYMONS

AVON BOOKS  NEW YORK

AVON BOOKS
A division of
The Hearst Corporation
1350 Avenue of the Americas
New York, New York 10019

Copyright © 1994 by Mitchell Symons
Published by arrangement with Headline Book Publishing, Ltd.
ISBN: 0-380-77444-5

First Avon Books Printing: August 1996

AVON TRADEMARK REG. U.S. PAT. OFF. AND IN OTHER COUNTRIES, MARCA
REGISTRADA, HECHO EN U.S.A.

Printed in the U.S.A.

RA   10 9 8 7 6 5 4 3 2 1

To Penny, as ever, and to Jack and Charlie
in the fervent hope that they'll never have
criminal records.

● CONTENTS

● INTRODUCTION

The months spent working on this book have, not unreasonably, made me consider my own attitude (which I have tried not to let influence what I've written or my choice of data) to crime. In so doing, I am reminded of an anecdote about US President Calvin Coolidge. He was renowned to be a man of few words. One Sunday he went to church on his own. When he returned home and his wife asked him what the vicar's sermon had been about, he replied "Sin." "And what did the vicar say about sin?" "He's against it," said the ever taciturn Coolidge.

I feel much the same way about crime. I'm against it. Oh, I've plenty of views about the causes of crime and many ideas how the crime figures might be reduced but this is not the appropriate forum for them. The bottom line is that I've always been a liberal on all matters to do with crime and punishment but, as I get older (I'm thirty-seven), I'm becoming increasingly more conservative, I'm still bothered by the fact that many British prisoners are obliged to "slop out" every morning and are "banged up" with two other men in cells designed by illiberal Victorians for one. But I'm now even more concerned about the victims of crime and, by victims, I don't just mean the "direct" ones but the "indirect" ones too: the old women who are frightened to go shopping during the day and the young women—and young men—who daren't travel on public transport at night. Meanwhile, I hang on to my moral opposition to the death penalty as the last great tenet of liberalism but even this I only sustain as an article of faith.

To some extent, this shift of opinion is inevitable

after months spent immersing myself in crime but, in reality, it probably has more to do with the inescapable fact that lawlessness—however they carve up the official figures—is on the increase.

I trust that readers will forgive me if things are not always as up to date as they (and I) would wish. I have used statistics and cases which are as recent as possible but there are always newer ones since crime, alas, is as remorseless as time itself. The truth is that crime figures for 1993 are not likely to be much different from the figures for 1991 or even 1990—especially when put in a fifty-year perspective or set in a global context.

However, until I started working on this book, I knew relatively little—beyond what everyone knows—about crime. This sets me apart from crime-writers whose whole lives are informed by their dedication to, and passion for, the world of crime. They are obviously better informed than me but, by the same token, there is always the possibility that they lack the fresh perspective that a newcomer can bring to bear on an area that has its own arcane and, to the outsider, downright strange, rules and customs.

As a writer who just happens to find himself writing about crime (as opposed to a crime-writer), I have attempted to redress the balance by selecting the facts and stats that I happen to find interesting rather than the accepted criminological agenda. Whilst largely omitting crimes to do with war and terrorism, I have aimed for eclecticism but not at the expense of the unusual and offbeat—lists which will, I hope, be more truly representative of what I've tried to achieve than those you might have expected to find.

Mitchell Symons
London, 1994

● ACKNOWLEDGMENTS

The author gratefully acknowledges the help of the following organizations and people:

The Howard League

The Criminal Injuries Compensation Board

The US Embassy

The United Nations

Madame Tussaud's

Central Office of Information

Interpol

The European Commission

The National Criminal Intelligence Service

The European Statistical Service

The Home Office

The British Library

Amnesty International

News International

John Ross of Scotland Yard's Black Museum

John Koski of *YOU* Magazine—for allowing me to pinch the odd list or three

Simon Rose—for being a mine of useful information

Bela Cunha—for doing a superb job on the copyediting and for adding vital information

Brian Lane—for providing additional research

Patrick Walsh—for his support and encouragement

Lorraine Jerram—for being a wonderful editor and for keeping her cool when I was losing mine

Justine Powell—for her research, her good humor and all her fabulous help. It is no exaggeration to say that I would never have been able to finish this book (well certainly not this side of the millennium) without her.

1
MURDER

The ten worst spree killers in the world

A spree (or mass) killer is different from a serial killer in that he (or, rarely, she) murders all his victims in a single day, whereas the serials murder their victims over a longer period of time—often years. For the purposes of this list, I have omitted arsonists and bombers—who would otherwise have qualified for inclusion—since they are an altogether different breed of murderer.

1. JOHN D. LEE (USA) 100+

In September 1857, a wagon-train transporting 140 men, women and children through Utah was attacked at a place called Mountain Meadows by what seemed to be Indians. During the skirmish twenty immigrants were killed and, but for the timely arrival of Bishop John D. Lee of the Mormon church and a large group of men, they might all have been massacred. Lee offered to escort the wagon-train to safety on condition that the settlers lay down their weapons. As soon as they had, Lee's men butchered them—with a little help from the "Indians." Only seventeen children—too young to give evidence—were left alive. It was not until 1876 that Lee was finally convicted of first-degree murder and sentenced to death. Back at Mountain Meadows, John D. Lee was seated on the edge of a prepared coffin. A firing squad sent a barrage of gunfire into his body which fell into the waiting coffin.

2. WOU BOM-KON (South Korea) 58

In an eight-hour orgy of violence twenty-seven-year-old Wou Bom-Kon killed fifty-eight people and wounded thirty-six in villages in the Kyong Sang-Namdo province of South Korea: On April 28, 1982, Wou, a former member of the Korean Marine Corps and at the time a serving policeman, had a row with his girlfriend, got drunk, stole guns, ammunition and hand-grenades from the police station armory and went on the rampage, shooting indiscriminately and detonating grenades. Eyewitnesses said the mutilated bodies of the dead littered the streets along with the wounded who were screaming out for help. The main difficulty in apprehending Wou was that the whole of the local police force was attending an obligatory "neighborhood association meeting." By the time they were alerted, Wou had backtracked toward his home village where, just two miles from the police station where he was based, he blew himself up with his last grenade.

3. DR. BARUCH GOLDSTEIN (Israel) 54

Forty-two-year-old Dr. Baruch Goldstein walked into the Ibrahim Mosque in Hebron on Friday, February 25, 1994 and opened fire on the Moslem worshipers. He emptied four magazines and threw three grenades. Fifty-four people were killed and many more injured. The massacre was halted when some of the congregation managed to knock Dr. Goldstein to the ground and he was beaten to death.

4. GEORGE HENNARD (USA) 22

With a victim count of twenty-two dead and eighteen wounded, it was America's worst mass shooting to date. At around 12:40 p.m. on Wednesday, October 16, 1991, George Hennard drove his pick-up truck through the plate-glass main entrance of Luby's cafeteria on Interstate 190 at Killeen, Texas, swung himself down from the driver's seat and yelled: "This is what Bell County has done to me." In the bloodbath which followed, Hennard, armed with a Glock-17 semi-automatic pistol, began methodically to slaughter the captive diners, always on the move, always shooting; and when one clip was exhausted, Hennard always had another one in his pocket. There is no telling how long the massacre might have continued if armed police had not arrived on the scene. During the mêlée one customer had hurled himself through a large unbroken side window and raised the alarm. Now Hennard's attentions were transferred to dueling with the police marksmen. It was a police bullet which slowed George down. Bleeding heavily from the wound, he made a last gesture of defiance: he raised the Glock to his head and put a bullet through his own left eye and deep into his brain.

5. JAMES OLIVER HUBERTY (USA) 20

Before Hennard took the crown at Luby's, America's worst gun massacre was committed by James Huberty at another restaurant—this time in California. In the early afternoon of July 18, 1984, Huberty, an unemployed security guard, drove to the crowded San Ysidro branch of McDonald's after telling his wife he was going "hunting humans." Opening fire with an arsenal of weapons, James Huberty killed twenty people and wounded another nineteen before police arrived and shot him dead.

6. CHARLES WHITMAN (USA) 17

It was on August 1, 1966 that the madness which had infected Whitman's mind decided to take him for a drive. The first stop was at his mother's home in Austin, Texas where he stabbed and shot her dead; back home, Charlie stabbed his wife three times in the chest before collecting his .30 M-1 carbine, a 12-gauge shotgun and several hundred rounds of ammunition. Then he picked up a survival kit, a few more guns and several knives which, neatly parcelled into a shopping cart, he carried to the 27th floor of the 307 ft office tower of the University of Texas. After beating the receptionist unconscious with the butt of a rifle, Charlie Whitman wheeled his death kit out on to the observation platform where he began sniping at passersby below. An ex-Marine sharpshooter, Whitman claimed seventeen lives and wounded another thirty people before he was cut down by police marksmen. Back at his home, detectives found Whitman's last message: "I've been having fears and violent impulses . . . After my death I wish an autopsy to be performed to see if there's any mental disorder." In fact the post-mortem revealed a small tumor in the back of his brain.

7= RONALD GENE SIMMONS (USA) 16

A former Air Force Master Sergeant, Simmons had already had charges filed against him alleging incest with his sixteen-year-old daughter when, just before Christmas 1987, he decided to dispose of the whole family. First he shot his wife and daughter, and then sat back and enjoyed a cold beer while he waited for his other children to arrive home—four died with their little heads held under the water in the rain barrel. Four days later, on December 26, the rest of the family arrived for their planned Christmas visit. The first to die were Simmons' son and daughter-in-law; then his grandson, followed by a daughter and son-in-law, and a couple more grandchildren. After this strenuous activity Gene Simmons spent the next couple of days relaxing in front of the television and drinking beer, apparently oblivious of the bodies piled up around him. Then on the Monday morning Simmons drove into the town of Russellville and shot and wounded a few local citizens and killed two more. And that was that. Simmons simply sat down and waited to be arrested. Ronald Gene Simmons was sentenced to death, refused to appeal, and on May 31, 1990 the then-governor of Arkansas signed his execution warrant—the governor's name was Bill Clinton. One month later Simmons died by lethal injection.

7= MICHAEL RYAN (UK) 16

The first victim was Susan Godfrey, shot dead by a man dressed in combat gear and flak jacket as she picnicked with her children. It was midday on August 19, 1987, and before the end of the day another fifteen people would lose their lives with fourteen injured, eight of them seriously. The killer, identified as twenty-seven-year-old Michael Ryan, next moved on toward the quiet Berkshire town of Hungerford, pausing to fill his car and take a couple of pot-shots at the filling station cashier. In town, Ryan made for his mother's home and shot her dead before setting fire to the house. Now the bloodbath began in earnest, with Ryan running and jogging, firing indiscriminately into the crowded market-day streets—shooting people in their gardens, in their cars, out shopping. By now the police had responded to the filling station cashier's emergency call and had sealed off the streets of Hungerford. With armed officers closing in on him, Michael Ryan holed up in the local secondary school where specialist siege negotiators tried to talk him out. At just after 7:00 p.m. a muffled shot sounded from within the school; Michael Ryan, like so many mass killers, had ended his spree by taking his own life. When Ryan was cremated on September 3, 1989, there was a single wreath on his coffin bearing the inscription: "Our savior will receive him fittingly."

9= MARC LEPINE (Canada) 14

Rejected by most women as "weird," Lepine had developed a deep hatred of what he called "feminists"—in effect, any female who found his attentions odious. Perhaps it was his violent bullying or his non-stop diet of war films; maybe it was the skull Lepine always kept in the window, but none of his girlfriends ever hung around long. But now it was different—his latest girl had become pregnant, she would *have* to stay. Not so. Sensing a bleak and squalid future with a psychotic gun-freak, she decided to have an abortion. This was the final straw for Marc Lepine. On December 7, 1989, Lepine burst into a classroom at the University of Montreal with an automatic gun in his hand. First he ordered the male students to one side of the room and the women to the other; then, still railing against feminists, Lepine opened fire into the crowd of terrified women students. He took fourteen lives before turning the gun on himself.

9= PATRICK HENRY SHERRILL (USA) 14

On the hot Wednesday morning of August 20, 1986, Patrick Sherrill drove to his job at Edmond, Oklahoma's main post office. The difference was that today he had two .45s and his trusty .22-caliber handgun in the car with him. He parked and walked across the car park, pausing just once to shoot dead a fellow worker before passing through the employees' entrance. After locking several doors to maximize his kill, Sherrill opened fire—in the words of the police, "shooting people as though they were sitting ducks." Although FBI marksmen surrounded the single-story building and there was no escape, Sherrill refused to talk with trained siege negotiators. When a special team eventually stormed the building they found the bodies of fourteen men and women, and seven other badly wounded victims. Patrick Sherrill lay dead where he had put a single bullet through his own head, his arsenal of guns and ammunition beside him.

9= CHRISTIAN DORNIER (France) 14

Well-known locally as a surly and violent man, Dornier worked a small farm near Luxiol on the French border with Switzerland, and was avoided by his neighbors; if only he had avoided them. On July 12, 1989, Christian Dornier, his slender grasp on reason broken, took up a double-barreled shotgun and shot dead the veterinarian who was working at the farm. Next to die were Dornier's own mother and sister, before the frenzied farmer climbed into his Volkswagen Golf and went rampaging through the village streets shooting anyone in sight— men, women and a number of children. Then Dornier turned his attention to the village of Autechaux where four more perished . . . on now to Verne, still shooting, still killing. The body count had risen to fourteen by the time the local gendarmerie put a stop to the bloodshed by seriously wounding Dornier. Later, one witness said: "He seemed completely out of his mind." And that was an opinion confirmed by the psychiatrists sent to examine him. Christian Dornier was certified insane and unfit to stand trial; he was instead committed to a mental institution indefinitely.

The eight most prolific serial killers in the world

1. THE BEANE (OR BEAN) FAMILY (Legendary) (UK) 1,000?

After a number of people had gone missing and a man had survived an attack by "savages" in the Galloway area of Scotland in the early seventeenth century, soldiers investigated and discovered a cave in which they found the remains of human bodies. The cave was inhabited by Sawney Beane and his wife and their eight sons, six daughters, eighteen grandsons and fourteen granddaughters. It is estimated that they murdered (and ate) one thousand people, but most sources disagree about the particulars of the case and, indeed, a question mark hangs over whether the Beanes really ever existed.

2. BEHRAM (India) 931

It is difficult to establish the exact origin of the Indian cult of Thugee or even its date, though it may be earlier than the eighth century. At the end of the eighteenth century and the early years of the nineteenth the British annexation of the Indian Continent produced a wealth of strange stories of eccentric faiths and religions. In his book *On the Murderers Called Phansigars,* a British doctor named Robert Sherwood first exposed the West to the cult of the *Phansigars* (*phansi* means "noose") or *Thugs.* According to Sherwood, the Thugs were for the most part of the year ordinary peasants and tradesmen, but at the time of the annual pilgrimage they would leave the village and infiltrate the bands of pilgrims on the road. This was done gradually until there were more Thugs than pilgrims; and then, at night, as the pilgrims sat in a circle around the fire the Thugs struck. At a given signal three assassins took up position behind a victim; one would pass the "strangling cloth" (yellow and white in color, called a *ruhmal*) around the pilgrim's neck, another would grasp his legs and lift them into the air, and the third would seize his hands or kneel on his back. Death was almost instantaneous. The bodies were quickly dismembered and buried in readiness for the ritual of *Tuponee*. A ceremonial axe (*kussee*) was placed on the grave and, as the Thugs sat in a circle around it, their leader offered prayers to the goddess Kali, called "the dark mother," in return for wealth and success. A symbolic strangulation followed, and then the "communicants" ate a piece of *goor* (a sweet, sugary substance) and drank consecrated water. Behram was the leader of a Thug gang in the Oudh district and between the years 1790 and 1840 is reputed to have strangled an estimated 931 victims—though whether this is a personal tally, or a collective one, cannot be reliably established. By the middle of the nineteenth century, the cult of Thugee had become almost totally corrupted, and the once "pure" religious aspects had given way to simple murder and robbery.

3. COUNTESS ELISABETH BATHORY (Hungary) 610+

According to tradition Elisabeth was born in 1561 and married at the age of fifteen to Count Ferencz Nádasdy, to become mistress of the castle at Csejthe. Utterly bored, the Countess experimented with torturing people; minor indignities to begin with—a little flagellation, a touch of flesh-tearing with pincers . . . But when her husband died in 1604, Elisabeth really discovered her talent for sadism. It is recorded that one day, after having drubbed a servant with such force as to draw blood she found to her horror that spots of gore had splashed on her skin. The horror was transformed to wonder when Countess Elisabeth wiped the blood off and became convinced that beneath the skin was that of a young woman. And so, henceforth, she would take a morning bath in virgins' blood, which, over a period of five years, quite decimated the local countryside. Having run out of peasant girls the increasingly desperate Countess turned to the daughters of the nobility, which is how she came unstuck. Having drained some girls of their rejuvenating fluid, the Countess had the corpses hurled over the battlements as a midnight snack for the wolves. But before all trace was eaten, some villagers recognized the victims and Elisabeth Bathory's reign of terror was over. Protected by her aristocracy from an ignominious death, the Countess was walled up in a small chamber of her castle where she died a few years later.

4. PEDRO ARMANDO LOPEZ (aka "THE MONSTER OF THE ANDES" (Colombia) 300+

At the age of eight little Pedro was discovered sexually fondling one of his younger sisters and was cast out of the family home onto the streets to fend for himself. And fend he did, after a fashion. At the age of eighteen, while in prison for car theft, he was brutally raped in his cell. Pedro's response was to make himself a crude knife; within weeks he had killed three of his attackers. They were probably his first killings—but by no means his last. Pedro Lopez traveled widely in Peru, and it is thought that, at a modest estimate, he was responsible for the deaths of more than one hundred women. It was a similar story in Ecuador, where the killing spree continued—in fact, so many women disappeared that the police in three countries began to think that a large organization was involved. It was in April 1980 that the full story began to unfold. A swollen river overflowed its banks near Ambato in Peru, exposing the remains of four missing girls. Then a woman working in the Plaza Rossa market noticed that her daughter was missing; she ran through the streets and eventually caught up with the girl walking hand in hand with a stranger. That man was Pedro Armando Lopez—caught in the act. In custody, Lopez made a confession describing how he

first introduced his young victims to sex and then
strangled them. Convicted of murder in Ecuador, Lopez
was sentenced to life imprisonment, that country having
long abolished the death penalty.

5. BRUNO LUDKE (Germany) 85

Born in 1909, young Bruno had already embarked on
an extravaganza of rape, murder and necrophilia before leaving his teens behind him. He played his part in
Adolf Hitler's grand plan by being rounded up—along
with other "mental defectives"—to help solve the
genetic problems of creating a master race. At the same
time as assisting with experiments, Ludke managed to
murder eighty-five women. His victims had invariably
been strangled or stabbed, and sex had been the
motivation—though, in an almost offended manner,
Ludke pointed out that they had been dead before he
violated them. Clearly as mad as a hatter, Bruno Ludke
was confined to hospital in Vienna and used as a
human guinea pig in "experiments." On April 8, 1944,
his participation in these experiments ended when an
injection proved fatal.

6. DANIEL BARBOSA (Ecuador) 71+

It was in 1986 that Daniel Camargo Barbosa embarked
on his career as a serial killer. He had just escaped from
prison in his native Colombia where he had been
convicted of the rape and murder of a nine-year-old girl.
Having fled over the border into Ecuador, Barbosa
abducted and killed fifty-five young girls in the port of
Guayaquil alone. The bodies of many remain undiscov-
ered, but those that were found revealed an extraordinary degree of brutality inflicted by bludgeoning and
slashing with a machete-type blade. At several of the
murder sites, police found one common clue—a dis-
carded sweet wrapper; from which it was deduced that
the killer was luring children with promises of sweets. In
June 1988 a further body was found holding the now
familiar candy wrapper; only this time there was a
fingerprint—smudged, but identifiable as belonging to

Daniel Barbosa, convicted killer. Under questioning, Barbosa admitted the killings, and in September 1989 he was sentenced to just sixteen years' imprisonment— the maximum punishment under Ecuador's criminal code.

7. KAMPATIMAR SHANKARIYA (India) 70+
In the late 1970s, Shankariya murdered at least seventy people in Jaipur. He was arrested, found guilty and executed on May 16, 1979.

8. ANDREI CHIKATILO (Russia) 55+
Called the "Rostov Ripper," Chikatilo was born near Rostov in 1936. After earning a degree in Russian literature he later became a lecturer in the school of Novo Shatinsk. It is probably here that sexual envy of the young men and women around him led to frustration and later to murder. The first victim was a teenage girl whose sexually abused and mutilated body was found hidden in some woods in 1978. Over the succeeding years the list of young people who disappeared grew longer, and in one year there were eight deaths in a single month. Then the outrage spread to neighboring Ukraine and Uzbekistan, coinciding with Chikatilo's new appointment as head of supplies at the Rostov locomotive repair shop—a post which enabled him to travel all over the south of the former USSR. Ironically Chikatilo had been arrested twice on suspicion of being responsible for the killings, once in 1979 and again in 1984. He was released the second time because his blood group differed from that of the semen samples found on the victims. What the police authorities did not know was that such a phenomenon *can* occur, and that Andrei Chikatilo was one of those one-in-a-million cases. It was not until November 1990 that the "Rostov Ripper" was taken into custody following an attempt to abduct a young boy. After a bizarre trial during which Chikatilo was confined like an animal in an iron cage in the center of the court, he was sentenced to death. In

March 1994, after President Yeltsin had refused to intercede on his behalf, Andrei Chikatilo was executed with a single bullet to the back of his head.

The ten most prolific serial killers in the USA

1. DONALD HARVEY 67+

During his employment as a hospital orderly in Kentucky and Ohio in the 1970s and 1980s Harvey is believed to have dispatched more than three score of the patients in his care. It was not until March 1987, when John Powell died suddenly and the autopsy revealed cyanide poisoning, that suspicion fell upon Donald Harvey. Under questioning, Harvey admitted to murder, and an investigation of his past showed that there were also an uncommon number of fatalities among his friends and homosexual lovers. Having plea-bargained his way out of the death sentence, Harvey pleaded not guilty to twenty-four murders in Ohio and was given twenty-five years to life on each. At a further trial he also pleaded guilty to killing one of his neighbors—effectively destroying his earlier claim that his murders had been mercy killings of the terminally ill. Then the action moved to Kentucky where Donald Harvey pleaded guilty to eight counts of murder and one of attempted murder at the Marymount Hospital; he picked up eight life sentences and twenty years. But it was not over yet; back in Ohio there were three more charges of murder to face, and three of attempted murder. It may never be known quite how many people Donald Harvey killed; what is sure is that he has earned enough prison sentences to keep him inside for the rest of his life.

2. THE ZODIAC KILLER 37

The death toll of thirty-seven attributed to "Zodiac" is almost certainly an exaggeration, and results from a letter to the San Francisco Police Department in 1974 making the claim and threatening to "do something nasty." What is known for sure is that the killer known as Zodiac (because his letters to newspapers, the police, and left at the scene-of-crime are signed with a cross superimposed on a circle—the symbol for the zodiac) has a body count of five dead and two wounded. On July 5, 1969, the Vallejo Police Department received a call from a man with a "gruff" voice, reporting a double murder: "If you will go one mile east on Colombus Parkway to a public park, you will find the kids in a brown car. They have been shot with a 9mm Luger. I also killed those kids last year. Good-bye." It was all true, except that one of the later victims survived and described his attacker as about twenty-five to thirty years old, stockily built, with a round face and wavy brown hair. Then the letters started to arrive, letters giving details of killings only the assassin could know. At the foot of each of the letters were lines of cipher (still undecoded) and the "Zodiac" signature of the cross on a circle. And so the pattern repeated itself until October 11, 1969 when a taxi driver named Paul Stine was shot dead in his cab and robbed in San Francisco. Now Zodiac began to manipulate the media as never before. He demanded air-time on a television chat show and via the telephone lines agreed to meet a lawyer in Daly City; Zodiac failed to turn up. There were a few more letters, but after the TV hype Zodiac went to ground. Nothing more was heard until 1971, when the *Los Angeles Times* received a letter commenting: "If the blue menaces are ever going to catch me, they had better get off their butts and do something." Then there was the letter of '74 claiming thirty-seven dead . . . and then, silence. Zodiac was never caught, nor, as far as we can know, did he kill again.

3. JOHN WAYNE GACY 33

John Wayne Gacy was arguably America's most notorious serial killer and certainly one of its most prolific multicides. Between 1972 and 1978 the man the press came to know as the "Clown Killer" (after Gacy's alter ego "Pogo," the lovable clown who entertained at children's parties) sexually abused, tortured then strangled thirty-three young men and boys and hid their bodies around his home and garden just outside Chicago. Gacy's reign of terror came to an end in December 1978 when police visited the house following leads to the disappearance of fifteen-year-old Robert Piest. In custody, Gacy admitted the murder of thirty-two teenage boys during or after sex (actually he had lost count, there were thirty-three) and at his trial a plea of insanity was rejected. From 1980 to 1994, he embarked upon the seemingly interminable process of appeals against his death sentence. Finally, in May 1994 Gacy was led to the death cell and a lethal injection was administered; it took eighteen minutes to kill him—twice the normal time. Outside the prison there was an almost carnival atmosphere as supporters of the death penalty—many of them dressed in clown costumes—sang and chanted such pieces of doggerel as "Turn that frown upside down, they have just fried the clown."

4. DAVID BROOKS, DEAN CORLL and ELMER WAYNE HENLEY 32

August 8, 1973. The telephone rang in the Pasadena Police Department and from the other end of the line a voice announced: "I just killed a man . . ." When officers arrived at the address in Lanar Street they found seventeen-year-old Wayne Henley standing beside the body of his one-time friend Dean Corll; Corll was lying face down with six bullets in him. The story Henley had to tell was one of the worst police had heard—even in a country where bizarre murder is no rare event. Henley, Corll and another youth named Brooks had systematically raped, tortured and killed thirty-two young men, most of them hitchhikers or vagrants. Corll, known locally as a "real nice guy" and nicknamed "The Candyman" because of his largesse with sweets, had designed a "torture board"—a plank of wood to which victims were handcuffed, then sodomized and subjected to other painful indignities before, sometimes days later, being killed. At Wayne Henley's trial some of the tortures were described: "pulling out their pubic hairs one by one, shoving glass rods up their penis and pushing a large bullet-like instrument in the victim's rectum." The showdown came when Corll decided that Henley should take his turn on the torture board. Wayne Henley was tried in 1974, convicted and sentenced to six ninety-nine-year terms; Brooks was jailed for life.

5. WAYNE WILLIAMS 28

Between 1979 and 1981, Williams, a black freelance photographer, murdered twenty-eight young black children in Atlanta. As all the victims were black it was the fear of the ethnic community that this was the work of a white racist. It was an unlikely theory for two reasons: first, all the children were taken in the kind of black neighborhoods where a white face would stand out; secondly, serial killers—indeed the majority of murderers—tend to kill within their own ethnic group. The break for a beleaguered police force came on May 22, 1981 when a man later identified as Wayne B. Williams was seen getting into a station wagon near the Chattahoochee river just after a loud splash had been heard. Two days later the body of Nathaniel Chater was recovered from the water. Williams was put on trial at the end of 1981 charged with just two counts of murder. In February the following year he was sentenced to two terms of life imprisonment. The so-called "Atlanta Child Murders" stopped abruptly after Williams' arrest, though it is fair to say that some doubt has been expressed over the safety of his conviction.

6. HERBERT MULLIN 27

It is difficult to pinpoint the cause of Herbert Mullin's eventual madness. Some say it was when his closest friend, Dean Richardson, was killed in a motoring accident in 1965. He turned his bedroom into a shrine to Dean, broke off his engagement and declared himself a conscientious objector. Taken into psychiatric care on the advice of his parents, Mullin was declared a paranoid schizophrenic. Released from hospital, Mullin began to lose what reason he still retained with the heavy use of hallucinogenic drugs. Then there were the voices in his head, voices telling him to kill. The first victim, in October 1972, was a tramp called "Old Whitey." A week later, Mullin stabbed to death college student Mary Guilfoyle, cut open her body and dragged out the innards with his bare hands. There followed a series of senseless shootings and stabbings, all ordered by the voices. In the middle of February 1973, Herbert Mullin shot down Fred Perez as he was working in his garden; unfortunately, the voices hadn't told him that Fred's neighbor was watching. At his trial in July 1973 Mullin's attorney advanced a plea of insanity—and when they heard Mullin's explanation, a jury might well have agreed. You see, Herbert Mullin had it on good authority that if he killed people he would avert the cataclysmic earthquake and tidal wave that were about to destroy California. Perversely, this jury decided that Mullin was fit to stand trial and eventually convicted him on two counts of first-degree murder and eight of second-degree murder. At present he is confined to San Quentin and eligible for parole in the year 2025.

7. JUAN VALLEJO CORONA 25

Having first arrived in California as a migrant fruit picker in the 1950s, Corona, by hard work and enterprise, built up a successful business hiring out Mexican migrants to local fruit-growers on commission. Then, in 1971, alerted by an anonymous tip-off, a squad of police arrived to search Corona's home and and the old bunkhouse where his workforce slept. Here in shallow graves the search team found the remains of twenty-five men, some migrants, others passing vagrants. All of them had been stabbed to death and their heads hacked with a heavy, sharp implement; in Corona's house was found the bloody machete with which the mutilation was carried out. The motive for the murders seems to have been at least partly sexual as many of the victims had been buried without their trousers. Tried at the California Supreme Court, Juan Corona was sentenced to twenty-five life terms. However, after strenuous appeals over the following ten years, Corona won a retrial on the basis of his claim that it was his brother Natividad (now conveniently deceased) who had committed the murders. The trial cost the taxpayers $5 million, featured nine hundred exhibits and two hundred and twelve witnesses, was the most expensive single-defendant trial in California's legal history, and resulted in Juan Corona being returned to prison to work out his life sentences.

8. THEODORE ROBERT BUNDY 23

The most remarkable thing about "Ted" Bundy was that he seemed such an unlikely killer. A well-educated, good-looking man, his charm and wit made him an attractive companion, and he experienced no difficulty in his relations with women—apart, that is, from his compulsion to kill them. In 1974, while Bundy was in Washington State (ironically as assistant director of the local crime commission) there was a spate of killings of young women. Later, when Bundy moved to Utah, the killings in Washington stopped and a new wave of disappearances began in Salt Lake. Eventually Bundy was arrested and imprisoned for kidnapping eighteen-year-old Carol DaRonch. It was while he was in custody that Bundy began to be linked with the murder of Caryn Campbell and he was extradited to Colorado. In 1977, while awaiting trial he escaped, was quickly recaptured, and then escaped again to carry out a further series of robberies, rapes and murders around Florida. It was not until February 1978 that Bundy was re-arrested—on a traffic violation. Under questioning he claimed his death toll had exceeded 100. This is almost certainly an exaggeration, but at his subsequent trial, Ted Bundy was sentenced to death; he was executed on January 24, 1989.

9. EARLE LEONARD NELSON (aka "THE GORILLA MURDERER") 22

Nelson acquired his nickname because of his dark complexion, receding forehead and general ape-like appearance. Between 1926 and 1927, he worked his way across the USA and Canada leaving in his wake a trail of twenty-two dead women. With only a couple of variations, all his victims were boarding-house landladies (the exceptions were a fellow lodger and the daughter of one of the landladies) who were strangled and raped. Nelson's killing spree ended in Winnipeg in June 1927. A man named William Paterson arrived home to find his wife murdered and a suitcase rifled and money and clothing stolen. At about the same time Nelson was selling off the Patersons' belongings in a second-hand clothes shop; this was followed by a trip to the hairdresser, where the barber noticed blood on his hair. The descriptions given of Nelson were sufficiently good for him to be recognized from a "Wanted" notice in a post office in Wakopa. Earle Nelson was tried before Mr. Justice Dysart at Winnipeg on the charge of murdering Emily Paterson, and was hanged on January 13, 1928.

10. PAUL JOHN KNOWLES 18
Knowles took to crime easily and early, rising in the ranks from juvenile delinquency through theft and robbery to multiple murder. The first killing was carried out on July 26, 1974, just two months after Knowles' release from Railford Penitentiary, Florida. Two young girls aged eleven and seven followed, then, during August, another three victims. In September five more. On October 16 he raped and killed a woman and her teenage daughter, and three days later shot a woman with her husband's gun. By November, Knowles had moved to Georgia where the killing rape continued. It was also in Georgia that Knowles (calling himself "Daryl Golden") met and began an extraordinary relationship with an English journalist named Sandy Fawkes. For six days they were inseparable, during which time "Daryl" hinted darkly that he might be a serial killer. What's more, he boasted, he had made a tape recording detailing all the murders. What would have happened to this bizarre liaison we will never know, because one evening Knowles pulled a gun on his

new companion and she wisely got out fast. As for Knowles he killed twice more, one of the victims being a police patrolman whose car he hijacked. In the chase that followed Knowles skidded off the road while trying to avoid a road block and was taken into custody. On the following day Paul John Knowles slipped his hand-cuffs and made a run for it; he got no further than the front office before an FBI agent shot him dead.

The ten most prolific serial killers in the UK

1. THE BEANE (OR BEAN) FAMILY 1,000?
(*see* World list).

2. WILLIAM BURKE and WILLIAM HARE 16
Burke and Hare were Irish immigrant laborers who arrived in Scotland around 1818, and met as fellow residents at Logue's lodging-house, a squalid building in Edinburgh's West Port. Sharing the same lodgings was Old Donald, an army pensioner who in November 1827 died; which was a source of great distress to William Hare, because the old fellow owed him £4. So between them Burke and Hare opened the coffin and substituted a sack of bark for the body, which they sold for the princely sum of seven pounds ten shillings to Dr. Knox at the Anatomy School. In fact over the next ten months Dr. Knox would be a very good customer of this newly formed body-snatching partnership. At first the corpses were resurrected from among the recently buried in the local graveyards. But as trade became more lucrative, Burke and Hare broadened the scope of their craft and began to create their own fresh supplies. It would happen like this: either Hare's "wife" Maggie Laird, or Burke's, Helen M'Dougal, would lure a victim back to the lodging-house and make them insensible with drink. Then out would pop Burke, kneel on the unfortunate drunk's chest, while stopping the nose and mouth with his hands—Hare would assist by restraining any victim who proved uncooperative. In honor of its inventor, this method of causing death became known as "burk-

ing." And long might the two resurrection men have continued in their enterprise had they not carelessly left the corpse of Margaret Docherty where other lodgers could find it. William Hare and Maggie Laird escaped prosecution by turning King's evidence, leaving Burke and M'Dougal to stand their trial at the High Court of Justiciary. The case against Helen M'Dougal was found "Not Proven" but Burke was found guilty and publicly hanged on January 27, 1829. M'Dougal was pursued through the streets of Edinburgh by a bloodthirsty mob and escaped lynching only through the intervention of the police.

3. DENNIS ANDREW NILSEN 15

Nilsen, a civil servant working at the Soho Job Center, was unmasked as one of England's worst serial killers in 1983 when his neighbors called a drain cleaning firm to do something about the toilets not flushing in the house they shared at 23 Cranley Gardens, Muswell Hill, London. The Dyno-Rod man found the main drain blocked with "meat"—possibly, he thought, human flesh. When he returned with his boss the drain expert found that most of the meat had gone—except for a few fragments and what looked like a human finger. It was, he decided, a job for the police. When "Des" Nilsen arrived home from work on the following evening he was greeted by three detectives. When he was told of the grisly finds in the drain, Nilsen replied: "Good grief, how awful." With an inspired guess, Chief Inspector Peter Jay turned to Nilsen and said simply: "Don't mess around, where's the rest of the body?" "In two plastic bags in the wardrobe. I'll show you," Nilsen answered. On the way back to Muswell Hill police station Detective Inspector McCusker asked Nilsen: "Are we talking about one body or two?" "Fifteen or sixteen since 1978," Nilsen replied. It was really all very simple; Dennis Nilsen proved to have a remarkable recollection of his crimes and proved most cooperative. At the end of a complex trial he was found guilty as charged of six counts of murder and two of attempted murder. Nilsen

is now serving a life sentence with a recommendation
that he serve at least twenty-five years.

4. MARY ANN COTTON 14

That rare creature in the annals of British crime, the
serial murderess, has as its figurehead Mary Ann Cotton, claimed to be the most prolific female multicide in
history. The majority of Mary's killings seem to have
been connected with her deep attachment to other
people's money, and she murdered her way through a
succession of husbands, often for the most paltry sums.
And when Mary wanted a new spouse she would
frequently kill off a few children, just so as not to
frighten the poor chap off. In those far off days (Mary
was active between about 1857 and 1872) the science of
toxicology was all but non-existent, and Mary Ann
Cotton's arsenic victims were almost always diagnosed
as suffering from "gastric fever." It was only in July
1872, when a post-mortem was ordered on the body of
Mary's stepson Charles Edward, that arsenic came to
light, and exhumations were ordered on many of the
others who had died in Mary Ann Cotton's company.
She was tried only for the death of little Charles Edward;
the jury at Durham Assizes announced their guilty
verdict in March 1873 and Mary died on the scaffold at
Durham County Jail on the 24th of that month.

5. DR. WILLIAM PALMER 13–16

Despite a dissolute start in life, when he was dismissed
from his apprenticeship with a druggist for embezzle-
ment, and then being obliged to flee yet another Master
after running a private abortion service from his premises, Palmer eventually qualified as a doctor. He set up
in practice in the town of Rugeley, in Staffordshire, and
married. However, it soon became clear that his love of
the racetrack was greater than that for medicine, and he
soon had so many gambling debts and so little income
that he started working his way through his family. First
his mother-in-law passed away; William inherited. Then
wife Annie died mysteriously, and brother Walter too,

both insured for hefty sums. As Palmer's racing losses increased, so his family decreased. Along the line four of his children died, plus an uncle and some of his more pressing creditors. In November 1855, Palmer visited Shrewsbury Races with a gambling companion named John Parsons Cook. Cook won, Palmer lost. So back at their hotel Palmer poisoned his companion and pocketed his winnings. Unfortunately for the deadly doctor, Cook's stepfather was a suspicious old fellow and insisted on an autopsy—the result of which proved that Cook died of antimony poisoning. Which is how Dr. William Palmer found himself on the scaffold at Stafford Jail before an audience of 50,000 people.

6. PETER SUTCLIFFE (aka "THE YORKSHIRE RIPPER") 13

The investigation of the Yorkshire Ripper case was a story of determination and frustration, of a police force desperate to put a stop to one of the worst serial murderers in Britain's history. Above all it is the story of a county gripped by terror, its women fearful of being out of doors at night. Thirteen of them paid with their lives for that freedom. Despite the largest manhunt ever mounted by British police, during which 250,000 people were interviewed and 32,000 statements taken, it was the very weight of all this paperwork that obscured the path to Sutcliffe. He had even been questioned a number of times in connection with the murders. The five-year hunt ended on January 2, 1981, when a suspicious police patrol picked up a man calling himself Peter Williams; it was Sutcliffe. The Yorkshire Ripper was a killer of the "evangelical" type, and his mission was to rid the streets of prostitutes—he had, so he said, become aware of the mission while he was working as a gravedigger and heard the voice of God coming from one of the graves.

7. PETER MANUEL 9

Typical of a certain type of 1950s Glasgow "hard man," Manuel was a dyed-in-the-wool criminal who engaged in a life of crime from the age of twelve until he was hanged in 1958. As a serial killer, Manuel was a comparative rarity in that all his murders were in pursuit of gain—to put it simply, he killed the people in the houses he burgled—or, in two instances sex. Both Manuel and his father were taken into custody over one family murder, and in exchange for his father's release, Manuel made a full confession. In fact they could not stop him confessing, and this uncontrollable eagerness to help the police with their inquiries earned him the nickname "The Man Who Talked Too Much." Although he was found guilty of nine killings at trial, he admitted to a further three. Peter Manuel was hanged at Barlinnie Prison on July 11, 1958.

8= JOHN GEORGE HAIGH 6

Haigh first came to the notice of the Murder Squad in 1949 when a wealthy fellow-resident at the Onslow Court Hotel suddenly disappeared. Haigh was in the frame because he was known to be the last person to have seen her and the one who was trying to interest her in a "business proposition." It was while Haigh was being interviewed by police that he made this extraordinary statement: "Mrs. Durand-Deacon no longer exists. I've destroyed her with acid. You can't prove murder without a body." Actually John George was wrong on both counts: a number of significant cases have been proved without the benefit of a corpse; and Mrs. Durand-Deacon (or at least identifiable fragments of her) existed in the greasy sludge that she had become in the acid bath. Not least important were her dentures, unaffected by the acid and recognizable by Mrs. Durand-Deacon's dentist. With his back against the wall, Haigh now confessed to a further five murders since 1944, and all the victims were disposed of in vats of sulphuric acid. The man who came to be known as the "Acid Bath Murderer" was put on trial and, despite his attempt to prove madness by claiming to have drunk his victims' blood, was found sane and guilty. He was hanged at Wandsworth Prison on August 10, 1949.

8= JOHN REGINALD HALLIDAY CHRISTIE 6

During the course of ten years between 1943 and 1953, Christie murdered six women at his home—the notorious 10 Rillington Place, in London. In 1949 a young man named Timothy Evans took over the top flat at No. 10 for himself, his wife and baby daughter Geraldine. On November 30 that year Tim Evans walked into a police station and announced that he had found his wife dead and disposed of her down a drain. Police found not only the body of Beryl Evans, but also that of baby Geraldine. After a trial in which John Christie was a leading prosecution witness, Evans was found guilty of murder and, on March 9, 1950, hanged. Two years later Christie killed his wife; a month later, in January 1953, he killed two prostitutes, and in March another woman. On March 19, Christie departed 10 Rillington Place, leaving the next tenant to trace the unpleasant smell to the corpses walled up in the kitchen. As well as the remains in the house, police diggers found evidence of a further two bodies buried in the garden. John Reginald Christie—"Reg"—confessed to the murders in a remarkably detailed document. He also, much later, admitted that it was he who had murdered Beryl Evans. Christie was hanged at Pentonville Prison on July 15, 1953. It was not until 1966 that Timothy Evans was granted a long-overdue posthumous pardon.

10= JACK THE RIPPER 5

For the three months from the end of August to the beginning of November in the year of 1888, the Whitechapel area of the East End of London was witness to a series of vicious—and still unsolved—murders. The slayings were characterized by an unparalleled savagery; each of the five victims—all prostitutes—had been attacked from behind and their throats cut; in four cases the bodies were afterwards subjected to such mutilation and dissection as to suggest a perverted sexual motive. Which leaves the question: who *was* Jack? Well, Jack has become something of an industry now and there are almost as many suspects—including members of the then-Royal Family—as there are "Ripperologists." In 1994 a "diary" was reputedly found which "proved" that Jack was none other than James Maybrick, victim of his wife Florence—so it is said—who poisoned him. Although this odd document has been exposed by some of the world's leading forensic experts as a fake, its publishers still claim Maybrick is the prime candidate— among so many other prime candidates . . .

10= COLIN IRELAND 5

Colin Ireland was one of those rare serial killers who set out to become one. He read books about it, and discovered that according to certain experts working with the FBI Offender Profiling Unit a figure of five determined whether one was a serial murderer or not. So Colin killed five. It helped that he wasn't too keen on homosexuals, because that gave him a perfect target group, a section of society that he could get angry enough with to kill. Ireland picked up five gay men from the notorious meeting place for homosexuals, the Coleherne pub in Earls Court, went back to their flats with them and committed murder. Finally identified, Colin Ireland, with some degree of self-satisfaction, confessed to the killings and pleaded guilty at his trial. Ireland was sent down on five life sentences, with a suggestion by the judge that he may never be safe enough to be released.

Postscript

During 1994 the house and garden belonging to Frederick West and his wife Rosemary at 25 Cromwell Street, Gloucester, were searched for human remains. At the time of writing, twelve bodies, or rather remains of bodies, have been uncovered at Cromwell Street and other locations associated with the West family. So far Frederick West has been charged with twelve murders relating to the corpses, and Rosemary has been named as co-defendant in nine. Since there has been no trial, no conviction, this case must remain, for the present, a footnote.

The twelve countries with the highest murder rates

1. Lesotho 532 (murders per million people)
2. The Philippines 425
3. The Bahamas 257
4. Zimbabwe 211
5. Lebanon 192
6. Thailand 166
7. Netherlands 123
8. Bermuda 108
9. Angola 103
10. Venezuela 99
11. Zambia 97
12. The Dominican Republic 93

The USA comes 15th with 79 murders per million inhabitants. In 13th and 14th place respectively are Papua New Guinea (92) and Tanzania (87).

The idea that Libya, the country which brought us state-sponsored terrorism, has a lower murder rate than the Bahamas reminds me of Tom Lehrer's comment about satire dying the day they gave Henry Kissinger the Nobel Peace Prize.

The most plausible explanation for Lesotho's extraordinary figure is inter-tribal hatred, though official sources were less than forthcoming when invited to comment.

The twelve countries with the lowest murder rates

1. Togo 1.6 (murders per million people)
2. Niger 2.1

"If poverty is the mother of crime, stupidity is its father."

JEAN DE LA BRUYÈRE

3. Morocco 7.8
4. Indonesia 9
5. Norway 9.2
6. Brunei 9.5
7= Kuwait 10.6
7= Zaire 10.6
9. Ireland 10.8
10. Gabon 11.2
11. Saudi Arabia 11.5
12. South Korea 13.6

The UK is in 13th place (13.7), confirming writer
Bernard Kops's assertion that Britain may not necessar-
ily be the best country to live in but is certainly one of
the best to go to sleep in.

The ten US States with the highest murder rates

1. District of Columbia 806 (murders per million
    people)
2. Louisiana 169
3. Texas 153
4. New York 142
5= Georgia 128
5= Mississippi 128
7. California 127
8. Nevada 118
9. Maryland 117
10. Alabama 115

The ten US States with the lowest murder rates

1. North Dakota 11 (murders per million people)
2. Maine 12
3. South Dakota 17
4. Idaho 18
5. Iowa 20
6. Vermont 21
7. Montana 26

8.   Utah 29
9.   Minnesota 30
10. Nebraska 33

Ten notorious poisoners

1. JANE TOPPAN (USA) 30+

Toppan worked as a nurse in Massachusetts where she poisoned at least thirty—and maybe as many as 100—patients with morphine and atropine over a period of about twenty years. She was caught and, in 1902, confessed to thirty murders. She was sent to a mental asylum for life.

2. SUZANNE FAZEKAS (Hungary) 26+

During the First World War, the women of a village near Budapest had affairs with prisoners of war. When the war ended, their husbands returned but the women were no longer satisfied with them and so, with the help of Fazekas, a midwife, they decided to murder them. The first murder had occurred as early as 1911—prior to the war—but it was in the ten years after the war that the murder rate accelerated. It is impossible to say how many poisonings took place but the figure could be as high as fifty. However, only twenty-six women were tried for murder of whom eight were sentenced to death and seven to life imprisonment. As for Fazekas, fittingly, she took poison and died.

3. ARNFINN NESSET (Norway) 22

Nesset obtained large quantities of the nerve poison curare between May 1977 and November 1980 and killed at least twenty-two (and possibly as many as 155) patients in the nursing homes where he worked in Norway. "I've killed so many I'm unable to remember them all," he boasted. At his trial in March 1983 he was convicted of twenty-two murders, one attempted murder and of embezzling funds from patients and was sentenced to twenty-one years in prison.

4. THE TOKYO MASS POISONING (Japan) 12

A man went into the Imperial Bank in Tokyo on January 26, 1948 and, saying that he was a public health official and that there had been an outbreak of dysentery, persuaded all sixteen bank employees to drink a solution of potassium cyanide and then robbed the bank. Twelve of the employees died. Sadamichi Hirasawa was arrested, convicted and sentenced to death (although the death sentence was never carried out and he died in prison in 1987 at the age of ninety-five). Doubts have been expressed about his guilt as police suspected that the real criminal was a soldier of the Imperial Japanese Army.

5. NANNIE DOSS (aka "ARSENIC ANNIE") (USA) 11

When an autopsy was carried out in Tulsa on Doss's fifth husband, Samuel, a huge quantity of arsenic was found in his body. This persuaded Doss to confess to having poisoned four of her five husbands and two children. However, investigators looking through the graveyard and exhuming other possible victims estimated the full tally to be eleven. Doss was sent to prison for life in 1964 but died a year later of leukemia.

Arsenic can be found in every part of the body of a person who has been poisoned with it. Even when someone has been dead and buried for years, it is still possible to find it in their hair and bones. In the nineteenth century, arsenic poisoning was so common in Britain that, in 1851, the Arsenic Act was introduced which made it illegal to sell any arsenic product unless the purchaser was known to the pharmacist and the arsenic was mixed with a colored powder (e.g. indigo or soot).

6. MARIE BECKER (Belgium) 10+

Marie Becker, a discontented housewife of Liège, poisoned her husband in 1932, her lover in 1934 and at least eight others with digitalis. Anonymous letters to the police in autumn 1936 triggered the investigation that led to her arrest and trial. She was sent to prison for life.

7. DR. THOMAS NEILL CREAM (UK) 4

In 1891 Cream poisoned a nineteen-year-old prostitute, Ellen Donworth, and was seen leaving her room in London a short while before she collapsed on the pavement of Waterloo Road. However, Cream covered his tracks by writing letters about his crime, signed "A. O'Brien," to the authorities and offering legal aid from "H.W. Bayne, Barrister." He then poisoned three more prostitutes, Matilda Clover, Emma Shrivell and Alice Marsh. This time, the police traced him from his letters and arrested him. He was hanged on November 15, 1892.

8=GRAHAM YOUNG (UK) 3

Young was sent to Broadmoor, the institution for the criminally insane, for nine years for poisoning his stepmother. After his release in 1971, he went to work for Hadlands, a photographic firm in Hertfordshire, but soon after he started there was a spate of mysterious illnesses which led to the death of two workers. When police came to the factory to question staff, Graham drew attention to himself by asking whether they had considered thallium poisoning as the cause of death. Graham was arrested, found guilty at St. Albans in July 1972 and sentenced to life imprisonment.

8=ANNA SCHONLEBEN (Germany) 3

Ex-prostitute-turned-housekeeper whose first job was working for a magistrate, Herr Glazer, who was separated from his wife and looked like a good catch. To remove any obstacle, Schonleben poisoned Frau Glazer. However, Glazer didn't want to marry her. Then she worked for Herr Grohmann, a lawyer, whom she poisoned when she heard he was going to marry someone else. Finally, when she was working for another lawyer, Herr Gebhard, she poisoned his wife and attempted to murder their baby and servants—all with arsenic. She eventually confessed and was beheaded in 1811.

10=PIERRE-DESIRE MOREAU (France) 2

Moreau, a Parisian herbal pharmacist, poisoned his first wife with copper sulphate three years after they married in order to marry a much more wealthy woman—to whom he also administered copper sulphate. Before dying, the second Mme. Moreau told friends that she believed she was being poisoned by her husband. Her corpse was examined, traces of copper sulphate were found and so the first Mme. Moreau's body was exhumed—with the same results. Moreau was found guilty of murder and guillotined in Paris on October 4, 1874.

10=CORDELIA BOTKIN (USA) 2

Botkin lured journalist John Presley Dunning away from his wife and into a life of whoring and gambling in San Francisco. Dunning was hired to report the Spanish-American war and Cordelia, worried that he might return to his wife, sent a parcel to Mrs. Dunning containing sweets and a lace handkerchief. Mrs. Dunning and her sister-in-law Mrs. Deane ate the sweets and both died that night. The sweets were traced back to Botkin, who had also bought the lace handkerchief. She was found guilty of murder on December 31, 1898 and sentenced to life imprisonment. She died at San Quentin in 1910.

10= SJEF RIJKE (Netherlands) 2

In January 1971, Sjef Rijke's fiancée Willy Maas died after suffering severe stomach pains. Rijke then proposed marriage to Mientje Manders—and she too died after severe stomach pains. Three weeks later he married Maria Haas who left him after only six weeks and told police later that she too had experienced stomach aches which had cleared up when she'd left. Rijke was arrested and explained that he enjoyed watching women suffer but that he hadn't wanted to kill them. He was

found to be legally sane, tried in January 1972 and given
two terms of life imprisonment.

Sixteen infamous murderers

1. CHARLES "LITTLE RED" STARKWEATHER and CARIL ANN FUGATE (USA)

Starkweather committed his first murder in 1957 at the
age of seventeen in Lincoln, Nebraska, when he shot a
gas station attendant in the head during a robbery. On
January 21, 1958, he killed the parents and younger
sister of his fourteen-year-old girlfriend, Caril Ann
Fugate. Charles and Caril Ann then sat down with some
sandwiches and watched TV. Neither Fugate's elder
sister nor her grandmother were allowed to come into
the house and they became suspicious and called the
police who entered the house to find it empty except for
the dead bodies. Over the next few days, Starkweather
and Fugate went on a killing spree, murdering seven
people before they were caught in Wyoming. Fugate was
sentenced to life imprisonment; Starkweather was electrocuted on June 24, 1959.

2. MICHAEL LUPO (aka "THE WOLF MAN") (UK)

Lupo, a thirty-three-year-old Chelsea fashion shop manager, caused widespread fear among London's homosexuals in 1986 when he murdered four gay men in a few
months. He was captured when one of his intended
victims, David Cole, got away and alerted police who
arrested Lupo in a gay bar. Lupo pleaded guilty to four
counts of murder and two of attempted murder on July
10, 1987 at the Old Bailey and was sentenced to life
imprisonment.

3. HERMANN WEBSTER MUDGETT (aka H.H. HOLMES) (USA)

In the early 1890s, Mudgett, now calling himself H.H.
Holmes, ran a Chicago hotel from which several guests
disappeared. When police searched the hotel they found
a death-house in which there were air-tight rooms with

gas inlets. In the basement, there were vats of acid and windowless rooms containing surgical instruments. Mudgett confessed to twenty-seven murders—although it is impossible to guarantee the accuracy of this figure—and was hanged on May 27, 1896.

4. CHARLES MANSON (USA)

On August 8, 1969, Manson, a schizophrenic sociopath whose followers treated him with messianic reverence, inspired a group of them, Susan Atkins, Linda Kasabian, Patricia Krenwinkel and "Tex" Watson, to break into the Beverly Hills home of the film director Roman Polanski, where they shot, stabbed and clubbed to death his pregnant wife Sharon Tate and four others. Two days later, Manson and a group of six "Family" members murdered supermarket owner Leno LaBianca and his wife Rosemary. The Family were arrested in December 1969 and several trials ensued involving the principal members, who had been charged with a series of murders. Manson, Atkins, Krenwinkel and van Houten were sentenced to death on April 19, 1971 for the Tate–LaBianca murders. Manson, of course, is still in jail, following the suspension of capital punishment in California. Kasabian and another Family member, Mary Brunner, were witnesses for the prosecution and were not charged.

It is interesting to note that Manson once auditioned (unsuccessfully) for The Monkees pop group. He—or, at least, members of his "Family"—might have performed an interesting rendition of *I'm a Believer* . . .

5. ALBERT DESALVO (aka "THE BOSTON STRANGLER," "THE GREEN MAN" and "THE MEASURING MAN") (USA)

In 1962, DeSalvo, thirty-three years old and recently released from prison, started a series of murders which, by the time of his capture in 1964, accounted for thirteen women between the ages of nineteen and eighty-five. He persuaded women to allow him into their Boston apartments by telling them that he was a representative of a modelling agency. He was arrested and, diagnosed as a schizophrenic, was sent to Boston State Hospital where he confessed to the murders. He was sentenced to life imprisonment but, on November 26, 1973, he was found stabbed through the heart at Walpole State Prison, Massachusetts.

6. DALE MERLE NELSON (Canada)

On the night of September 5, 1970 in West Creston, British Columbia, Nelson went on a rampage. He got into the home of Shirley Wasyk and killed her and her youngest daughter, Tracey. He then went to the home of Ray Phipps and killed him, his common-law wife, Isabelle St. Amand, and their four children. He was tried for murder in March 1971, found guilty and sentenced to life imprisonment.

7. ROBERT NIXON (aka "THE BRICK MORON") (USA)

In Chicago in 1936, Nixon used a brick to beat a cocktail waitress to death but left his fingerprints on it. He moved to Los Angeles, where he snatched purses and killed four more people with bricks. He was arrested in May 1938, soon after his last murder, and put on trial in Chicago, where he was electrocuted on June 15, 1939.

8. WILLIAM THOMAS ZEIGLER (USA)

On Christmas Eve 1975, Zeigler walked into his father's furniture shop in Orange County, Florida, and went on a shooting spree. The victims were his wife Eunice, her mother and father, and a customer. On December 29, Zeigler was charged with murder. He was found guilty on July 2, 1976 and sentenced to death.

9. CALVIN JACKSON (USA)

Between April 1973 and September 1974, nine elderly women were murdered at the Park Plaza Hotel in Manhattan, New York. Some were also raped and robbed. On September 12, 1974, the police received a phone call from a woman who had just found her employer murdered in the hotel. They also learned of a suspicious-looking man who had been seen climbing down a fire-escape with a TV set. Later that day, police arrested twenty-six-year-old Calvin Jackson. In May 1976, he was tried for the nine murders, found guilty and sentenced to life imprisonment. He will not be eligible for parole until the year 2030.

10. THE BENDER FAMILY (USA)

In 1872, the Bender family lived in Cherryvale, Kansas, in a long log cabin which was divided by a curtain. They would offer meals to travelers, who were seated with their backs to this curtain from behind which Pa Bender or his son would then attack the traveler who would be killed, robbed and buried. After the disappearance of Dr. William H. York, the Benders' cabin was searched and eleven graves were discovered. However, the Bender family disappeared and was never found.

11. NEVILLE GEORGE CLEVELY HEATH (UK)

On June 21, 1946, Margery Gardner's body was found in the Pembridge Court Hotel, in London. She had been strangled, beaten with a whip and her breasts had been bitten till they bled. A rough object had been forced into her vagina. Her killer, Heath, then went to Bournemouth where, posing as Group-Captain Rupert Brooke, on July 3 he met and murdered Doreen Marshall, whose body was found on July 8 lying in some bushes. Heath was tried for murder at the Old Bailey in September 1946, was convicted and was hanged on October 16, 1946 at Pentonville Prison. His last wish was for a whiskey—or, as he said, "in the circumstances, you might make that a double" . . .

12. DONALD NEILSON (aka "THE BLACK PANTHER") (UK)

Neilson abducted seventeen-year-old Lesley Whittle on January 13, 1975 from her home near Kidderminster, murdered her and hid her body in a nearby underground shaft. Her body was found on March 7, 1975.

Nine months later his house in Bradford was searched and police found guns and black hoods. He was tried in June 1975 for the murder of Lesley Whittle, and in July for the murders of three post-office workers during armed raids between 1971 and 1975. He was sentenced to twenty-one years in the Whittle case and to life for each of the other murders.

13. KENNETH ERSKINE (aka "THE STOCKWELL STRANGLER") (UK)

Erskine sodomized and strangled four elderly men and three elderly women over a three-month period in 1986. Police had great difficulty in tracing him as he kept moving from one empty flat to another. He was eventually caught in 1988 because he was still claiming unemployment benefit. On interviewing him, the police found him to be half-witted and, when he was put on trial, his arms had to be restrained to prevent him from masturbating in the court. He was sentenced to life imprisonment—with a recommendation from the judge that he serves a minimum of forty years.

14. SYLVESTRE MATUSCHKA (Hungary)

Having failed in two previous attempts to blow up trains, Matuschka succeeded on Saturday, September 13, 1931 at 11:30 p.m. in blowing up the Budapest–Ostend train: twenty-five people were killed and 120 were seriously injured. Eventually, after some more attempts to derail trains, Matuschka was arrested and told detectives that he "wrecked trains because I like to see people die. I like to hear them scream. I like to see them suffer." The sight of trains crashing also, apparently, brought him enormous sexual gratification. He was sentenced to death but this was commuted to life imprisonment in 1935 and some sources say that he escaped ten years later during all the confusion at the end of the Second World War.

15. JEFFREY DAHMER (USA)

Dahmer committed his first murder in 1978 when he picked up Stephen Hicks and invited him back to his house in Milwaukee, Wisconsin, for a few beers. When Stephen said he had to leave, Dahmer hit him over the head, stripped off his skin and smashed up the skeleton. Over the next years, he murdered at least fifteen more young men and butchered them. When, in July 1991, police broke into Dahmer's apartment, they found nine severed heads (two in the fridge), a pot full of male genitalia and bits of bodies scattered everywhere. In 1992, he was tried in Wisconsin, found guilty of murdering fifteen men and, later that year, he was tried in Ohio for murdering another man in that state. He was sent to jail for life, where he was murdered by another inmate.

16. THE KRAY TWINS (UK)

During the 1950s and 1960s, the Kray twins ruled the criminal world in London. In 1965 a case was brought against them, but the jury was so scared that the case collapsed. The only threat to the brothers came from the Richardson gang in South London. One of the gang, George Cornell, taunted Ronnie about his homosexuality. Bad move. Ronnie shot him between the eyes. In 1967, Reggie tried shooting Jack "The Hat" McVitie but the gun jammed and so he killed him with a carving knife. Eventually, the twins were brought to book for these murders and, in 1969, were sentenced to life imprisonment.

And let us not forget perhaps the most extraordinary *non*-murderer of all time in the UK. Oliver Styles, a watchmaker, was upset after falling out with his wife and so he went into a pub in Coventry late in May 1880 and shot a man in the hand, another man in the thigh and the landlady in the back. He then went home and shot his mother-in-law in the head, his wife in the back and their child in the arm. Amazingly, *all* his victims survived.

Nine significant murders

1. FRANZ MÜLLER (UK)

Müller, a German-born tailor, had the dubious distinction of committing the first ever murder on a British train, on the North London line on July 9, 1864, when he killed Thomas Briggs and took his gold watch and chain. However, by mistake, Müller got off the train wearing Briggs's hat while leaving behind his own which was traced to him. By this time, however, he had departed for New York. So Chief Inspector Tanner and Detective Sergeant George Clarke sailed for New York on a faster ship and arrived there before him. He was brought back, convicted of the murder at the Old Bailey in October 1864 and hanged on November 14, 1864.

2. KIM NEWELL (UK)

Newell fell in love with Eric Jones, an older man, when she was working as an assistant in a confectionery shop. She then took a job in a Berkshire hospital where she met Raymond Cook who was also older and married to a wealthy woman. On March 2, 1967, Cook took his wife out for a drink. On their way back home, they were stopped by Jones, who dragged Mrs. Cook out of the car and battered her to death. The car was then driven into a tree to make her death look like an accident. However, the felicitously named P.C. Sherlock realized that the "crash" had been far too gentle to be consistent with Mrs. Cook's injuries and Jones, Newell and Cook were arrested for murder. All three were found guilty and were sentenced to life imprisonment.

3. PIERRE VOIRBO (France)

In Paris in 1869, a craftsman named M. Bodasse disappeared. Later, his legs were found in a well in the Rue Princesse. Gustave Macé, a Parisian policeman, discovered that the house to which the well belonged was often visited by Voirbo, a tailor, who had known Bodasse. M. Macé visited Voirbo's apartment and found some stolen securities belonging to M. Bodasse. Convinced that Voirbo had murdered and dismembered the body in his apartment, M. Macé poured a jug of water over the tiled floor. Where the water gathered, he lifted the tiles and discovered coagulated blood.

Voirbo confessed that he had killed M. Bodasse when he had refused to lend him money. He was sent for trial, but killed himself before the case could come to court.

4. THE ZEBRA KILLINGS (USA)
Over a six-month period in 1973–4, fifteen men and women were shot dead in San Francisco. The murders became known as the Zebra Killings as all the victims where white and all the attackers black. The worst night was that of January 28, 1974 when five people were killed. Following the announcement of a reward, Anthony Harris confessed to his part in the killings and named his associates. On May 1, 1974, seven people were arrested of whom four, Larry Green, J.C. Simon, Jesse Cook and Manuel Moore, were sent for trial. After the longest trial in California's legal history, the jury found them guilty and each received a life sentence.

5. JOHN MERRETT (UK)
On March 17, 1926, Mrs. Bertha Merrett was shot by her son, John. Although he had cleverly made it look like suicide, and despite his insistence that she had taken her own life, John Merrett was tried at Edinburgh in February 1927 for both his mother's murder and forging her checks. A verdict of Not Proven was returned on the murder charge, but he spent eight months in jail for forgery. On his release, he took the name of Ronald John Chesney and married a woman named Vera. On February 3, 1954, he murdered her by drowning her. The police soon realized that Chesney and Merrett were the same person, but before they could arrest him, he committed suicide in a forest near Cologne, Germany, on February 16, 1954.

6. MARGARET DUNBAR (UK)
Christine Offord was a prostitute and dominatrix known to her clients as "Miss Whiplash." She was also a lesbian and had a relationship with Dunbar, another

prostitute. However, in 1986 when Christine Offord ended the relationship, Dunbar hired two men to rough her up. Unfortunately, they went too far and murdered her by crushing her throat with one of the iron bars in her dungeon. Dunbar was sent to prison for seven years.

7. ST. VALENTINE'S DAY MASSACRE (USA)

On St. Valentine's Day 1929, five members of "Bugs" Moran's gang—together with a dentist and a garage mechanic who just happened to be there—were lined up against the wall of a garage in North Clark Street on Chicago's North Side and machine-gunned to death. The gunmen were never caught but it is known for sure they were members of Al Capone's gang.

8. BRIAN TEVENDALE and SHEILA GARVIE (UK)

Maxwell Garvie, aged thirty, the erstwhile proprietor of a flying club in Aberdeen, decided to start a nudist colony and began a relationship with a woman whose brother, Brian Tevendale, aged twenty-two, had been having an affair with Garvie's wife, Sheila. On May 14, 1968 Maxwell Garvie was battered with a gunstock and then suffocated to death with a pillow. In November 1968, Sheila Garvie and Tevendale stood trial, were found guilty of murder and sentenced to life imprisonment.

9. MARTIN PANCOAST (USA)

Vicki Morgan was the mistress of the department store millionaire, Alfred Bloomingdale, who gave her a monthly allowance of $18,000. Ms. Morgan had a gay lodger, Pancoast, whom she decided to evict from her apartment. However, on July 6, 1982 he beat her to death. What made the case hit the headlines was the fact that Pancoast had video tapes of Alfred Bloomingdale and Vicki Morgan playing sexual games with distinguished people. Pancoast pleaded insanity, but on September 14, 1984 he was found guilty of murder and sentenced to twenty-six years in prison.

Five macabre murders

1. ALBERT EDWARD BURROWS (UK)

Married already, Burrows bigamously "married" another woman named Hannah Calladine in Nantwich, Cheshire. This was discovered and he was fined and imprisoned. However, to avoid paying two lots of maintenance, he murdered both wives (and their children) and threw the bodies down an air shaft. He was found guilty and hanged on August 8, 1923 in Nottingham.

2. RICHARD SPECK (USA)

On July 14, 1966, Speck entered the nurses' home at South Chicago Community Hospital and tied up all the nurses before taking Pamela Wilkeming into a room and killing her. Twenty minutes later he returned for his next victim and then again twenty minutes later for his next. Corazon Amurao escaped and the description she gave to the police led to Speck's arrest. In 1967, he was convicted of murder and eventually given a sentence of 400 to 1,200 years in jail.

3. MARTIN DUMOLLARD (France)

Martin Dumollard and his wife lured young girls back to their cottage near Lyons by pretending to be the owners of a local château and by promising them well-paid domestic work. In twelve years, Dumollard murdered ten girls while his wife kept their clothes for herself. He then buried his victims around the cottage or dumped them in the Rhône. The Dumollards were tried at Bourg in January 1862 and found guilty. He was hanged; she was sent to the galleys for life.

4. THE PORNOGRAPHIC CINEMA ARSON ATTACK (UK)

On Saturday, February 26, 1994, the Dream City gay cinema club, near Smithfield Market, London, went up in flames. Eight men died in the blaze and several more were seriously injured. A man was charged but, at the point of writing, no one has been convicted.

5. MARTHINUS ROSSOUW (South Africa)

Rossouw was employed by Baron Dieter von Schauroth as a bodyguard. In March 1961, the Baron was found dead, having apparently been robbed. Police inquiries showed that the Baron's marriage was unhappy, that he had recently insured his life heavily and that he was suspected of being involved in illegal diamond trading. Rossouw confessed to killing the baron but claimed that his unhappy victim had asked him to do it. Nevertheless, Rossouw was hanged in 1962.

Seven headless corpse murders

1. EDMUND KEMPER (USA)

In April 1973, Kemper confessed to being the killer who had mutilated and decapitated (and then tried to have sex with) six college students in Santa Cruz, California, in 1972. When the police went to Kemper's house, they found his mother's decapitated head on the mantelpiece. In the lounge, also decapitated, was her best friend. Kemper was convicted of eight counts of first-degree murder and, though he asked for the death penalty, was sentenced to life imprisonment.

2. REGINALD DUDLEY and ROBERT MAYNARD (UK)

Billy Moseley's head was discovered in a North London public toilet in 1977. His headless and handless body had been found in 1974 on Rainham Marshes. Dudley and Maynard had been convicted of Billy Moseley's murder in 1977, just before the discovery of their victim's head and it was believed at the time that the head was put where it could be found in order to cast doubt on the guilt of the convicted men.

3. JAMES GREENACRE (UK)

Greenacre murdered his fiancée, Hannah Brown, when he found out that she wasn't very wealthy. Over the Christmas week of 1836, Greenacre cut up her body and dumped various parts of it around London. Her torso was found at a building-site in the Edgware Road, her legs in a field in Brixton and her head was discovered blocking a canal lock-gate in Stepney. Greenacre was arrested, tried and hanged in 1837.

4. DANIEL GOOD (UK)
When, in 1842, Good found another mistress, he murdered his common-law wife, Jane Jones, and cut up her body. Her headless corpse was discovered in a pile of hay by a policeman who was questioning Good about a minor theft offense at the stables in Putney where he worked. Good was tried at the Old Bailey, found guilty and hanged at Newgate before one of the largest crowds ever assembled for an execution.

5. PATRICK BYRNE (UK)
On December 23, 1960, Margaret Brown was molested by a man in the YWCA hostel in Birmingham but he ran away when she screamed. The police launched a search for the intruder and found the headless body of Stephanie Baird with her head lying separately on a blood-stained bed. In 1961, Patrick Byrne, an Irish laborer, was arrested in Warrington and confessed to the murder. His conviction for murder was subsequently reduced to manslaughter on the grounds of insanity but he was still sentenced to life imprisonment.

6. JIM EDWARDSON (Victim) (UK)
In 1994, Jim Edwardson, a sixty-eight-year-old widower and grandfather from Corby, Northamptonshire, was stabbed more than forty times and beheaded. Detectives working on the investigation formed the impression that the murder was the result of a feud between two families. However, in March 1994 the police had still not found the victim's head.

7. CAPTAIN WILLIAM BUTT (Victim) (UK)
In 1938, Captain William Butt's decapitated and dismembered body was found in the River Severn near Cheltenham. The case has remained a mystery ever

since as there seemed to be no motive for the murder of the fifty-four-year-old retired army officer. One possibly salient factor was the fact that the body of Brian Sullivan, a twenty-seven-year-old dancer and gigolo friend of Captain Butt's, was found ten days before the discovery of Captain Butt's torso (although, he might very well have been murdered *after*—to keep him quiet). Police at the time also discovered the captain's coat in a garden at the home of Sullivan's mother and it was in this garden that David Gladstone dug up a skull in 1978. He called the police but they did nothing about it. In 1994, Mr. Gladstone, who had recently moved, decided to contact the police again and they have reopened the case—not least because it was, until recently, Gloucestershire's only unsolved murder.

It was this type of murder that prompted what is possibly the greatest headline ever to appear in the USA's mass-circulation tabloid the *New York Post*. The headline read: "Headless Body Found in Topless Bar" . . .

Ten gruesome sex murderers

1. RANDY KRAFT (USA)
Before being arrested in California in 1983, Kraft murdered a series of gay men. He would invite men—especially Marines—to have sex and, afterward, would murder and mutilate them. He was finally convicted in 1989 of sixteen murders and he was sentenced to die in the gas chamber at San Quentin.

2. AILEEN ("LEE") WUORNOS (aka "THE DAMSEL OF DEATH") (USA)
Wuornos lived in Florida's east coast in a run-down trailer with her girlfriend and made her money soliciting men. Half-clothed dead men with condoms beside them began to turn up along Highway I-52 and police concluded that it must be the work of a prostitute. When

they caught her in 1992, Wuornos confessed to six murders but gave details of seven. She was found to be insane and unfit to plead.

3. HERMAN DRENTH (USA)

In West Virginia in the 1920s, Drenth gassed women to death in his concrete blockhouse which he'd fitted with a plate-glass partition so that he could watch them die and experience sexual gratification. It is not known for certain how many women he murdered—although the figure could be as high as fifty. The only killings he admitted to were those of Mrs. Lemke, Mrs. Eicher and her children, but no bodies were found. He was convicted of murder and hanged on March 18, 1932.

4. DR. TEET HAERM and DR. ALLGEN LARS THOMAS (Sweden)

From 1984 onwards, three Swedish prostitutes were strangled and their bodies mutilated in and around Stockholm's red light district. Five other prostitutes disappeared—also presumed murdered. Haerm was arrested but denied involvement. However, the police found pictures in his house of his deceased wife with a cord around her neck. Meanwhile, Haerm's medical colleague, Allgen Thomas, accused of sexually molesting his four-year-old daughter, also confessed to helping Haerm murder the prostitutes. In September 1988, both Haerm and Thomas were convicted and sentenced to life imprisonment.

5. PETER KURTEN (aka "THE VAMPIRE OF DÜSSELDORF") (Germany)

From 1929 until 1931, Kurten murdered—in a variety of ways—as many as twenty-three people. In many instances, he drank his victims' blood—hence his nickname. He was eventually caught when a putative victim escaped and gave the police Kurten's address. At his trial in April 1931 Kurten was found guilty of nine murders and he was beheaded on July 2, 1931.

6. THOMAS PIPER (USA)

For three years from 1873 to 1876, young women and girls were raped and killed in Boston, Massachusetts, by a man who wore a black cape. At least five women were murdered (and many more raped) before Piper was witnessed taking a small girl into a Baptist church where she was later found raped and strangled. Piper confessed upon his arrest and, after his trial, was executed.

7. HEINRICH POMMERENCKE (aka "THE BEAST OF THE BLACK FOREST") (Germany)

Pommerencke started molesting girls in 1955 before "graduating" to rape and murder. He killed ten women before being arrested in Freiburg in 1960. He made a full confession in which he stated that watching pornographic films had made him "tense." He was tried in October 1960 and found guilty of ten murders with rape, twenty cases of rape and thirty-five assaults and burglaries. He was sent to jail for 140 years.

8. GORDON CUMMINS (UK)

In February 1942, Cummins, a young airman, murdered four women (including a prostitute) in London for his sexual gratification. On February 13, 1942, he offered Mrs. Greta Haywood a drink in a pub and then attacked her. He ran away when she started screaming but she was able to identify him to the police. Cummins was convicted of murder and hanged on June 25, 1942 at Wandsworth Prison.

9. MELVIN REES (aka "THE SEX BEAST") (USA)

On January 11, 1959, Carroll Jackson, his wife and their two daughters were stopped in their car in Apple Grove, Virginia, by Rees who murdered Carroll Jackson and his younger daughter on the spot but took Mrs. Jackson and the elder daughter to Fredericksburg, Virginia, where he raped and murdered them. Rees, who had killed before, was tried for these murders in Virginia and he was executed there in 1961.

10. MAGDALENA and ELEAZOR SOLIS (Mexico)

In 1963, prostitute Magdalena Solis and her hustler brother, Eleazor, posed as incarnations of gods to help persuade Mexican villagers of the authenticity of a bizarre cult which involved regular sex orgies. When Magdalena saw cult member Celina Salvana (whom she herself desired), having sex with a male cult member, she ordered her crucifixion and beat her unconscious while she hung on the cross. She was then killed and ritually burned. On June 13, 1963 the Solis brother and sister each received thirty-year sentences for this and for several other ritual murders.

The gentler sex? Ten women killers

1. EUGENE FALLENI (aka "HARRY LEO CRAWFORD") (Australia)

At the age of sixteen, Falleni passed herself off as a cabin boy on a ship where she had a relationship which, in 1899, resulted in her falling pregnant and giving birth to a girl named Josephine whom she gave to an Italian couple to look after. Falleni then adopted the alias of Harry Crawford and started to date Annie Birkett, an unwitting widowed cook and housemaid who fell in love with Falleni and agreed to use her life savings to buy a sweet shop in Balmain, a Sydney suburb. In 1914, Falleni and Annie Birkett "married" and Josephine came to live with them—all the time keeping her mother's secret. However, Annie Birkett found out so Falleni murdered her "wife." The murder wasn't discovered until 1919 when, confronted by the police, Falleni confessed her identity and was imprisoned for ten years.

2. BELLE GUNNESS (aka "THE FEMALE BLUE-BEARD") (USA)

On April 28, 1908, Gunness's farm near Laporte, Indiana, was burned down. Police suspected arson and so started inquiries which led them to unearth the remains of fourteen men. A farm worker revealed that Gunness, having lured the men through "lonely hearts ads," used to drug her victims and then murder them with a cleaver. There was a charred body found in Gunness's room but, judging by the size, it wasn't Gunness but probably a vagrant whom Gunness had placed there in order to fake her own death. Belle was never found.

3. HENRIETTE CAILLAUX (France)

The first wife of Joseph Caillaux, the French Finance Minister, was given some love-letters written by her husband to Henriette, who became his second wife. Meanwhile, Gaston Calmette, the editor of *Le Figaro,* started to criticize Caillaux for his pacifist stance. Caillaux, in turn, came up with some less than complimentary facts about Calmette who, on March 16, 1914 published one of Caillaux's love letters to Henriette on the front page of *Le Figaro.* Henriette went around to Calmette's office and killed him with five shots. However, she was found not guilty, after evidence was produced which implicated Calmette in anti-French propaganda.

4. MINNIE DEAN (New Zealand)

In 1895, Dean was sentenced to death in Invercargill for murdering children in her care. There was nothing much to "distinguish" her from hundreds of other murderers except for the amazing fact that Minnie Dean was the first and only woman ever to be hanged in New Zealand.

5. WINNIE RUTH JUDD (aka "THE TIGER WOMAN") (USA)

In 1931, Judd murdered her flatmates Agnes LeRoi and Helga Samuelson in Phoenix, Arizona. Then, with the help of her friend Carl Harris she put their bodies into two large trunks which she took with her on a train to Los Angeles. When asked to open one of her trunks, Judd disappeared. Police opened the trunks and found the bodies in various stages of dismemberment. Judd was tracked down, and at her trial in January 1932 was found guilty and sentenced to death, while Harris was charged with being an accessory. However, at Judd's retrial she was found to be insane and sent to the Arizona State Hospital for the Insane. She was paroled in 1971.

6. SHARON KINNE (USA)

On March 19, 1960, Kinne, aged nineteen, shot dead her husband James Kinne in their Kansas home. However, her story—that her two-year-old daughter, playing with a gun, had accidentally killed him—was believed. On May 27, 1960, Patricia Jones's body was found in a lovers' lane. Thanks to several coincidences, Kinne was charged with murder in September 1960 but was later acquitted. Then, after witnesses had come forward to say that Kinne had put out a $1,000 contract on her husband, she was found guilty of murdering her husband and sentenced to life imprisonment. The verdict was challenged and she was freed. In 1964, she went to Mexico City where she met Franciso Paredes Ordonez in a bar. She took him to her motel room and later shot him—along with the motel owner. Sharon Kinne was found guilty in October 1965 and sentenced to ten years in jail. She appealed, whereupon the courts added three years to her sentence.

7. NAN PATTERSON (USA)

On the morning of June 4, 1904, gambler Francis "Caesar" Young was in the back of a cab with his mistress, Nan Patterson, a twenty-two-year-old chorus girl in the Broadway musical, *Floradora*. She told him that she was pregnant and asked him to leave his wife and certainly not to take her on the European holiday that they were supposed to be going on. Patterson and Young had a row. A shot was fired inside the cab and "Caesar" Young was taken to hospital where he was dead on arrival with a bullet in his chest. Despite Patterson's claims that Young had committed suicide, she was arrested, charged with murder, tried and sent to prison but in a third trial in April 1905, the jury was deadlocked and she was discharged on a wave of popular sentiment. Her innocence in *law* is undoubted; her innocence in *fact* can be judged by her inclusion here . . .

8. SUSAN NEWELL (UK)

On June 23, 1923 Newell was seen pushing a handcart with a bundle in it along a Glasgow street. The police inspected the bundle and found it to be the body of John Johnston, a thirteen-year-old newspaper seller. Newell was found guilty of his murder and was hanged at Glasgow's Duke Street Prison on October 10, 1923.

9. RUTH ELLIS (UK)

The name of Ruth Ellis will never be forgotten as she was the last woman to be executed in Britain—and, indeed, her execution gave a huge fillip to the whole abolition cause. In 1954 Ellis, a good-time girl who made the tragic mistake of having sex across the class system, was seeing both David Blakely and Desmond Cussen which provoked violent arguments between Blakely and Ellis. On April 6, 1955, Blakely told Ellis that he was going to Hampstead to see someone about a car. Believing that he was going to meet another woman, Ellis followed him. On April 10, Ellis went to the Magdala Pub in Hampstead and shot Blakely when he came out. Her trial began on June 20, 1955, she was found guilty and was hanged on July 13, 1955 at Holloway Women's Prison in London.

10. LOUISA MERRIFIELD (UK)

In 1953, Merrifield and her third husband, Alfred, became live-in housekeepers to Mrs. Sarah Ann Ricketts in her Blackpool bungalow. Merrifield started boasting to people that she had worked for a woman who had died and left her a bungalow worth £3,000. When asked who this woman was, she said "She's not dead yet, but she soon will be." Mrs. Ricketts died on April 14, 1953 from phosphorus poisoning. The Merrifields were tried for murder in July 1953. Louisa was hanged on September 18, 1953. Her husband was sent to jail for being an accomplice but was eventually released.

Eight biblical homicides

1. CAIN

The first son of Adam and Eve, Cain was a farmer who brought as an offering to God a gift of his harvested crops. The second son, Cain's brother Abel, was a shepherd and brought as an offering a sacrificial lamb. God accepted Abel's offering but refused Cain's:

> And it came to pass, when they were in the field, that Cain rose up against Abel his brother, and slew him. And the Lord said unto Cain, Where is Abel thy brother? And he said, I know not: Am I my brother's keeper? And he said, What hast thou done? The voice of thy brother's blood crieth unto me from the ground . . . *(Genesis 4; 8-10)*

2. EHUD

A Benjamite, son of Gera and one of the earliest Judges of Israel (and, for those who collect such facts, "left-handed"), Ehud was chosen by God to end the servitude of the Israelites:

> But Ehud made him a dagger which had two edges, of a cubit length; and he did gird it under his raiment upon his right thigh. And he brought a present unto Eglon King of Moab; and Eglon was a very fat man . . . And Ehud came unto him; and he was sitting in a summer parlor, which he had for himself alone. And Ehud said, I have a message from God unto thee. And he arose out of his seat. And Ehud put forth his left hand, and took the dagger from his right thigh, and thrust it in his belly. And the haft also went in after the blade; and the fat closed upon the blade, so that he could not draw the dagger out of his belly; and the dirt came out. Then Ehud went forth through the porch, and shut the doors

of the parlor upon him, and locked them. *(Judges 3; 16–23)*

3. DAVID

One of the best known and best loved stories of the Bible, and perhaps its greatest metaphor for the triumph of right over wrong. The Philistine armies were ranged against the Israelites. Goliath of Gath, the Philistines' champion, was challenged by David who, having refused armor, went forth to do battle with the giant, armed with just five stones and a sling:

> And it came to pass, when the Philistine arose, and came and drew nigh to meet David, that David hasted, and ran toward the army to meet the Philistine. And David put his hand in his bag, and took thence a stone, and slang it, and smote the Philistine in his forehead, that the stone sunk into his forehead; and he fell upon his face to the earth. So David prevailed over the Philistine with a sling and with a stone, and smote the Philistine, and slew him. But there was no sword in the hand of David. Therefore David ran, and stood upon the Philistine, and took his sword, and drew it out of the sheath thereof, and slew him, and cut off his head therewith. And when the Philistines saw their champion was dead, they fled. *(1 Samuel 17; 48–51)*

4. HAZAEL

Senior officer in the court of King Ben-hadad of Syria, Hazael took the ailing king's greetings to Elisha, who prophesied that Ben-hadad would die and that Hazael would be king over Syria. Hazael was rather surprised at this because he thought he was the only one who knew of his plan to suffocate the sovereign:

> And it came to pass on the morrow, that he took a thick cloth and dipped it in water and spread it on his face, so that he died: and Hazael reigned in his stead. *(2 Kings 8; 15)*

5. HEROD ANTIPAS (HEROD THE GREAT)

At the time of Christ's birth Herod, King of Judaea, learned of the rumor of the child who was destined to become "King of the Jews" and, fearing for his own power, ordered the "Massacre of the Innocents":

> Then Herod, when he saw he was mocked of the wise men, was exceeding wroth, and sent forth and slew all the children that were in Bethlehem, and in all the coasts thereof, from two years old and under, according to the time which he had diligently inquired of the wise men. *(Matthew 2; 16)*

The Holy Family, forewarned by an angel, fled to safety in Egypt.

6. JOAB

David's most successful general both before and after the death of Saul. When David made peace with Saul's people, Joab enticed Abner (who had killed Joab's brother Asahel on the field of battle at Gibeon) back to David's headquarters and slew him:

> And when Abner was returned to Hebron, Joab took him aside at the gate to speak with him quietly, and smote him there under the fifth rib, that he died for the blood of Asahel, his brother. *(2 Samuel 3; 27)*

He also killed Absalom, son of David. Despite their kinship Absalom raised an army in order to usurp his father, but was defeated by David's army and met his own death in a rather dramatic fashion. Riding his mule under an oak tree, Absalom's hair became entangled in the branches and his mount carried on, leaving the unfortunate man dangling:

> Then, said Joab, I may not tarry thus with thee. And he took three darts in his hand, and thrust them through the heart of Absalom, while he was yet alive in the midst of the oak. And ten young men that bore Joab's

armor compassed about and smote Absalom and slew him. *(2 Samuel 18; 14–15)*

A prolific murderer, Joab also killed Amasa:

And Joab said to Amasa, art thou in health my brother? And Joab took Amasa by the beard with the right hand to kiss him. But Amasa took no heed to the sword that was in Joab's hand: so he smote him therewith in the fifth rib, and shed out his bowels to the ground and struck him not again, and he died. *(2 Samuel 20; 9–10)*

7. JUDITH

The Assyrian army had laid siege to the Jewish city of Bethulia, when Judith, a rich and beautiful widow, hatched a plan to save the inhabitants. Having "dressed herself so as to catch the eye of any man who might see her," she made her way, with a servant, into the Assyrian camp. On the pretense that she had deserted her people, she gained the confidence of the general Holofernes; indeed, he began to be quite enamored of Judith and held a huge banquet in her honor, hoping afterward to seduce her. However, Holofernes had consumed so much liquor that when they were alone in his tent he fell into a drunken slumber. This was Judith's big opportunity; she seized the general's sword and, with two blows, severed his head and took it back to Bethulia. The death of their commander threw the Assyrians into such disarray that they fled.

8. PHINEHAS

When the people of Israel began to worship Baal and "to commit whoredom with the daughters of Moab," God inflicted a plague on the Israelites of the Sinai Desert region. In a symbolic murder, Phinehas slew Zimri, "the man of Israel," and his Midianitish prostitute called Cozbin, appeasing God's wrath:

And behold one of the children of Israel came and brought unto his brethren a Midianitish woman in the sight of Moses, and in the sight of all the congregation of the children of Israel who were weeping before the door of the tabernacle of the congregation. And when Phinehas, the son of Eleazar, the son of Aaron the priest, saw it, he rose up from among the congregation, and took a javelin in his hand. And he went after the man of Israel into the tent and thrust both of them through, the man of Israel and the woman through her belly. So the plague was stayed from the children of Israel. *(Numbers 25; 6–8)*

Two men who instigated mass suicides

1. JIM JONES (Guyana)

The "Reverend" Jim Jones founded the commune–colony of Jonestown in Guyana and about 1,000 of his followers moved there from San Francisco. Then on November 14, 1978, Congressman Leo Ryan visited the colony on a fact-finding mission. Just as he was about to leave—with three journalists and one of Jones's followers—some of the remaining followers opened fire and killed them all. Realizing that the game was up, Jones put his suicide plan into operation. Security guards rounded up his 913 followers and, to the sound of messages on the loudspeakers saying, "We're going to meet again in another place," they all took cyanide. In all, nearly 1,000 people killed themselves and Jim Jones was found dead with a bullet in his head.

2. DAVID KORESH (USA)

Koresh led a cult religious commune in Waco, Texas. On the morning of Sunday, February 28, 1993, federal agents and officials attached to the Bureau of Alcohol, Tobacco and Firearms turned up with a warrant to arrest Koresh for breaches of gun-control law. Backed up by three helicopters, they tried storming Koresh's commune but came up against heavy automatic gunfire which killed four agents and injured sixteen others. A siege then started and, after three weeks, people began to leave the cult headquarters. Then on April 19 the FBI told David Koresh that this was his last chance to surrender. At the same time an armored combat vehicle moved up to the gates of the buildings. As it did so, gunfire was heard from inside the building and then a fire broke out. This was the start of the mass suicide. Many people died—around eighty-eight—but it isn't clear how many took their own lives and how many may have been murdered by Koresh and other cult members.

Ten unsolved murders

1. JACK THE RIPPER (UK)
This name was given to an unknown killer(s) who stabbed to death five (or more) prostitutes in the White-chapel area of London in 1888.

2. THE ZODIAC KILLER (USA)
American serial killer nicknamed "Zodiac" who claimed to have murdered 37 people between 1968 and 1974 (*see* The Ten Most Prolific Serial Killers in the USA).

3. LIZZIE BORDEN (USA)
In a famous case, thirty-two-year-old Lizzie Borden was accused of killing her father and stepmother with an axe on August 4, 1892 in Fall River, Massachusetts. All the evidence was against her and yet she was found not guilty. Which begs the question: who did it?

4. THE NEW ORLEANS AXE MAN (USA)
In 1918–19, at least eight people were murdered with a hatchet. These murders stopped suddenly in 1919, and nothing much is known of the killer.

5. THE CLEVELAND TORSO KILLER (USA)
From 1933 to 1937, this unknown murderer struck several times. He often killed two people at a time, cut up their bodies and kept their heads. The killer, who had a car, was probably someone with a house in a quiet street and may also have been a homosexual, but that is all that is known about him.

6. THE BRIGHTON TRUNK MURDER (UK)
On June 17, 1934, the torso of a woman was found in a trunk at Brighton train station. Meanwhile, her legs were found in another suitcase at King's Cross station. The girl was in her middle twenties, about three months pregnant, and was—if her sun-bleached hair was anything to go by—upper class and yet she was never identified. Nor was her murderer ever found.

7. THE BLACK DAHLIA MURDER (USA)
Elizabeth Short, an actress known as the Black Dahlia, was found murdered in Los Angeles in January 1947. Her body had been cut in two at the waist. Her murderer sent the police his victim's address book and birth certificate—with one page of the address book torn out. The killer was never found.

8. THE WALLACE CASE (UK)
On January 19, 1931, there was a mysterious phone call to the Liverpool Central Chess Club, asking William Herbert Wallace (who hadn't yet arrived) to go and see a man in Mossley Hill the following evening. While Wallace was out trying to find this address—which, in fact, didn't exist—his wife was brutally murdered. Wallace was tried, found guilty and sentenced to death. However, on appeal, his conviction was overturned and he was freed. So who did kill Mrs. Wallace?

9. THE THAMES NUDES MURDERS (UK)
These began in February 1964, when a woman's body was washed up by Hammersmith Bridge. In April, another appeared at Dukes Meadow, Chiswick. The police located the murderer's secret lair in West Acton where they found the body of Bridie O'Hara. However, the police closed the case when one of their last suspects, a security guard, committed suicide. Nevertheless, these murders must still be classified as unsolved.

10. SUZY LAMPLUGH (UK)
Estate agent Suzy Lamplugh left her office in Fulham at lunchtime on July 28, 1986 to show a "Mr. Kipper" a

house. A huge search started when she didn't return—although her car was found a mile away from the house. Neither Suzy Lamplugh nor her abductor were found, so perhaps this is an unsolved "case" rather than an unsolved "murder." It is interesting to note that, sometime later, there was a convicted rapist who was nicknamed "Mr. Kipper" by his fellow prisoners because of his love of kipper ties.

Seven people who have killed in their sleep

1. WILLS EUGENE BOSHEARS (UK)
In 1961, Wills Boshears was serving with the US Air Force at Wethersfield in England when he invited a twenty-year-old girl named Jean Constable to his flat on New Year's Eve. Boshears passed out and when he woke up he found himself on top of the strangled body of Jean Constable.

2. WASYL GNYPIUK (UK)
In 1960, Gnypiuk broke into his British landlady's house, helped himself to her drink and went to sleep. He had a nightmare and woke up to find his landlady dead. He tried getting rid of the body, and stole some money from her house. His story was not believed and he was hanged.

3. WILLIAM POLLARD (USA)
One night in 1946, Pollard from Little Rock, Arkansas, had a dream in which he was fighting a stranger. His wife's screams woke him up and he realized that he had killed her.

4. JO ANN KIGER (USA)
During a nightmare one night in 1943, sixteen-year-old Jo Ann Kiger from Kentucky shot at a human monster that wanted to murder her family. She woke up to find that she had in fact killed her father and her younger brother. Her mother, who was shot in the hip but survived, testified at the trial that Jo Ann had always been a sleepwalker.

5. ROBERT LEDRU (France)

In 1888, Ledru, a Parisian cop, was asked to investigate the murder of a businessman who had been shot at night on a beach in Le Havre where Ledru had been resting after some hard work. He found the following clues: a bullet from a Luger, and some footprints which indicated that the murderer had been wearing socks and that the right foot lacked a toe. Ledru himself had a toe missing on his right foot and his socks had been damp that morning. He checked his own Luger, found a bullet was missing and, realizing that he must have committed the crime while sleepwalking, turned himself in.

6. SIMON FRASER (UK)

In 1878 in Glasgow, Fraser dreamed of "a white beast flying through the floor," so he grabbed it and fought with it. He woke up and realized with horror that he had killed his son.

7. ESTHER GRIGGS (UK)

In 1859 in London, Griggs dreamed that her house was on fire and so threw her baby out of the window into the street—killing it. The arrival of the police prevented her from throwing her two other children.

In the conservatory with the lead piping . . . The ten most common murder methods in England and Wales

Male victims			*Female victims*		
1.	Sharp instrument	40%	1.	Strangulation	25%
2.	Hitting, kicking, etc.	24%	2.	Sharp instrument	24%
3.	Shooting	9%	3.	Hitting, kicking, etc.	15%
4.	Blunt instrument	8%	4.	Blunt instrument	10%
5.	Strangulation	7%	5.	Burning	9%
6=	Burning	3%	6.	Shooting	6%
6=	Poison or drugs	3%	7.	Poison or drugs	4%

Male victims (Cont'd)

6= Motor vehicle 3%
6= Other 3%

Female victims (Cont'd)

8. Motor vehicle 3%
9= Drowning 2%
9= Other 2%

The commonest relationships of homicide victims to their killers in the UK

Male victims

1. Friend or acquaintance 31%
2. Stranger 28%
3. Unknown 11%
4= Son or daughter 7%
4= Parent 7%
6= Spouse or cohabitant (inc. ex-) 4%
6= Other family 4%
6= Lover or former lover 4%
6= Other associate 4%
10. Official on duty (e.g. police or prison officer) 2%

Female victims

1. Spouse or cohabitant (inc. ex-) 36%
2= Son or daughter 15%
2= Friend or acquaintance 15%
4. Stranger 13%
5. Unknown 8%
6. Lover or former lover 5%
7. Parent 3%
8. Other family 2%
9= Other associate 1%
9= Official on duty (e.g. police or prison officer) 1%

The figures don't add up to 100% because they've been rounded up.

Two striking things are: 1) just how many victims know their killers and 2) the difference in the number of men and women killed by their spouses/cohabitants.

––––––––––

"Murder is always a mistake: one should never do anything that one cannot talk about after dinner."

OSCAR WILDE

The relationship of homicide victims to their killers in the USA

Victims		*Of 22,540 total:*
1.	Unknown relationship	8,818
2.	Acquaintance	6,102
3.	Stranger	3,053
4.	Wife	913
5.	Friend	843
6.	Girlfriend	519
7.	Other family	393
8.	Husband	383
9.	Son	325
10.	Boyfriend	240
11.	Daughter	235
12.	Neighbor	217
13.	Father	169
14.	Brother	167
15.	Mother	121
16.	Sister	42

Of these 22,540 homicide victims, 17,576 were male, 4,936 were female and twenty-eight were, apparently, "unknown."

There are many more—both in terms of numbers and percentage—homicides committed by strangers in the USA than there are in the UK.

Nine cases of murder for the insurance money

1. JOHN GILBERT GRAHAM (USA)

One of the most cynical insurance murderers of modern times, Jack Graham took out a policy on his mother's life in the sum of $37,000 (he also stood to inherit a further $150,000 when she died) and then planted dynamite in her suitcase as she set off on one of her periodic trips from Denver to Alaska to visit her daughter. United Airlines flight 629 was blown out of the sky just ten minutes after take-off on November 1, 1955; all forty-four passengers and crew were killed. Graham, who had nurtured a hatred of his mother ever since she placed him in an orphanage for the first eight years of his life, readily confessed and was sent to the gas chamber at Colorado Penitentiary in January 1957.

2. WILLIAM YOUNGMAN (UK)

In 1860 William Youngman insured his fiancée's life for £100—a considerable sum at the time—and when she came to London to visit with his family, William killed her. Unfortunately his mother saw what had happened, so she too had to die; and just for good measure William slew his two younger brothers as well. William Youngman subsequently paid for his crimes at the end of the hangman's rope.

3. EDMOND DE LA POMMERAIS (France)

In 1859 de la Pommerais was in medical practice in Paris—a lively little business, but sadly too modest to support the extravagant lifestyle to which he felt entitled. In 1861 Edmond married a Mademoiselle Duibiczy, whose ample dowry seemed so attractive. Another advantage was that her mother was also rich, and when she died suddenly it was Edmond and his wife who inherited. Inherited enough for de la Pommerais to take a mistress who, being as crooked as Edmond himself, entered into an elaborate insurance swindle. A sizeable insurance policy was taken out in the name of Séraphine de Pauw—that was the lady's name—and the plan was that she should feign a fatal illness to scare the insurance company into paying an annuity in order to be able to cancel the policy. All went according to plan, except that Madame really did die; which, far from encouraging the insurance company to pay up, led them to investigate this unexpected death. The result of an autopsy was that Séraphine de Pauw had died from a massive intake of digitalis. Edmond de la Pommerais was tried for the double murder of his mistress and his mother-in-law: he was found guilty of the former, but not guilty of the latter. Despite pleas for clemency to Emperor Napoleon III himself, de la Pommerais lost his head to Madame Guillotine in 1864.

4. EUGENE MARIE CHANTRELLE (UK)

A French national, Chantrelle arrived in England, via America, in 1862, and thence removed to Edinburgh where he enjoyed some distinction as a teacher of his native language. It was in this capacity that he met fifteen-year-old Elizabeth Dyer, made her pregnant and, on August 11, 1868, married her. An addiction to drink and women soon eroded what money Chantrelle could earn, and his general demeanor was rapidly rendering him unemployable. In October 1877, with the specter of ruin shadowing him, Chantrelle insured his wife's life for £1,000. On New Year's Day 1878 Elizabeth fell ill and was admitted to the Royal Infirmary, where she died. Meanwhile, Eugene Chantrelle had been trying to persuade the maid who had found Elizabeth that there was a gas leak—which might have explained his poor wife's untimely demise. However, an above-averagely bright physician, Dr. Maclaglan, had been analyzing samples of vomit scraped from Mrs. Chantrelle's nightdress and found it to contain an uncommonly large quantity of opium. Eugene Chantrelle was tried for the murder of his wife by opium poisoning, found guilty and hanged. In fact Chantrelle was the first prisoner to be executed in Edinburgh after the passing of the Capital Punishment Amendment Act of 1868, making execution within the walls of the prison mandatory.

5. THE BOLBER-PETRILLO-FAVATO GANG (USA)

In 1932 Dr. Morris Bolber decided to profit a little more grandly from the medical practice he ran among the poor Italian immigrants of Philadelphia. And so, with the assistance of the Petrillo brothers, Paul and Herman, he set about defrauding the insurance companies. It worked like this: Paul Petrillo would pose as a number of fictitious Italian gentlefolk and take out insurance policies on Bolber's less healthy patients. When these patients "unfortunately" died, Petrillo would collect. When a new recruit joined the gang—Carino Favato, the "Philadelphia Witch"—things became more straightforward. No more waiting for people to die: they were simply whacked over the head with a canvas bag filled with wet sand and died of "cerebral hemorrhage." Over five years it is probable that the gang eliminated thirty victims to their gain. And it might have gone on, had not the talkative Herman Petrillo confided to an ex-convict friend what a good scheme he was in. Of course he did not know that his friend was also a police informer. Paul and Herman Petrillo were sentenced to death and executed; Bolber and Favato were imprisoned for life.

6. MARTHA MAREK (Austria)

Martha Marek was, by any standard of wickedness, in a class of her own. She worked up to the "ultimate crime" via a most grotesque insurance fraud. Martha had taken out a policy on her husband's safety against accident; she then chopped away at one of his legs with an axe (with his agreement, of course) and put in a claim. The surgeon treating Emil Marek's leg injuries was suspicious because the angles of the cuts were not entirely consistent with his account of the story, and the couple were charged with fraud. Martha later tried to bribe the hospital staff, which did nothing other than earn her a longer prison sentence. On her release, Martha went on to poison her husband, her children, the old lady to whom she had become companion and a couple of lodgers—all of whose lives had been comfortably insured in Martha's favor. It could only end in sadness: Martha Marek's luck ran out and she was beheaded in December 1938—with an axe.

7. FREDERICK SMALL (USA)

Small was hanged in the Concord State Prison, New Hampshire, on January 15, 1918. His crime? He killed his wife to collect the $20,000 life insurance.

8. WILLIAM UDDERZOOK (USA)

It was in February 1873 that a cottage in Baltimore burned down. The owner of the dwelling was William E.

Udderzook; the man who died in the blaze was Winfield Scott Goss, his brother-in-law. Despite the fact that the coroner attributed the blaze to a faulty kerosene lamp, the insurance company refused to pay out on Goss's $25,000 policy, claiming that as the corpse was unrecognizable it may not have been Goss. How right they were. Four months later William Udderzook was seen in the company of another man who subsequently disappeared—in fact he vanished at about the same time that a farmer came across a shallow grave containing the body of a man, later identified as Winfield Goss. It transpired that, having faked his own death, Goss threatened to expose the scheme and Udderzook's part in it; which is why he had to die. Udderzook was tried and convicted, and in November 1874 he was executed. His last wish was to be buried close to Goss—so that "our spirits may mingle together."

9. GEORGE JOSEPH SMITH (aka "THE BRIDES IN THE BATH MURDERER") (UK)

George Smith dispatched three unwanted spouses to a watery grave, netting, it is estimated, some £3,800 in insurance claims. He also plundered the worldly goods of a further six bigamous "wives" who, though they lost their savings, were fortunate to escape with their lives. Smith was a totally amoral killer, whose only motive was personal profit; and, despite the services of the legendary Edward Marshall Hall as his defense counsel, a jury found him guilty and a judge sentenced him to death. Friday the thirteenth was a very unlucky day for George Joseph Smith—on that date in August 1915 they hanged him at Maidstone Prison.

Twelve cases of child murder

It almost seems absurd to compile such a list while omitting men like Hitler and Pol Pot—and, yet, the thought of the death of millions of children is (thankfully) too abstract to contemplate which renders the individual cases detailed below all the more gruesome.

After all, wasn't it Stalin who said: "A single death is a tragedy; a million deaths are a statistic." He should know.

1. MYRA HINDLEY and IAN BRADY (UK)
From 1963 till 1965, Myra Hindley and Ian Brady carried out a series of horrendous murders—known as "The Moors Murders"—during which they even tape-recorded their victims' screams. The two met as fellow office workers at a Manchester chemicals' firm. Brady, a former juvenile delinquent, was obsessed with sadism and Nazism. Hindley became obsessed with Brady. Together, they murdered Pauline Reade (sixteen), John Kilbride (twelve), Keith Bennett (twelve), Lesley Ann Downey (ten) and Edward Evans (seventeen). Brady and Hindley were caught after David Smith, Hindley's brother-in-law, witnessed the killing of Edward Evans and called the police. Brady and Hindley were convicted on May 6, 1966 and sent to jail for life. Let us hope that for once life means life.

2. HOLY CHILD ORPHANAGE CASE (China)
In 1951, five French-Canadian Catholic nuns, Germaine Gravel, Elizabeth Lemire, Germaine Tanguay, Antoinette Couvrette and Imelda Lapierre, were arrested for murder. Children had been brought regularly to the orphanage in Canton for medical treatment but from October 1950 to February 1951, 2,116 died while only 135 survived. The nuns were also charged with illegally selling the babies who survived. All five nuns were found guilty. Couvrette and Gravel were each sentenced to five years in jail; the other three were deported.

3. FREDERICK BAKER (UK)
On a hot August day in 1867, Baker, a solicitor's clerk, was walking through fields in a Hampshire village when he came across three small girls playing. He took seven-year-old Fanny Adams and battered her to death in a nearby hopfield before mutilating her body. He then returned to his office and wrote in his diary "Killed a

young girl. It was fine and hot." Her dismembered
remains were found by villagers. Baker, who had no
explanation for the bloodstains on his shirtcuffs, was
tried and hanged at Winchester.

4. WILLIAM GOULDSTONE (UK)

Mr. and Mrs. Gouldstone of Walthamstow, London
already had three sons when, in August 1883, Mrs.
Gouldstone gave birth to twins. Her husband couldn't
bear the thought of supporting five children so he
murdered the week-old twins with a hammer and
drowned the other three children in a cistern containing
just fourteen inches of water.

5. BEVERLEY ALLITT (UK)

On February 21, 1991, Nurse Beverley Allitt killed her
first victim, baby Liam Taylor, soon after starting work
at Grantham and Kesteven General Hospital in Nottinghamshire. On March 5, eleven-year-old Tim Hard-
wick died and epilepsy was given as the cause of death.
On April 5, nine-week-old Becky Phillips died at home
after being discharged from the hospital. Her parents
were so grateful for Allitt's support that they made her
godmother to Becky's twin sister, Katie. When Katie
was in hospital, Beverley Allitt caused her permanent
brain damage. There were several non-fatal attacks on
other children, before the blood of Paul Crampton, a
five-month-old who had suffered three near-fatal attacks
in March, was analyzed and found to contain a massive
overdose of insulin. Allitt was arrested and charged. In
May 1993 she was found guilty of murder, attempted
murder and grievous bodily harm. She was diagnosed as
having the extreme attention-seeking disorder Mun-
chausen Syndrome by Proxy and sent to Rampton, a
secure mental institution.

6. ESTHER HIBNER (UK)

In 1829, Esther Hibner ran an embroidery business
in Camden Town, London, using orphans from the

workhouse as cheap labor. Frances Colpitts, a little girl employed by her, was taken away from the business by her grandmother when she was discovered suffering from starvation and abscesses on the lungs. The girl died within days. Hibner was found guilty of causing the death of the child by starvation and was executed.

7. MARYBETH ROE TINNING (USA)

In New York from 1972 to 1985, Tinning murdered nine of her children. In 1978, after six of their children had died, the Tinnings applied to the state adoption service and were in the process of adopting thirty-one-month-old Michael when he died of pneumonia. Jonathan died in February 1980 and then Tami Lynne in December 1985. Suspicion fell on Marybeth Roe Tinning who confessed to the police, "I smothered them each with a pillow because I'm not a good mother . . ." On July 17, 1987 she was found guilty (her husband was not charged as he knew nothing of his wife's actions) and sentenced to twenty-years-to-life.

8. JEANNE WEBER (France)

On March 2, 1905, a child left in Weber's care died. Within a month, three more children died, all with marks on their throats. Then, while relatives were visiting two weeks later, Weber's nephew died. Weber was charged with murder but a brilliant lawyer convinced the jury that the children had died of various medical problems and she was acquitted. She left Paris and resurfaced in the village of Chambon as Madame Mouliner; living with a man called Bavouzet, who had three children. One of his sons died but, once again, the same defense team got Jeanne acquitted. She returned to Paris as Madame Bouchery, where she killed another boy. She was arrested and this time found guilty. She was declared insane and sent to a mental hospital, where she died in 1910 of injuries sustained trying to strangle herself.

9. RAYMOND MORRIS (aka "THE A34 MURDERER") (UK)

Seven-year-old Christine Ann Darby was kidnapped in Coronation Street, Walsall, on August 19, 1967 by a man driving a gray car. She was suffocated and sexually assaulted. On November 4, 1968 a man tried to entice a ten-year-old girl into his car, but he drove off when he realized a woman was watching him. She took down his car registration number and the car was traced to Morris's home where police discovered pornographic photographs. He was found guilty and sentenced to life imprisonment in February 1969.

10. ARTHUR ALBERT JONES (UK)

In December 1960, twelve-year-old Brenda Nash was found murdered in some Hampshire woods. An assault on another girl had taken place in the same area a couple of months before but the girl had been released unharmed. The police used her description to track down Jones but they could only charge him on the assault. He was tried in March 1961 and sentenced to fourteen years. However, while he was in jail, Jones confessed and he was successfully charged with Brenda Nash's murder and sentenced to life imprisonment.

11. LOUISE MASSET (UK)

In 1899, the body of a three-year-old boy was found, still warm, in the women's toilets at a London train station. The boy was identified as Manfred Louis Masset. His mother told the police that she had taken on a new lover and had therefore put her son in the care of a "Mrs. Browning." However, this woman could not be traced. Louise Masset was found guilty of the child's murder and was hanged at Newgate on January 9, 1900.

12. ROBERT BLACK (UK)

In May 1994 Black, who was born near Edinburgh, Scotland, in 1947, received ten life sentences for the murder of three young girls between 1982 and 1986. Van driver Black was caught in July 1990 after abduct-

ing and sexually assaulting a six-year-old girl in the
Borders village of Stow, for which he was already
serving a life sentence when convicted of the murders of
Susan Maxwell (aged eleven), Caroline Hogg (five) and
Sarah Harper (ten). The biggest criminal investigation
in British legal history is to be followed by a Europe-
wide inquiry into a series of disappearances and murders involving children in Britain and on the continent.

Nine cases of children who killed

1. MARY FLORA BELL (UK)

On May 25, 1968, four-year-old Martin Brown's body
was found in a derelict house in Scotswood, Newcastle.
The next day, a nursery school was broken into and a
note in a child's handwriting, "We did murder Martin
Brown," was left there. Then, on July 31 three-year-old
Brian Howe went missing. Eleven-year-old Mary Bell
was arrested, found guilty on two counts of manslaughter and sentenced to life detention. She was released in
1980.

2. NATHAN LEOPOLD and RICHARD LOEB (USA)

In a famous case which inspired the classic Hitchcock
film, *Rope,* two Americans from wealthy Chicago families, Leopold, aged eighteen, and Loeb, aged nineteen,
kidnapped fourteen-year-old Bobby Franks, gagged him
and killed him with four blows of a chisel to the head.
They then left him in their unlocked rental car and
returned later to pour hydrochloric acid over his face to
impede identification. The motive for this murder was
the desire of Leopold and Loeb to demonstrate their
supposed superiority—over their victim, the police and,
indeed, society in general. In fact, they made a series of
elementary mistakes—including dropping a pair of
traceable spectacles at the scene of the crime. Thanks to
the legal skills of Clarence Darrow, they were spared the
electric chair but were sentenced instead to life imprisonment. Although Leopold and Loeb were in their late
teens rather than children, they belong in this list if only

because their awful crime was born out of the immature amorality ordinarily associated with sociopathic children.

3. JON VENABLES and ROBERT THOMPSON (UK)

In 1993, Venables and Thompson, both aged eleven, abducted two-year-old James Bulger from a shopping center and dragged him through Liverpool before beating him to death on a railway line. The case, and the way it made us rethink our attitudes to evil, touched a raw nerve throughout Britain—not least because the security cameras caught the abduction on tape and so we were all able to witness the tragic moment when James was lured to his death.

4. BILLY ISAACS (USA)

On May 14, 1973, with his brother, Carl, their half-brother and a friend, Isaacs killed five members of a family in a mobile home in Georgia. Billy Isaacs, aged sixteen, testified for the prosecution to avoid the death penalty but the other three older boys were sentenced to death.

5. HAROLD JONES (UK)

In 1921, just two weeks after being acquitted of the killing by strangulation (and attempted rape) of eight-year-old Freda Burnell, fifteen-year-old Harold Jones, from Abertillery, Wales, murdered eleven-year-old Florence Irene Little by cutting her throat. After being tried for this crime—and found guilty—he confessed to the earlier killing. He was sentenced to be detained at His Majesty's Pleasure.

6. PAULINE PARKER and JULIET HULME
(New Zealand)

Early in 1954, Juliet Hulme's father decided to take her from New Zealand to South Africa, but the fifteen-year-old didn't want to be separated from her friend, Pauline Parker, aged sixteen, and so the two girls decided that

Pauline should go too. However, in the belief that Parker's mother would oppose this plan, they killed her. They were found guilty of murder and were sentenced to be detained at Her Majesty's Pleasure. They have since been released.

7. MICHAEL QUERIPEL (UK)

On April 29, 1955, Mrs. Currell didn't return from taking her dog for a walk on Potter's Bar golf course. Her battered body was found the next day near the seventeenth tee where she had been killed with a heavy iron tee marker which lay near her and which still had a bloody hand-print on it. Palm-prints were taken of all the local employees and checked against the print on the tee marker. Finally a matching print was found—that of seventeen-year-old Michael Queripel. He was charged with murder and pleaded guilty on October 12, 1955 at the Old Bailey. The judge ordered that he should be detained at Her Majesty's Pleasure.

8. STEVEN TRUSCOTT (Canada)

In 1959, twelve-year-old Lynne Harper was found raped and strangled in Goderich, Ontario. As fourteen-year-old Truscott was the last person to be seen with her, he was medically examined and found to have scratches and sore genitals. He was charged, found guilty and sentenced to death but, because of his youth, the Canadian Prime Minister commuted the sentence to life imprisonment. As he was too young to be put in an adult jail, he was sent to the Ontario Training School for Boys. He has since been released.

9. BRENDA SPENCER (USA)

On January 29, 1979, sixteen-year-old Brenda Spencer went to her school in San Diego, California, and shot dead her headmaster and the caretaker. She also wounded nine pupils. When eventually apprehended and asked why she had done such a terrible thing, she merely replied: "I don't like Mondays: they give me the blues. I wanted to liven up a dull Monday." Her statement—and her murders—inspired the song *I Don't Like Mondays,* by the Boomtown Rats.

Hippocratic hypocrites: Ten murdering doctors

The shadow of the Nazis hangs over this list. Josef Mengele, the chief doctor at Auschwitz—assisted by many other doctors—performed the most hideous experiments on people (including children) without anaesthetic which led to them suffering agonizing deaths. Consequently, the following cases must be seen in that context—albeit using Mengele as the template for evil. Having said that, very often the extent of a man's cruelty is one of scope. Who knows how barbaric the men below would have been if they had found themselves in Mengele's position at Auschwitz?

1. DR. HAWLEY HARVEY CRIPPEN (UK)
In 1910, the mild-mannered, American-born Crippen killed his overbearing wife Belle in London with an overdose of hyoscine, then cut up the body and hid it in the cellar. He sailed to Canada, one step ahead of the law, with his young mistress Ethel Le Neve dressed (unconvincingly) as a boy. Crippen was identified on board ship by the captain who sent a wire back to England. A British detective was immediately dispatched on a fast ship to Quebec where he arrested Crippen and brought him back to England. Crippen was tried for murder, found guilty and hanged at Pentonville on November 23, 1910.

2. DR. ROBERT GEORGE CLEMENTS (UK)
The British doctor's first wife died of "sleeping sickness" in 1920, his second of "endocarditis" in 1925, his

---

"The study of crime begins with the knowledge of oneself."

HENRY MILLER

third of "cancer" in 1939 and his fourth of "myeloid leukaemia" in 1947. At his fourth wife's autopsy, morphine was found in the body but Clements committed suicide at his home in Southport before he could be arrested.

3. DR. WILLIAM PALMER (aka "THE RUGELEY POISONER") (UK)

Dr. Palmer's friend, John Parsons Cook, collapsed while celebrating his horse's win at Shrewsbury Races. Dr. Palmer tended to his friend and collected the winnings on his behalf. John Cook died and the post-mortem revealed antimony in his corpse. Palmer was arrested for murder, tried and hanged on June 14, 1856 outside Stafford Jail. However, this does not seem to have been the full extent of Palmer's criminality because there were some fourteen deaths—all in suspicious circumstances—within Palmer's immediate family circle from which Palmer collected insurance payouts.

4. DR. ARTHUR WARREN WAITE (USA)

This American doctor wanted to murder his wife's millionaire parents. In the winter of 1916, he tried killing his mother-in-law by driving in the pouring rain with the windows open to give her pneumonia; he sprayed her throat with anthrax, diphtheria and influenza and put ground glass in her marmalade. All to no avail. Eventually, he had to give her an overdose of Veronal before she would die. Then he turned his attention to his father-in-law. Once again, he tried the cold, wet car treatment and attempted to infect him with typhoid and diphtheria. These didn't work and so Waite tried a huge dose of arsenic—but even that didn't work and he ended up suffocating his father-in-law with a pillow. The venal and persistent Waite was executed in the electric chair in 1917 in Sing Sing.

5. DR. ALFRED WILLIAM WARDER (UK)

Although the British Dr. Warder was only tried for the murder of his third wife, Ethel, in 1866, all three of his wives died under suspicious circumstances. He had given Ethel a tincture of aconite even though he knew it should only be used externally. But before the jury could return a verdict of guilty, Warder committed suicide.

6. DR. BUCK RUXTON (UK)

Indian-born Dr. Ruxton's wife, Isabella, and their family maid "disappeared" in September 1935. He reported that his wife had deserted him but, at the end of the month, pieces of flesh were found wrapped in newspapers—including a Morecambe and Lancaster edition of the *Daily Graphic* which helped to pin the murder on Ruxton who was tried at Manchester Assizes in March 1936, found guilty and hanged on May 12, 1936 at Strangeways Prison.

7. DR. WILLIAM BURKE KIRWAN (Ireland)

In 1852, Kirwan was sentenced to life imprisonment for the murder of his wife whose body was found on a small island off the coast of Ireland where the couple had taken a day-trip, Dr. Kirwan to sketch the landscape, Mrs. Kirwan to swim. Medical examination found that she had been suffocated with a wet sheet to simulate drowning. Kirwan was found guilty and sentenced to hang but the complicated medical testimony eventually reduced the punishment to penal servitude for life.

8. DR. MARCEL PETIOT (France)

In 1944, after the liberation of France, the police were called to Dr. Petiot's Parisian home by neighbors complaining about the smell. In the cellar, the police found the dismembered, decomposing bodies of twenty-seven Jews whom Petiot had promised to help but had instead murdered for their money and valuables. Petiot was executed by the guillotine in May 1946.

9. DR. GEZA DE KAPLANY (aka "THE ACID DOCTOR") (USA)

De Kaplany was a Hungarian refugee working in a hospital in San Jose, California, when he married twenty-five-year-old Hajna, a model and beauty queen. Unfortunately, he was sexually impotent. On August 28, 1962, de Kaplany decided to "operate" on his wife—to disfigure her to the extent that no other man would look at her. He stripped her, tied her up and made small incisions all over her body and then poured acid into the open cuts—completely destroying her face, breasts and genitals. The police were alerted when neighbors heard Mrs. de Kaplany's screams. The poor woman was taken to hospital where she eventually died. After a trial, de Kaplany was sentenced to life imprisonment but was released in 1975 to work as a cardiac specialist in a missionary hospital in Taiwan.

10. DR. WALTER WILKINS (USA)

On February 27, 1919, Dr. and Mrs. Wilkins returned to their Long Island, New York home and, according to Dr. Wilkins, surprised a gang of house-breakers who beat and robbed them. The next day, Mrs. Wilkins, who had been hit on the head seventeen times, died from her injuries. Some two weeks later, Wilkins was charged with his wife's murder: there had been no gang of robbers and his fingerprints had been found on the weapons used in the attack. He was found guilty but committed suicide in jail.

"Why murder is the greatest of all crimes is not that the life taken may be that of an Abraham Lincoln, but because it might be yours or mine."

F. TENNYSON JESSE

Three cases of bigamists who killed

The record number of bigamous marriages is 104 by Giovanni Vigliotto, a man who used so many aliases (over fifty) it is difficult to establish his true identity. Between 1949 and 1981, this lothario married women in fourteen countries and twenty-seven US States. In 1983, he was sent to jail for six years for bigamy (and twenty-eight years for fraud). He died in 1991 (absolutely exhausted, I shouldn't wonder).

1. GEORGE ALBERT CROSSMAN (UK)

Crossman "married" seven times under different names. His fifth "marriage" was to Ellen Sampson, a nurse and widow, in January 1903 but the morning after the "wedding" night, he killed her by hitting her over the head. He then hid the body in an upstairs room as the fourth Mrs. Crossman (Edith Thompson) was due to return that evening. However, Crossman's lodger, aware of a bad smell, became suspicious and went to the police who found the body. Crossman ran off and killed himself by slitting his throat.

2. JOHANN HOCH (USA)

Between 1892 and 1905, Hoch, a German immigrant, married at least twenty-four women—fifteen of whom died. These women's bodies were exhumed and they all contained arsenic. Hoch was found guilty of murder in Chicago in May 1905 and was hanged in February 1906.

3. ARTHUR GOSLETT (UK)

Arthur Goslett had two wives. As Captain Goslett he lived with Evelyn Goslett, in London NW11. As Captain Arthur Godfrey he lived with Daisy Godfrey in Kew, Surrey. He "married" again—a woman from Richmond, Surrey. In May 1920, he murdered Evelyn Goslett. He was hanged on July 27, 1920, after a visit from his Richmond "wife"—who forgave him.

Ten cannibal killers

We're not talking about those poor souls who are obliged to eat people to stay alive—say, in the aftermath of an airplane crash (such as the one in the Andes which was featured in the film *Alive*)—or even about native tribes which have eaten human flesh out of superstition. No, instead, we're looking at those sick, twisted people who murder their victims and then eat them (or serve them up to other people to eat). The fact is we're into Hannibal Lecter territory here—and pretty stomach-churning it is too . . .

1. EDWARD GEIN (USA)

Police searching for the missing Bernice Worden came upon her gutted body hanging from the ceiling of Gein's garage in Plainfield, Wisconsin, where they also found a bag of women's noses, a bag of women's vulvas, four skulls and a belt of women's nipples. Gein confessed to murder and to having eaten parts of the corpses. He was sent to a mental institution for life in December 1957. He died in 1984 at the age of seventy-seven. It is said that Robert Bloch based his novel *Psycho* (later a Hitchcock film) on the Ed Gein story.

2. FRITZ HAARMANN (Germany)

Haarmann's cannibalism came to light when two separate police enquiries dovetailed. His arrest, in the summer of 1924, for indecently assaulting a boy in the street coincided with the discovery of human bones in the river at Hanover, Germany. Police searching his apartment found piles of his victims' clothing waiting to be sold. The game was up: Haarmann confessed, implicating his homosexual lover Hans Grans, and it emerged that the two had butchered their victims—young male refugees made homeless by the First World War—and sold the flesh as horsemeat. He was charged with the murder of twenty-seven boys but confessed to killing around forty. He was beheaded, while Grans was sentenced to twelve years' imprisonment.

3. GEORGE GROSSMAN (Germany)

In 1921, tenants in a Berlin boarding-house heard screams coming from one of the rooms and discovered Grossman in the act of murdering a young woman. He later confessed to having picked up and killed many young women whose flesh he would later sell as "meat" in Berlin. He was sentenced to death, but hanged himself in his cell.

4. ALBERT HOWARD FISH (USA)

Fish attacked and molested children. On March 3, 1928, Fish abducted twelve-year-old Grace Budd whom he strangled, decapitated and sawed in half in Westchester County, New York. He then carved up her body and made a stew out of it which he lived on for several days. He was tried in March 1934, found guilty of murder and electrocuted on January 16, 1936 at Sing Sing.

5. ISSEI SAGAWA (France)

Renee Hartwelt, a twenty-five-year-old Dutch student studying in Paris, went missing on June 12, 1981. The next day, witnesses saw an Asian man dumping two very large suitcases and alerted the police who looked inside the suitcases and found most of the remains of a woman. A few days later the Asian man was tracked down and identified as a thirty-three-year-old Japanese named Issei Sagawa, who was studying at the university in Paris. The police searched Sagawa's flat where they found the dead girl's lips, her left breast and both buttocks in the fridge. Sagawa was asked what he'd done with the rest and replied that he'd eaten it. "Cooked?" asked the police. "No," replied Sagawa, "sliced thin and raw." On July 13, 1982 Sagawa was found mentally incompetent to stand trial and in 1984 he was transferred to a mental hospital in Japan. He was released in September 1985, when he was pronounced "cured." He has subsequently written a best-selling book, *In the Fog*, about his terrible exploits.

6. LIZZIE HUGHES (USA)

In 1891, a member of the black community of Washington, Georgia, returned home having made a name for himself. The local community laid on a large banquet in his honor at Lizzie Hughes's Cookhouse. Everything was going well until someone asked about the "delicious" meat which was pale and tender—a bit like veal. Before Hughes could say what the meat was, her little daughter replied, "My sister . . ."

7. ADOLPH LUETGERT (USA)

Adolph Luetgert, a German immigrant to the United States, was a sausage manufacturer. His wife, Louisa, found his many mistresses intolerable. On May 1, 1897, Louisa went missing and a police search of the sausage factory turned up human bone fragments. Luetgert had stabbed and boiled down the body of his wife and then put it through the sausage grinder. He was sentenced to life imprisonment. He died in Joliet State Penitentiary in 1911, never having confessed.

8. KATE WEBSTER (UK)

Webster, a thirty-year-old Irish servant, was dismissed by her employer (a Mrs. Thomas, who lived in Richmond) and so killed her. She boiled up the body and packed it into a trunk which she persuaded an unknowing acquaintance to help her dump in the Thames. The trunk eventually washed up near Barnes Bridge. Webster was tried at the Old Bailey and hanged on July 29, 1879. However, what gives the story an even more disgusting twist is that after boiling up the body, Webster sold Mrs. Thomas's boiled fat as dripping.

9. JOACHIM KROLL (aka "THE RUHR HUNTER") (Germany)

From 1955 until 1976, the German Joachim Kroll murdered fourteen women. His first victim was nineteen-year-old Irmgard Strehl whom he knocked unconscious and raped. Because he was a necrophiliac, his victims had to be unconscious or dead before he could have sex with them. Later, he started taking flesh from his victims' buttocks and thighs to eat so that he could, as he readily admitted after he was caught, save money on food. He was tried and sentenced to life imprisonment.

10. JACK THE RIPPER (UK)
As well as being an evil serial sex murderer, there is also the strong possibility that "Jack" was a cannibal. He removed a kidney from one of his victims and sent half of it to the chairman of the Whitechapel Vigilance Committee with a note stating: "T'other piece I fried and ate it was very nice."

JACK THE RIPPER

In 1888, from the end of August to the beginning of November, there was a series of gruesome murders in the Whitechapel area of London. All the victims had their throats slashed from behind and some of the bodies were mutilated afterward. No one knows for sure the identity of the man/men responsible, but given the massive interest in the subject (and the money to be made from speculating about it) there is no shortage of theories.

Five known Ripper victims

1. MARY ANN NICHOLS (aka "POLLY," 42)
August 31. Murdered in Buck's Row.

2. "DARK ANNIE" CHAPMAN (47)
September 8. Murdered in Hanbury Street.

3. ELIZABETH STRIDE (aka "LONG LIZ," 45)
September 30. Murdered in Dutfield's Yard.

4. CATHARINE EDDOWES (aka "KATE KELLY," 43)
Also September 30. Murdered in Mitre Square.

5. MARY JANE KELLY (25)

November 9. Murdered in Miller's Court. This was the most horrific murder of all. Her liver and entrails were removed and laid out between her feet, while flesh from the thighs and legs as well as the breasts and nose had been placed on her bedside table.

Four other possible Ripper victims

1. EMMA ELIZABETH SMITH (45)

Killed on April 3, 1888 in Osborn Street, Whitechapel.

2. MARTHA TABRAM (39)

Killed on August 7, 1888 in George Yard, Whitechapel.

3. ALICE "CLAY PIPE" McKENZIE (40)

Killed on July 16, 1889 in Castle Alley. Her throat was stabbed and she had some abdominal injuries. However, Police Commissioner Monro said that this was *not* the work of the Ripper.

4. FRANCES COLES (26)

Killed on February 14, 1891 in Swallow Gardens (now Royal Mint Street). She was still alive when she was found but bled to death from a cut throat. A ship's fireman named Sadler was charged with her murder by the police but later cleared in court.

Ten Ripper suspects

Given that forensic science was not nearly as well developed as it is today, the chances are that the murders "credited" to Jack the Ripper were probably committed by more than one man. Which means, of course, that not just one but any number of the men below could have been the murderer(s).

1. HRH PRINCE ALBERT VICTOR, DUKE OF CLARENCE

Queen Victoria's grandson was often put forward as a suspect as contemporary gossip suggested that a member of the royal family was involved—though the Duke was at Sandringham at the time of the last murder.

2. SIR WILLIAM GULL

The doctor of the Duke of Clarence, he was often to be found with blood on his clothing and it's possible that his patient, who is also a suspect, might have been framed by Gull, the real murderer.

3. JOSEPH BARNETT

He was victim Mary Jane Kelly's lover and it's been suggested that he might have committed the other murders to frighten Kelly off the streets before finally killing her.

4. MONTAGUE JOHN DRUITT

Many police involved in the case suspected Druitt, a barrister. Against this theory is the fact that Druitt drowned himself in 1888—before the final Ripper murder(s). However, notwithstanding the fact that many Ripper investigations have tried to identify Jack by concentrating on when the killings stopped, the fact is that "Jack" may have died, been imprisoned, or sent to a mental hospital before the later killings ascribed to him but carried out by a copy-cat murderer. He was also named by Sir Melville Macnaghten, the head of CID at Scotland Yard, as the probable Ripper.

5. ANDERSON'S SUSPECT

Dr. Anderson never actually named the man whom he believed to be Jack the Ripper. All he said was that the man was a poor Polish Jew who lived in the part of London where the murders took place. Either of the following two men—both violent lunatics—could have been the one he had in mind: **AARON DAVIS COHEN (aka DAVID COHEN)** or **AARON KOSMINSKI.**

6. THOMAS HAYNES CUTBUSH

Suffering from paranoid delusions after contracting syphilis, he used to wander about at night—often coming home in dirty clothes. Once when he was taken to Lambeth Infirmary, he escaped with a knife and killed a woman named Florence Johnson.

7. SEVERIN KLOSOWSKI
A Pole who had taken the name of George Chapman, he lived in Whitechapel where he practiced as a "barber-surgeon." His mistress told the police that he frequently didn't come home till the early hours of the morning.

8. DR. THOMAS NEILL CREAM
A doctor and murderer of four prostitutes, his last words as the trapdoor of the Newgate gallows opened under his feet were, "I am Jack the . . ." Yet at the time of the Whitechapel murders he was in jail in Chicago. Maybe he was going to say Jack the lad?

9. DR. ALEXANDER PEDACHENKO
In 1888, when he was known to the Russian secret police as the "greatest and boldest of all Russian criminal lunatics," he was living with his sister in Walworth, London. The theory goes that he committed the Ripper murders while working for the Russian secret police in order to discredit the Metropolitan Police.

10. ROBERT DONSTON STEPHENSON
The son of a Yorkshire seed-oil mill owner, he was a heavy drinker who, despite his "genteel" appearance (he called himself Dr. Roslyn D'Onston), was physically strong—and he often used to go to Whitechapel at the time of the murders. But this description probably fitted thousands of men.

Suspicion also fell upon a group of freemasons—led by Sir William Gull and Walter Sickert under the aegis of Lord Salisbury—of having carried out the Whitechapel murders. However, this can to a large extent be put down to the hatred and fear that freemasonry has always inspired in people.

2
POLITICAL CRIMES

Cold war warriors I: Sixteen significant Soviet spies*

1= GUY BURGESS, DONALD MACLEAN, KIM PHILBY and **ANTHONY BLUNT**—who were turned by the Russians at Cambridge University in the 1930s—spied for Russia until Burgess and Maclean defected in 1951. Amazingly, Philby didn't defect for another twelve years (although he was interrogated by MI6 in 1954). Blunt was granted immunity from prosecution in return for co-operation. However, when this deal became public in 1979, he was sacked from his job as art advisor to the Queen and stripped of his knighthood. After much speculation a KGB agent named John Cairncross as the "Fifth Man" in 1991. There are some serious spywatchers who genuinely believe that the late Sir Roger Hollis, the former head of MI5, was actually a KGB mole.

5. ALDRICH AMES
In 1994, Aldrich Ames of the US CIA was charged with spying for the Soviet Union (and later for Russia). He was said to have received more than £1 million for his activities.

---

*That is to say, the most significant Soviet spies *who've been found out* . . .

6= Three Canadians, **GORDON LONSDALE** and **PETER** and **HELEN KROGER,** and two British civil servants, **HARRY HOUGHTON** and **ETHEL GEE,** formed a spy ring in the 1950s which passed secrets from the British Navy's Underwater Warfare establishment in Portland, Dorset, to the Russians.

11. GEORGE BLAKE
In 1961 Blake, a British diplomat who was captured by the Communists during the Korean War and apparently brainwashed, was sent to jail for forty-two years for passing secret documents to the Soviets. He escaped from London's Wormwood Scrubs jail in 1966.

12. WILLIAM VASSALL
In 1962, Vassall, a British Admiralty clerk, was sent to jail for eighteen years for passing secrets to the Soviets.

13= ETHEL and JULIUS ROSENBERG
The Rosenbergs were sent to the electric chair in 1953 for stealing atomic secrets and giving them to the Soviets. They were the first married couple to be executed in the U.S.A. and also the first Americans to be executed for treason in peacetime.

15. KLAUS FUCHS
Fuchs, a scientist at the Harwell weapons research center in Berkshire, Britain, passed atomic secrets to the Soviets and was sent to prison for fourteen years in 1950.

16. GEOFFREY PRIME
In 1982, Prime, a linguist at the British secret communications center in Cheltenham, was sentenced to thirty-five years in jail for spying for the USSR. His activities were discovered when he was charged with sexual assault.

Cold war warriors II: Four men who spied — or allegedly spied — on the Soviets

1. OLEG GORDIEVSKY

In 1985, it was revealed that Gordievsky, the KGB chief at the Soviet embassy in Britain, had, in fact, been working for British Intelligence. He named twenty-five Soviet spies operating in London and they were immediately expelled. In retaliation, the Soviet authorities expelled twenty-five Britons (including journalists who were manifestly *not* spies) from the USSR. Gordievsky is the only spy I've ever knowingly met (we were guests on the same TV program) and someone less like James Bond — or, at any rate, Sean Connery — would be harder to imagine.

2. FRANCIS GARY POWERS

In 1961, Powers, an American U-2 pilot, was sent to jail by a Soviet court for flying a spy mission over the USSR.

3. GREVILLE WYNNE

In 1962, the British businessman Greville Wynne was arrested in Hungary and flown to Moscow where he was tried for being a spy. He was sentenced to eight years in jail but was swapped for Soviet spy Gordon Lonsdale in 1964. Meanwhile, Wynne's alleged Soviet colleague, Colonel Oleg Penkovsky, was sentenced to death and shot.

4. GERALD BROOKE

In 1965, Brooke, a British university lecturer, was sentenced to five years in a Soviet prison for smuggling pamphlets from a Soviet anti-Communist group into the USSR.

Fourteen terrorist groups (since 1960) and where they have operated

1. IRISH REPUBLICAN ARMY (IRA): Ireland and Britain

Aims: A unified Ireland

2. THE ANGRY BRIGADE: Britain
Aims: Anarchy

3. EUZKADI TA ASKATASUN (ETA): Spain
Aims: A separate Basque state

4. POPULAR FRONT FOR THE LIBERATION OF PALESTINE (PFLP): Israel/worldwide
Aims: The destruction of Israel in favor of a Palestinian state

5. RED BRIGADE: Italy
Aims: Anarchy

6. ARMED REVOLUTIONARY NUCLEI: Italy
Aims: Anarchy

7. MAU MAU: Kenya
Aims: Independence from British rule

8. SOUTH MOLUCCANS: Holland
Aims: Independence from Indonesia for these inhabitants of a former Dutch colony

9. ORGANISATION DE L'ARMÉE SECRÈTE (OAS): Algeria and France
Aims: Stop Algerian independence

10. SYMBIONESE LIBERATION ARMY (SLA): USA
Aims: Anarchy

11. RED ARMY FACTION: West Germany
Aims: Anarchy

12. BLACK SEPTEMBER: Worldwide
Aims: See PFLP

13. PALESTINE LIBERATION ORGANIZATION (PLO): Israel/worldwide

Aims: Initially those of the PFLP; recently for a Palestinian state to exist alongside Israel

14. BAADER-MEINHOF: West Germany
Aims: Anarchy

The twenty-five most important assassinations in history

A lot of it is about timing. Much in the same way that yesterday's terrorist is today's statesman, so too is one era's assassination another era's execution. If Benito Mussolini had been killed by a mob in 1935, this would have counted as assassination, but by 1945, when he and his mistress were strung up by a mob, we have to consider this execution.

Actually, the point about timing is fascinating when you apply it to Mussolini's ally, Hitler. There were two attempts made on his life: one in 1939 and the other in 1944. With hindsight, if the 1939 attempt had succeeded, it is quite possible that the Second World War and the Holocaust wouldn't have happened. However, if the 1944 attempt had succeeded, it is also entirely possible that Germany would have managed to achieve some sort of negotiated peace which would have left many Nazis and much of Nazism still intact.

The most frequently assassinated heads of state in modern times have been the Tsars (or, if you prefer, Czars) of Russia. In the 200 years from 1718 to 1918, four Tsars and two heirs were assassinated and there were many other unsuccessful attempts.

In modern times, the holder of the invidious record for being the target of the greatest number of assassination attempts is Charles de Gaulle, the former President

---

"Assassination is the extreme form of censorship."

GEORGE BERNARD SHAW

of France. He is said to have survived thirty-one plots against his life between 1944 and 1966.

1. PRESIDENT ABRAHAM LINCOLN (1865)

During the American Civil War, actor John Wilkes Booth plotted with other conspirators to kidnap President Lincoln and take him in chains to the Confederate capital, Richmond. As we all know, the plan failed [trust a bunch of luvvies to screw up]. When the war finished, Booth and his gang decided instead to murder Lincoln, his Vice-President and other Cabinet members. During a performance of *Our American Cousin* at Ford's Theater in Washington, Lincoln was shot by Booth who then threw himself over the box-rail on to the stage but misjudged the leap and broke his leg. He managed to escape arrest for twelve days (after his leg was treated by a doctor named "Mudd"—hence the expression "His name is mud") but was then found in a tobacco shed in Virginia and was shot by soldiers. The following question posed by the comedian Tom Lehrer (fortunately some 100 years later) is still considered to be the paradigm of tastelessness: "But how did you enjoy the *play,* Mrs. Lincoln?"

2. PRESIDENT JOHN KENNEDY (1963)

Never mind where *you* were, we all know where *he* was on November 22. More than thirty years later, we are, it seems, no nearer to knowing the truth. My own feeling is that Oswald and A.N. Other did it, aided and abetted by Cuban exiles and organized crime but your theory is as good as mine—and probably a lot better than Oliver Stone's. On the morning of his assassination, JFK told his wife Jackie, "If someone wants to shoot me from a window with a rifle, nobody can stop it, so why worry about it?" (See the spine-tingling list of coincidences between the assassinations of Lincoln and Kennedy on pages 101–102.)

3. DR. MARTIN LUTHER KING Jr. (1968)

The greatest civil rights leader in American history was

shot dead in Memphis on April 4 as he stepped on to the balcony of the Lorraine Motel. The murderer, James Earl Ray, then fled to Canada where he got hold of forged documents and traveled to England where he was eventually arrested. He was sentenced to ninety-nine years in jail but managed to escape for three days in 1977. One doesn't have to be a conspiracy theorist to believe that Ray, previously a minor criminal, wasn't acting off his own bat. More specifically, one can detect in this the hand of King's bitter adversary (and closet transvestite) J. Edgar Hoover. King knew the stakes he was playing for. He once said: "I live each day under a threat of death: I know that I can meet a violent end"—but this didn't make his assassination any less tragic.

4. INDIRA GANDHI (1984)
The Indian Prime Minister was assassinated by Sikh extremists as she was walking from her home to her office to meet the British actor Peter Ustinov. Given the often "robust" way that Mrs. Gandhi had ruled India—not to mention the state of relations with Pakistan and the Sikhs—her assassination was not entirely unexpected and yet it is no overstatement to say that the world was deeply shocked by the news.

5. REINHARD HEYDRICH (1942)
Heydrich was the ruthless (even by Nazi standards) "Protector" of Czechoslovakia and Hitler's heir apparent. He was assassinated in a grenade attack by two Czech soldiers who had been parachuted in from Britain. The Nazis retaliated by murdering the entire adult population of Lidice (in Czechoslovakia) and razing the village to the ground.

6. MOHANDAS "MAHATMA" GANDHI (1948)
In an extraordinary end to an extraordinary life, Gandhi was shot dead by Nathuram Godse, a Hindu fanatic who resented the great man's tolerant attitude toward Muslims.

7. ARCHDUKE FERDINAND (1914)

The Archduke was assassinated (along with his wife Sophie) on June 28, 1914 when Gavrilo Princip shot him through the jugular vein with a bullet which lodged in his spine. People say that this was the most important assassination in history as it precipitated the start of the Great War—and there's something to be said for that view. But the truth is that most European countries were itching for a war—well they hadn't had one since 1870—and, in retrospect, Ferdinand's assassination was the excuse rather than the cause.

8. ROBERT F. KENNEDY (1968)

During the extraordinary Presidential primaries, Bobby Kennedy was assassinated in the Los Angeles' Ambassador Hotel as he was leaving a meeting of campaign supporters. In a crowded room, the tautologically named Sirhan Sirhan stepped forward and shot Kennedy at point-blank range. The tragedy was that Bobby had finally stepped out of his hawkish elder brother's shadow—and away from his own right-wing, McCarthy-supporting past—to become an international statesman actively working for peace.

9. LEON TROTSKY (1940)

The Russian revolutionary was assassinated in Mexico by Ramon Mercader with an ice-pick he had hidden under his raincoat. There is no doubt that this assassination was on Stalin's direct orders.

10. ANWAR EL-SADAT (1981)

Like so many other victims of assassination, Egyptian President Sadat was murdered by extremists—specifically Muslim fundamentalists who bitterly resented his liberal, Western stance. Sadat had won the Nobel Prize (with Menachem Begin) for securing the Egyptian-Israeli peace deal. Thirteen years later, the peace holds—a fitting tribute to the life of this extraordinary statesman.

11. JULIUS CAESAR (44 B.C.)

"Beware the Ides of March," he was told. Casca, Cassius and the other conspirators wounded Caesar before Brutus—"Et tu, Brute"—finished him off.

12. SPENCER PERCEVAL (1812)

Amazingly, Spencer Perceval is still the only British Prime Minister to have been assassinated. The interesting thing is that Perceval is not really one of those Prime Ministers you remember such as Gladstone or Disraeli, though nothing much happened to them. Perceval was assassinated by one John Bellingham who had been sentenced to prison in Russia and appealed to the British Ambassador there. His appeal doubled his sentence and ruined Bellingham's business as a merchant. When he returned to England, Bellingham wrote to the Prime Minister seeking damages. When these weren't forthcoming, Bellingham shot the Prime Minister in the lobby of the House of Commons. He was convicted of murder and hanged even though he was clearly insane. However, I guess if there's one crime which needs a deterrent, it's killing Prime Ministers.

13. PRESIDENT WILLIAM McKINLEY (1901)

McKinley became the third US President to be assassinated in thirty-six years when Leon Czolgosz, a bizarrely nomenclatured anarchist, shot him at the Pan-American Exposition with a gun he'd hidden under a false bandage. "I done my duty," yelled Leon, thereby scoring full marks for effort but very few for grammar. As a result of McKinley's death, Teddy Roosevelt became President.

14. LIAQUAT ALI KHAN (1951)

Pakistan's first Prime Minister died in almost exactly the same way—and for the same reasons—as Mahatma Gandhi. A well-known moderate and a friend of Nehru, he incurred the hatred of the Muslim fundamentalist Syed Azbar Khan, who shot him several times. The

Prime Minister died in hospital; his murderer was torn apart by a mob.

15. SALVADOR ALLENDE (1973)

The President of Chile died during an attack on his Santiago palace by right-wing gunmen. The question remains, however, whether he was indeed assassinated or, as his personal physician (and the only man to see him die) declared, he committed suicide. Either way, his death represented a tragedy for Chile and its hopes for democracy.

16. SOLOMON BANDARANAIKE (1959)

A great Ceylonese Prime Minister who was assassinated by a Buddhist monk. Perhaps the most important result of his assassination was that he was succeeded by his wife, Sirimavo, who became the world's first female Prime Minister.

17. PRESIDENT JAMES GARFIELD (1881)

During the 1880 election campaign, Charles Julius Guiteau wrote an unsolicited campaign speech for Garfield. But Garfield didn't use it, so Guiteau handed out copies of it at meetings. When Garfield won the election, Guiteau reckoned that his "contribution" entitled him to be appointed ambassador to France. Not unreasonably, Garfield's people thought nothing more of it. But Guiteau, aggrieved by the thought of doing all that work for nothing, decided to shoot the President and did so.

18. KING UMBERTO I (1900)

An anarchist called Gaetano Bresci fired three shots into King Umberto I of Italy, who fell back saying, "I think it is nothing." He reminds me of General John Sedgwick in the American Civil War whose last words were "Why, they couldn't hit an elephant at this dist—"

19. RAJIV GANDHI (1991)

The former Indian Prime Minister—who took office when his mother Indira was assassinated—was killed while attempting a political comeback. His assassin was a woman who approached Gandhi and detonated a bomb—killing both of them. She has never been identified but her Tamil co-conspirators committed suicide after a gun battle.

20. OLAF PALME (1986)
You don't really associate Swedes with political assassination, but the Swedish Prime Minister—who had no guards as such precautions seemed unnecessary in Sweden—was gunned down by a person (or persons) unknown as he walked home with his wife after having been to the cinema in Stockholm.

21. BENIGNO AQUINO (1983)
Aquino was assassinated as he stepped off the plane in the Philippines, having returned from political exile in the USA. As with Solomon and Sirimavo Bandaranaike, the most important consequence of Aquino's assassination was the political emergence of his widow, Corazon.

22. MICHAEL COLLINS (1922)
Collins was right at the forefront of the (mostly successful) Irish struggle for independence in 1919–21 but some of his more extreme colleagues decided that he'd sold out in not securing the six counties of Northern Ireland as well and so they assassinated him.

23. AIREY NEAVE (1979)
This Tory MP was assassinated by the Irish National Liberation Army by means of a car bomb. He was one of Margaret Thatcher's greatest supporters and was clearly destined for Cabinet office—probably as Secretary of State for Northern Ireland—after the forthcoming General Election. He was the first MP to be assassinated since Spencer Perceval. Unfortunately, with the murder of Ian Gow by the IRA in 1990, he wasn't the last.

24. EARL MOUNTBATTEN OF BURMA (1979)
The Queen's cousin was blown up on his boat in County Sligo, Ireland, by the IRA as (in their words) "a discriminate act to bring to the attention of the English people the continuing occupation of our country." Nothing was achieved—beyond the senseless murder of a harmless old man.

25. MALCOLM X (1965)
Civil rights leader Malcolm X (born Malcolm Little) was shot dead as he was about to address a rally of his followers in Harlem, New York. His assassins were Black Muslim extremists, members of the sect to which he belonged until a year before his death. In 1964, following a rift with leader Elijah Muhammad, he broke away from the Black Muslims to form the Organization of Afro-American Unity, a movement preaching racial solidarity. Malcolm X was gunned down on February 21, 1965; he was thirty-nine at the time of his death and would only be in his late sixties if he were alive today.

Two racists who were shot and survived but were then assassinated in the 1960s

1. HENRIK VERWOERD (1966)
Prime Minister Verwoerd was the architect of apartheid in South Africa—having been an enthusiastic supporter of Hitler in the Second World War. He was shot by a farmer just a few weeks after the Sharpeville massacre but survived. Six years later, he was assassinated by Dimitrio Tsafendas, a parliamentary messenger, who was subsequently sent to a mental asylum.

2. GEORGE LINCOLN ROCKWELL (1967)
Rockwell, the founder of the American Nazi Party, was shot at by snipers in Arlington, Virginia, but was unhurt. A couple of months later, John C. Patler, a former Rockwell aide who'd been expelled from the

American Nazi Party for being too extreme (if you can get your head around that) assassinated him.

Two men whose deaths may have been murder . . .

1. DAG HAMMARSKJOLD (1961)
Dag Hammarskjold, the Swedish Secretary-General of the United Nations, was traveling on a DC airliner which crashed in the Zambian jungle. Two facts suggest sabotage: the Soviets were highly critical of Dag's handling of the Congo crisis and wanted him replaced; two of the bodies from the plane were riddled with bullets. You can make up your own mind . . .

2. POPE JOHN PAUL I (1978)
On September 28, 1978, the newly elected Pope John Paul I went to bed. He never woke up again. His death was put down to cardiac arrest but there have been several allegations (not least in the film *The Godfather Part III*) that he was murdered—possibly because he couldn't be trusted not to uncover scandals.

A glossary of the fifteen most important attempted assassinations

Most modern American Presidents have had to endure attempts on their lives. This possibly explains why Richard Nixon and George Bush chose Vice-Presidents like Spiro Agnew and Dan Quayle. After all, you'd have thought that the prospect of either of them becoming President would have been a pretty powerful deterrent to any would-be assassin. But you'd have been wrong as Nixon and Bush are featured in this list along with fellow twentieth-century Presidents Roosevelt (both of them), Truman, Johnson, Ford (shot at by Lynette "Squeaky" Fromme, a member of Charles Manson's gang and the first woman to try to assassinate a President) and Reagan (shot at by the J.D. Salinger/Jodie Foster-loving John Hinckley).

1. YASSER ARAFAT
Fortunately for the Middle East peace process, none of the many attempts on his life has thus far worked. Now they say he's protected by Mossad, the Israeli Secret Service.

2. FIDEL CASTRO
The CIA made many attempts on Castro's life: exploding cigars, poisonous pens and infected clothes being just three of the bizarre methods used.

3. CHARLES DE GAULLE
The most important figure in French politics during and after the Second World War, he was subjected to thirty-one attempted assassinations.

4. QUEEN ELIZABETH I
Good Queen Bess was the target of any number of Catholics who wanted to see Mary, Queen of Scots on the throne.

5. HUGH FRASER
Tory MP (one-time husband of the author Lady Antonia Fraser) and outspoken critic of the IRA which attempted to kill him with a car bomb but instead murdered the eminent cancer specialist, Gordon Hamilton-Fairley. We use the word tragedy so often that it has lost its meaning but if ever there was a genuine tragedy, this was it. Who's to say that this great man wouldn't have found a cure for cancer? Ross McWhirter who, with his twin brother Norris, was the instigator of *The Guinness Book of Records,* started a "Beat the Bombers" campaign as a result of this murder, and was himself assassinated by the IRA.

6. GENERAL ALEXANDER HAIG
When he was Supreme Commander of NATO, Haig

narrowly survived an attempted bomb assassination in 1979. I suppose if it had succeeded, we'd have been spared Haig's ludicrous "I'm in charge" (when Vice-President George Bush clearly would have been) when Ronald Reagan was nearly assassinated by John Hinckley.

7. HASSAN II
In 1972, Hassan II, King of Morocco was traveling in his Boeing 727 when it was met by five Moroccan Air Force jets, three of which started firing at his plane. A radio appeal—supposedly from a mechanic—asked that the shooting stop as the king was "mortally wounded." The shooting stopped and the king was landed uninjured. The mechanic was none other than . . . King Hassan II.

8. ADOLF HITLER
Hitler survived two attempts on his life. On November 8, 1939, he left a Munich beer cellar twelve minutes before a would-be assassin's bomb exploded. On July 20, 1944 another attempt to assassinate Hitler failed when a bomb planted by Lieutenant-Colonel von Stauffenberg only succeeded in killing four of his aides but not the dictator himself. He had the devil's own luck but then doesn't the devil always look after his own?

9. POPE JOHN PAUL II
On May 13, 1981, Pope John Paul II was being driven through the great piazza in front of St. Peter's Basilica when twenty-three-year-old Mehmet Ali Agca opened fire, hitting him twice. The pope was seriously injured, but recovered to forgive his would-be assassin.

10. VLADIMIR ILYICH LENIN
On August 30, 1918, Lenin had just finished making a speech to the workers at the Michelson factory in Moscow when Fanya Kaplan pulled out a revolver from under her clothes and shot him in the neck and shoulder. Neither bullet was removed, but Lenin recovered and lived for another six years.

11. NAPOLEON BONAPARTE
Apparently, there were many attempts made on his life but he chose to suppress any news about them and there wasn't too much freedom of the press in Napoleon's day.

12. SIR ROBERT PEEL
The attempted assassination of the British Prime Minister by Daniel McNaghten in 1843 is important because it is from this case—in which the mad McNaghten mistook Peel's Private Secretary William Drummond for Peel and murdered him—that we get the McNaghten Rules defining the degree of sanity required for criminal responsibility. [And anyone who can't tell the different between a secretary and a Prime Minister must be one or two apples short of a picnic.]

13. MARGARET THATCHER
This was the IRA bombing of the Grand Hotel in Brighton in 1984 during the Tory Party Conference. Four people were killed and over thirty injured but the Iron Lady was unharmed and she addressed the Conference later that day as planned.

14. QUEEN VICTORIA
There were many attempts on the Queen's life during her long reign and all the perpetrators were either committed to mental institutions or transported to Australia. Which probably explains why these days there are so many Republicans down under.

15. GEORGE WALLACE
In 1972, the segregationist Wallace, Governor of Alabama and maverick Presidential candidate, was stopped in his tracks by Arthur Bremer whose bullet put him in a wheelchair. When, a few years later, Wallace ran again for Governor, it was on a much more racially liberal platform and he won—with a large proportion of the black vote. So it could be argued—at least by all except Governor Wallace and his family—that Bremer (who

was sent to jail for life) didn't do Alabama too much of a disservice.

Sixteen extraordinary links between the assassinations of Abraham Lincoln and John Kennedy

As everyone knows, both Lincoln and Kennedy were assassinated but there's more that links them than that . . .

1. Lincoln was elected President in 1860; Kennedy was elected President in 1960.
2. Lincoln and Kennedy each had seven letters in their names.
3. Lincoln had a secretary named Kennedy; Kennedy had a secretary named Lincoln.
4. Both Presidents were shot in the head.
5. Both Presidents were with their wives at the time.
6. Both assassinations took place on a Friday.
7. Both Presidents were warned that they might be assassinated but both refused to change their schedules.
8. Two of Lincoln's sons were named Edward and Robert: Edward died when he was young and Robert lived on; two of Kennedy's brothers were named Edward and Robert: Robert died when he was young and Edward lived on.
9. Lincoln was shot in a theater by a man who hid in a warehouse; Kennedy was shot from a warehouse by a man who hid in a theater.
10. John Wilkes Booth (Lincoln's assassin) was a Southerner in his twenties; Lee Harvey Oswald (Kennedy's assassin) was a Southerner in his twenties.
11. John Wilkes Booth and Lee Harvey Oswald each had fifteen letters in their names.
12. Booth and Oswald both died before they were tried.

13. Lincoln was succeeded by Andrew Johnson; Kennedy was succeeded by Lyndon Johnson.
14. Andrew Johnson was born in 1808; Lyndon Johnson was born in 1908.
15. Andrew Johnson and Lyndon Johnson each had thirteen letters in their names.
16. Kennedy was riding in a Lincoln when he was shot.

Doesn't that make the hairs on the back of your neck stand up?

Eight cases of politicians who came up against the law

1. GENERAL MANUEL NORIEGA
The former dictator of Panama, Noriega was sentenced to forty years in jail in 1992 by an American court for drug trafficking.

2. TERRY FIELDS
A left-wing British Labor MP, Fields was sentenced to sixty days in jail in 1991 for refusing to pay his poll tax (community charge).

3. BERNADETTE DEVLIN
Devlin, the twenty-three-year-old MP from Northern Ireland, was sent to jail for six months in 1970 for "incitement to riot."

4. WATERGATE
In 1973–74 the Watergate affair accounted for many political careers—notably those of **Richard Nixon, John Mitchell, Bob Haldeman, John Ehrlichman** and **John Dean.**

5. JOHN STONEHOUSE
A British former Cabinet Minister, Stonehouse faked his own suicide in 1974 (by pretending to have drowned

while swimming off a Miami beach) after his business affairs went awry. He was later sent to jail for seven years for theft. His faked suicide provoked a fellow politician to comment: "This proves that old politicians never die: they simply wade away."

6. JEREMY THORPE
In 1979 Thorpe, a former leader of the British Liberal Party, was tried for conspiring to murder his alleged ex-lover, Norman Scott. Thorpe, who didn't take the stand, was found not guilty, but his political career was over.

7. SPIRO AGNEW
The American Vice-President under Nixon, in 1973 Agnew was forced to resign for taking bribes and evading taxes.

8. JOHN POULSON
Poulson was an architect who used bribery and graft to win contracts. He and a provincial politician, T. Dan Smith, went to jail in 1974. Reginald Maudling, a leading British Conservative politician, saw his career hampered as a result of his links with Poulson.

Ten people who were imprisoned before going on to lead their countries

1. Benazir Bhutto (Pakistan)
2. Menachem Begin (Israel)
3. Archbishop Makarios (Cyprus)
4. Adolf Hitler (Germany)
5. Nelson Mandela (South Africa)
6. Fidel Castro (Cuba)
7. Jomo Kenyatta (Kenya)
8. Mário Soares (Portugal)
9. Vaclav Havel (Czechoslovakia)
10. Ahmed Ben Bella (Algeria)

3
ROBBERY, THEFT
AND BURGLARY

Seven notorious robbers

1. JOHN DILLINGER (USA)

Dillinger, the one-time FBI Public Enemy No. 1, committed many successful bank robberies and used some of the proceeds to smuggle guns into the prison that was holding his associates, Harry Pierpoint and Homer Van Meter, so that they could break out and join him. However, when Dillinger and "Baby Face" Nelson robbed the First National Bank in Mason City on March 13, 1934, they only managed to get $50,000 of the bank's $240,000, because the brave cashier handed the money over very slowly and in huge sacks of cents and bundles of $1 notes. Eventually, Dillinger was forced to lie low in Chicago but his girlfriend's friend tipped off the police and they gunned him down outside a cinema on July 22, 1934.

2. NED KELLY (Australia)

The most infamous bandit in Australian history owes most of his notoriety to the bizarre armor he wore. In reality, his criminal career was almost as short as it was inglorious. From 1878 to 1880, he and his brother Dan and their "colleagues" went on a somewhat manic spree during which they robbed prospectors, murdered policemen and robbed banks. In June 1880, Kelly's gang was finally cornered at the Glenrowan Hotel. Ned Kelly was shot in the leg but carried on shooting at police until he eventually collapsed from loss of blood. He recovered from his wounds and was hanged on November 11, 1880.

3. COLONEL BLOOD (UK)
In the late seventeenth century, Colonel Blood—posing as a clergyman—got into the treasure room of the Tower of London and stole the Crown Jewels. He was eventually captured but instead of punishing him, King Charles II rewarded his audacity with a pension for life.

4. WILLIAM SUTTON (USA)
From 1925 to 1952, Sutton was a notorious robber. As "Willie the Actor," in various guises such as a window-cleaner and a policeman, he robbed several banks. He was arrested and imprisoned more than once but in 1947 he escaped and got a job at an old people's home where he worked happily for five years. However, in 1952 he was recognized and once again arrested. The police found $7,000 in his suit and asked him why he didn't put his money in a bank to which he replied, "It's never safe in a bank." He was sentenced to thirty years in prison but was released after seventeen because of ill-health.

5. HENRY "FLANNELFOOT" VICARS (UK)
Possibly the most prolific burglar of all time was Henry Vicars who burgled houses in the London suburbs—usually on a Friday night when they would be empty and the pay-packets would be lying around. His *modus operandi* was to force a window open and then pad about in his socks—hence his nickname. After a thousand burglaries, he was eventually caught red-handed with pliers and keys. He was found guilty on December 2, 1937 and sentenced to five years in prison.

6. THE KING OF THE KEYS (UK)
In 1976, Lennie Minchington (aka "The King of the

Keys") masterminded a robbery from deposit boxes in London which netted him £8 million—and a twenty-five-year prison sentence.

7. THE MOLASSES GANG (USA)

In the 1870s, this gang went into New York shops—always following the same routine: one of the gang would take off his hat and ask the shopkeeper to fill it with molasses because they were having a bet on how much molasses it would hold. The shopkeeper would oblige and then the gang would pull the hat down over his eyes which would blind him while they then proceeded to rob the shop. You wouldn't have thought that they could have got away with a stunt like that more than once or twice, but apparently they did. And that is why, despite the fact that they don't really belong in the big league, they are included in this list.

The twelve greatest robberies of all time

1. THE GREATEST ART ROBBERY OF ALL TIME

Vincenzo Peruggia stole the (literally) priceless *Mona Lisa* from the Louvre Museum in Paris on August 21, 1911. He took the painting back to his native Italy where he and his associates forged copies which they then sold to US dealers and collectors. However, Peruggia was caught when he tried selling the original to a local art dealer. He was arrested and the *Mona Lisa* was safely returned to France. Or was it? There is a school of thought that says that the original *Mona Lisa* wasn't returned, just a copy.

2. THE WORLD'S BIGGEST TRAIN ROBBERY

This took place in the early hours of August 8, 1963 when a gang of men, led by Bruce Reynolds, ambushed the Glasgow to London mail-train near Mentmore, Buckinghamshire, and stole £2.6 million worth of bank notes. The gang was caught after police found their hideout which was, according to the detective in charge of the case, "one big clue." The gang members were given various sentences totalling 307 years and not only were they all the subject of a film based on their exploits (*Robbery*) but Ronnie Biggs and Buster Edwards have had films devoted to them. And who could forget Ronnie with Sid Vicious and the boys in *The Great Rock 'n' Roll Swindle*?

3. THE FIRST TRAIN ROBBERY
On October 6, 1866, the Reno gang of Indiana, brothers Frank, John, Simeon and William Reno—who ordinarily restricted themselves to burglaries, robberies and saloon-bar hold-ups—held up a train near Seymour, Indiana, and forced the guard to open the safe in the express coach. They took $10,000 and made their getaway on horseback.

4. THE CENTRAL PACIFIC EXPRESS
In 1870, Big Jack Davis and his men stopped a train bound for Reno and got away with $40,000. Many hours later, the train was robbed again—of another $4,500 that the earlier robbers had missed! Both sets of criminals were caught and sent to jail.

5. BRITAIN'S GREATEST ROBBERY
On November 26, 1983, a gang of six men broke into the Brinks-Mat warehouse at London's Heathrow Airport. They took nearly £26 million in gold bullion. Gang members "Colonel" Brian Robinson and Michael McAvoy, together with their accomplice "on the inside" Anthony Black, were arrested, convicted and sent to jail—without revealing the whereabouts of their booty. In 1989, Michael Relton, a solicitor, was sentenced to twelve years in prison for laundering part of the proceeds. By this time, after a search spanning six countries, police had traced most of the gold and frozen the gang's assets.

6. THE BRINK'S ROBBERY
On January 17, 1950, nearly $3 million was stolen from

Brink's, the Chicago security firm by a gang of thieves—
led by Joe McGinnis—who wore Brink's uniforms and
thus aroused no suspicion. They had keys to all the
doors and managed to get away within fifteen minutes.
They left absolutely no clues or fingerprints but were
eventually caught five years later when one of the gang,
Joseph "Specs" O'Keefe, turned them in because they
refused to reimburse him for the money he'd given to a
fellow gang member who then wouldn't let him have it.
So much for the proverbial honor among thieves . . .

7. THE WORLD'S BIGGEST BANK ROBBERY
In January 1976, during the civil war in Lebanon, a
guerrilla force blew up the vaults of the British Bank of
the Middle East and took approximately $50 million.
Note also the 1945 robbery from the German Reichs-
bank which netted its perpetrators less than $50 million
but still the 1994 equivalent of some £2,500 million.

8. THE WORLD'S GREATEST INSURANCE THEFT
Between 1964 and 1973, 64,000 faked insurance policies were created on the computer at the Equity Funding
Corporation in the USA. Each of these policies then
paid out a check for $2,000.

9. THE WORLD'S GREATEST JEWEL THEFT
In 1980, jewels valued at $16 million were stolen from
the bedroom of Prince Abdul Aziz bin Ahmed Al-
Thani's villa near Cannes, France.

10. BRITAIN'S GREATEST JEWEL THEFT
In 1983, £6 million worth of jewels were stolen from a
Conduit Street, London jewellers.

11. THE WORLD'S GREATEST BRIEFCASE THEFT
In May 1990, a robber snatched a briefcase containing
nearly £292 million in negotiable bonds from a City
of London messenger. The robber couldn't do anything with his ill-gotten gains because the Bank of
England immediately warned the City, but his crime did

manage to wipe £300 million off the City's money market liquidity. And *you* were worried about being mugged . . .

12. THE £115,000 CASH WITHDRAWAL

A man (as yet unnamed) whose job it was to refill bank cash machines took £115,000 of cash from machines in Manchester and at Manchester Airport on February 6, 1994. What made his crime work so well (and led to his inclusion in this august list) was the fact that he didn't just put blank paper in the machines, but put some cash in as well in such a way that the machines were initially dispensing cash which gave him time to make his getaway—on a plane for Islamabad.

The ten countries with the highest incidence of theft

When it comes to theft, Western countries top the league tables. But it's fair to say that this has more to do with people having things worth stealing than with greater innate dishonesty. There is also the matter of people having enough confidence in their police officers to make it worthwhile reporting the theft so that the countries at the top of the list are just as likely to be those with the best police forces as those with the most villains.

1. New Zealand 72,451 (thefts per million people)
2. Denmark 71,103
3. Sweden 69,310
4. Netherlands 55,885

"Thieves respect property. They merely wish the property to become their property that they may more perfectly respect it."

G.K. CHESTERTON

5. UK 51,232
6. Canada 51,141
7. USA 46,975
8. Australia 46,105
9. Switzerland 45,857
10. Bermuda 44,794

Just outside this top ten are Germany (42,687), Israel (41,136) and France (41,116).

The ten countries with the lowest incidence of theft

This list looks like a mixture of places where either they don't have too many police, or they don't have much confidence in their police or they cut off the hands of thieves.

1. Togo 37 (thefts per million people)
2. Niger 102
3. Burundi 253
4. Egypt 362
5. Syria 376
6. Gabon 482
7. Saudi Arabia 549
8. The Philippines 555
9. Indonesia 570
10. Nigeria 632

But I never felt a thing . . . The ten European countries where you are most likely to have your pocket picked

1. Spain
2. France
3. Holland
4. Switzerland
5. Belgium
6. Germany

7. Finland
8. England and Wales
9. Scotland
10. Northern Ireland

Twelve countries and their people's desire for imprisonment for recidivist burglars

1. USA 52.7%
2. Northern Ireland 45.4%
3. Scotland 39%
4. England and Wales 38.2%
5. Australia 35.6%
6. Canada 32.5%
7. Spain 27%
8. Netherlands 25.6%
9. Belgium 25.5%
10. Norway 13.8%
11. France 12.8%
12. Switzerland 8.6%

This is a somewhat unusual list so I suppose I should reveal my source. It was: *Experiences of Crime across the World; Key Findings from the 1989 International Crime Survey* by J.J.M. van Dijk, P. Mayhew and M. Killias (1990).

The areas of the UK with most burglaries

1. North 35.04 (per 1,000 people in a year)
2. Yorkshire and Humberside 32.14
3. North West 27.06
4. Greater London 26.37

"A kleptomaniac is a person who helps himself because he can't help himself."

ANON.

5. West Midlands 25.83
6. East Midlands 22.83
7. Scotland 22.77
8. South East (excluding Greater London) 21.3
9. Wales 20.47
10. South West 19.23
11. East Anglia 16.94
12. Northern Ireland 10.39

England 24.26

The North is particularly bad—worse even than London—and more than twice as bad as East Anglia.

N.B. Burglary is when someone enters premises illegally with intent to steal. Robbery includes purse-snatching, car theft, shop-lifting and burglary. Therefore, all burglaries are robberies but not all robberies are burglaries.

The best clear-up rates for burglaries in the UK

1. North West 35%
2. North 30%
3. West Midlands 29%
4. East Anglia 27%
5. Wales 26%
6. East Midlands 25%
7. Yorkshire and Humberside 24%
8. Northern Ireland 22%
9. South West 20%
10. Scotland 15%
11. South East (excluding Greater London) 14%
12. Greater London 11%

England 23%

The clear-up rates are obviously worse for burglary than for other offenses because, unlike other offenses, burglaries are nearly always reported—if only for insurance purposes.

Percentage increases in burglaries in the UK in the last decade

1. Northern Ireland—22%
2. Scotland 23%
3. Greater London 33%
4. North West 40%
5. South East (excluding Greater London) 55%
6. Wales 60%
7. West Midlands 62%
8. East Midlands 72%
9. North 88%
10. East Anglia 93%
11. Yorkshire and Humberside 100%
12. South West 121%

England 66%

The top ten values of goods stolen during burglaries in England and Wales

	Value of goods stolen	*Burglaries*
1.	£101–£500	321,354
2.	Nothing of value	305,881
3.	£1,001–£5,000	170,735
4.	£501–£1,000	147,940
5.	£26–£100	124,057
6.	£5–£25	66,675
7.	Under £5	54,472
8.	£5,001–£10,000	18,489
9.	£10,001–£50,000	9,306
10.	£50,001 and over	555
	Total burglaries	**1,219,464**

The average value of property stolen was £976. Property recovered (as a total percentage of the total value) was 7%.

Even allowing for the fact that people tend to overestimate (for insurance purposes) the value of goods stolen, the average figure of £976 seems rather high—especially as in roughly a quarter of the burglaries, the burglar walked away with nothing.

The areas of the UK with most robberies

1. Greater London 3.01 (per 1,000 people in a year)
2. South East (excluding Greater London) 1.47
3. Scotland 1.22
4. Northern Ireland 1.16
5= North West 0.89
5= West Midlands 0.89
7. Yorkshire and Humberside 0.57
8. East Midlands 0.54
9. South West 0.44
10. North 0.39
11. East Anglia 0.29
12. Wales 0.2

   England 0.94

Interesting that Wales is substantially lower than the other UK countries. Note also that the North has a much better record (in comparison with the other regions) for robbery than it has for burglary.

"A burglar who respects his art always takes his time before taking anything else."

O. HENRY

The best clear-up rates for robberies in the UK

1.   Wales 48%
2.   East Anglia 45%
3.   North 35%
4= South West 34%
4= Yorkshire and Humberside 34%
6= East Midlands 33%
6= West Midlands 33%
8.   North West 29%
9.   Scotland 27%
10. Northern Ireland 17%
11. South East (excluding Greater London) 16%
12. Greater London 13%

England 23%

Percentage increases in robberies in the UK in the last decade

1.   Northern Ireland −35%
2.   Scotland 51%
3.   Wales 58%
4.   Greater London 95%
5.   South East (excluding Greater London) 96%
6.   North West 142%
7.   North 146%
8.   East Anglia 151%
9.   West Midlands 160%
10. East Midlands 179%
11. Yorkshire and Humberside 191%
12. South West 212%

England 120%

The areas of the UK with most offenses of theft and handling stolen goods

1.   North 65.24 (per 1,000 people in a year)
2.   Greater London 62.99

3. Yorkshire & Humberside 61.02
4. North West 57.55
5. East Midlands 56.53
6. Scotland 55.74
7. South East (excluding Greater London) 54.36
8. West Midlands 49.01
9. South West 48.74
10. Wales 48.25
11. East Anglia 44.77
12. Northern Ireland 20.09

England 54.81

The best clear-up rates for theft and handling stolen goods in the UK

1. North West 38%
2. East Anglia 37%
3= North 34%
3= Northern Ireland 34%
3= Wales 34%
6. Yorkshire and Humberside 31%
7. West Midlands 30%
8= East Midlands 28%
8= South West 28%
10. Scotland 23%
11. South East (excluding Greater London) 19%
12. Greater London 13%

England 27%

Percentage of Americans whose homes have been illegally entered during the year

1987
Yes   6%
No   94%
1988
Yes   7%
No   93%

Dr. Baruch Goldstein, the Israeli settler who walked into a Hebron mosque and massacred fifty-four Moslem worshippers in one of the worst spree killings of recent times. *(Hulton Deutsch Collection)*

American serial killer John Wayne Gacy spent fourteen years on Death Row. He was finally executed by lethal injection in May 1994. *(Topham)*

When Dr. William Palmer, "The Rugeley Poisoner," went to the gallows at Stafford Gaol on June 14, 1856, thousands turned up to watch him hang.
(*Peter Newark's Historical Pictures*)

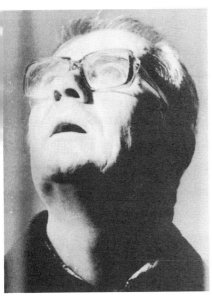

"Rostov Ripper" Andrei Chikatilo, executed in March 1994 for the sex-and-torture murders of over fifty-five young people during a twelve-year rampage through the south of the former USSR. (*Popperfoto*)

Prostitute Aileen "Lee" Wuornos admitted murdering seven men and by the time of her trial in 1992 had earned herself the label of "America's First Female Serial Killer." (*Popperfoto*)

Police search the house and garden at 25 Cromwell Street, Gloucester, home of Frederick and Rosemary West. Human remains have been found here and at other locations associated with the West family.
(*Topham*)

Dubbed "The Gay Slayer," Colin Ireland preyed on homosexual men in London, killing five between March and June 1993.
(*Hulton Deutsch Collection*)

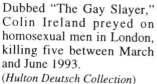

The so-called "Co-ed Killer" Edmund Kemper, convicted in 1973 of eight murders including that of his mother. He asked to be executed but the court in Santa Cruz sentenced him to life imprisonment.
(*Topham*)

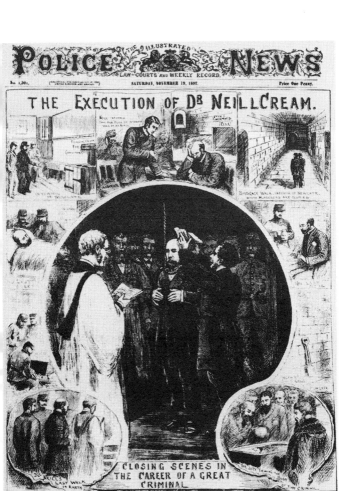

Briefly suspected to be Jack the Ripper, Dr. Thomas Neill Cream poisoned four prostitutes and was hanged at Newgate Prison on November 15, 1892.
(*Peter Newark's Historical Pictures*)

Child-killer Robert Black is led away from Newcastle Crown Court in May 1994 after being found guilty of the murders of schoolgirls Susan Maxwell, Caroline Hogg and Sarah Harper. (*Press Association*)

Houskeeper Louisa Merrifield making the bed in which Mrs. Sarah Ann Ricketts died. Found guilty of poisoning the elderly widow with phosphorus, Louisa Merrifield was hanged at Strangeways Prison on September 18, 1953. (*Popperfoto*)

Charles Manson arrives at court in Los Angeles to stand trial for the Tate-LaBianca murders. (*Topham*)

Actress Sharon Tate, who was pregnant at the time of her murder by members of Manson's "Family" in 1969. (*Popperfoto*)

John Gilbert Graham, the cynical insurance murderer who planted dynamite in his mother's suitcase. She became one of forty-four people to die when United Airlines flight 629 exploded in midair on November 1, 1955. (*Topham*)

The twisted wreckage of the United Airlines plane blown out of the sky by John Graham's bomb. (*Topham*)

Police discover the body of another Ripper victim.
(*Peter Newark's Historical Pictures*)

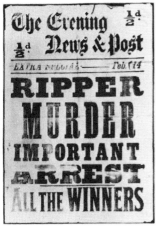

Despite this optimistic contemporary newspaper headline, the identity of Jack the Ripper remains one of crime's greatest unsolved mysteries.
(*Peter Newark's Historical Pictures*)

Among the men suspected of being the Ripper was HRH Prince Albert Victor, Duke of Clarence.
(*Hulton Deutsch Collection*)

Dr. Geza de Kaplany, "The Acid Doctor." Jealous paranoia drove him to mutilate his wife with acid so that no other man would look at her. (*Topham*)

The beautiful Hajna de Kaplany, whose mother prayed for her to die following the vicious attack by her husband. (*Topham*)

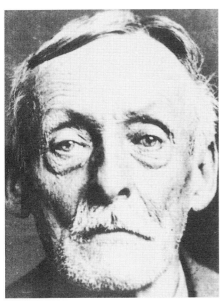

Albert Howard Fish, the child molester, murderer and cannibal who short-circuited the electric chair. (*Topham*)

Violent riots erupted in Los Angeles following the acquittal of four police officers accused of beating black motorist Rodney King. (*Popperfoto*)

"Son of Sam" David Berkowitz, the American serial killer instructed by "voices" to kill. (*Popperfoto*)

Former policeman and mass murderer Dennis Nilsen. (*Syndication International*)

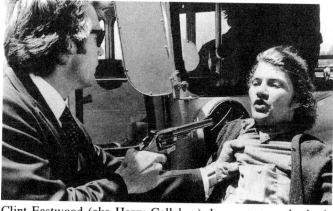

Clint Eastwood (aka Harry Callahan) demonstrates why he is arguably the greatest movie cop of all time. (*The Kobal Collection*)

The assassination of Abraham Lincoln. (*Peter Newark's Western Americana*)

American actress Mae West, charged in 1926 with "corrupting the morals of youth." (*Topham*)

Dutch forger Han Van Meegeren painting his seventh "Vermeer" under police supervision.
(*Peter Newark's Historical Pictures*)

Kidnap victim John Paul Getty III arrives at police headquarters in Rome, his right ear clearly missing.
(*Topham*)

Stern journalist Gerd Heidemann holds aloft the fake Hitler diaries. (*Popperfoto*)

Bushranger Ned Kelly, Australia's most famous criminal and the subject of the world's first ever feature-length film, *The Story of the Kelly Gang* (1906). (*Peter Newark's Historical Pictures*)

Kenneth Erskine (center), the killer who stalked elderly residents of south London during 1986 and became known as "The Stockwell Strangler." (*Topham*)

Timothy Evans, hanged for his wife's murder in 1950 and posthumously pardoned in 1966. Serial killer John Christie, the Evans' landlord, confessed in 1953 to the murder of Beryl Evans. (*Popperfoto*)

1989
Yes   6%
No   94%
1990
Yes   6%
No   94%
1991
Yes   5%
No   95%

This list is based on a survey and while there is no reason to suppose that respondents haven't been truthful, it should be pointed out that the "Nos" include nonrespondents.

Injuries, deaths and hostage-taking during US bank and other robberies

Victim	Injuries	Deaths	Hostages taken
Customer	24	1	31
Employee	67	1	87
Employee's relative	0	0	2
Perpetrator	20	16	N/A
Law officer	8	0	0
Guard	9	6	2
Other	4	3	13
Total (1991)	**132**	**27**	**135**

4
FRAUD, FORGERY AND CONS

The ten greatest art and literary forgeries of all time

1. WILLIAM HENRY IRELAND

Ireland managed to convince the scholars of England (including James Boswell) that he had discovered hitherto unknown letters and two plays written by Shakespeare. One of the plays was actually performed at London's Drury Lane Theater in 1796. In fact, Ireland had manufactured his entire Shakespearean "find" and written all the material himself on paper specially dyed to simulate age. He admitted his forgery in 1797 but went unpunished.

2. YVES CHAUDRON

In 1911, six Americans each paid $300,000 for the *Mona Lisa*. All six paintings had been painted by Frenchman Yves Chaudron.

3. CLIFFORD IRVING

In 1971, Irving convinced his New York publisher that he had been commissioned to ghostwrite the autobiography of the famous reclusive billionaire Howard Hughes. People believed it to be genuine. His wife, pretending to be Mrs. Helga R. Hughes, opened a bank account in Switzerland. After sixty-seven days, the hoax was discovered and Irving was sent to prison for seventeen months.

4. ALCIBIADES SIMONIDES
In 1853, Simonides sold collections of ancient Greek, Egyptian and Assyrian manuscripts and letters to scholars—as well as an ancient manuscript of Homer to the King of Greece. They were all found to be forgeries but Simonides didn't go to prison.

5. THOMAS CHATTERTON
In 1767, Chatterton, an articled clerk with a Bristol law firm, forged the work of a fifteenth-century monk named Thomas Rowley, producing letters, poems and diaries. He was subsequently forced to admit the forgeries and committed suicide by taking poison.

6. FRITZ KREISLER
In the 1890s, Kreisler, a famous violinist from Vienna, wrote salon pieces which he ascribed to composers such as Couperin, Pugnani and Vivaldi. What made Kreisler a great forger was that he wasn't actually discovered: he himself confessed to the forgeries in 1935.

7. ELMYR DE HORY
Reckoned by experts to be the greatest (discovered) art forger of all time, he did forgeries of paintings "by"— among others—Chagall, Matisse, Modigliani and Picasso. He was exposed in 1967 and committed suicide in 1976.

8. HAN VAN MEEGEREN
In the 1930s, Dutch artist Van Meegeren painted forgeries of pictures including *The Last Supper* and *Isaac Blessing Jacob* and sold them for a total of 750,000 florins. At first police thought he had stolen *Christ and the Adulteress* but eventually he admitted that he had painted it himself. They didn't believe him until he painted a picture for them. He became a national hero during his trial and was given the minimum sentence of one year in jail.

9. JOHN PAYNE COLLIER

In the nineteenth century, Collier—an expert on the literature of Tudor England—wrote a book, *History of English Dramatic Poetry in the Time of Shakespeare,* in which he added invented details of his own. He also gained access to literary items held at Dulwich College, where he tampered a great deal with letters and a diary. However, a colleague in the Shakespeare Society blew the whistle on him and he was publicly exposed as a forger.

10. TOM KEATING

Keating faked pictures by great artists such as Rembrandt, Goya and Samuel Palmer—indeed, the first Palmer painting Keating faked sold for £94,000. In all, he faked more than 2,000 works in the style of more than 120 artists. In July 1976, he was exposed as a faker but the case against him was dropped because of his deteriorating health. However, he recovered enough to present his own TV series on Britain's Channel 4.

Six great financial forgeries

1. JAMES TOWNSEND SAWARD

In 1857, Saward, a London barrister, operated a complex scam in which he forged signatures on other people's checks, employed solicitors to collect prearranged debts and then forged his own debt-collectors' signatures while pocketing the money himself. He was transported to Australia for a life of penal servitude.

"I came to the conclusion many years ago that almost all crime is due to the repressed desire for aesthetic expression."

EVELYN WAUGH

2. WILLIAM DODD

Dodd, an Essex clergyman, frittered away his wife's legacy and was struck off the list of chaplains in 1774. So he became a forger. He got a stockbroker to dispose of a bond—worth £4,200—supposedly signed by Lord Chesterfield. However, it became clear that the signature had been faked and, on June 27, 1777, Dodd was hanged.

3. HENRY FAUNTLEROY

At a young age he was made a partner of the private bank his father had founded. In 1815, he lent a lot of money to a speculative builder but the money was lost and so he forged documents which authorized transferrals into the bank to cover the loss. Once he'd done that, he started forging for his own gain. He was eventually found out and he was hanged at the Old Bailey on November 30, 1824.

4. IVAR KREUGER (aka "THE MATCH KING")

By the end of the First World War, Kreuger's company, the Swedish Match Company, had a monopoly in Sweden but he wanted a world monopoly and so he gave loans to countries that had run into difficulties in return for the match monopoly (for example, in 1927, he lent £15 million to France). However, in 1930 several of the countries that owed him money defaulted on their payments so, to raise cash, he forged forty-two Italian Treasury bills to the value of £20 million. They were discovered to be forgeries and he shot himself in Paris on March 11, 1932.

5. THOMAS WAINEWRIGHT

In 1821, he married Frances Ward but continued with his expensive bachelor lifestyle. To augment his income, he forged the signature of his trustees on documents that would allow him to sell £2,000 worth of stocks. He got the money but his forgery was eventually discovered and in 1837 he was transported from Britain to Van Diemen's Land (Tasmania) for life.

6. ARTUR ALVES REIS

Reis forged letters and documents which convinced the British firm, Waterlow and Sons, which printed money for the Bank of Portugal, that he was personally authorized to receive some $10 million worth of escudos for "the Portuguese colony of Angola." With all this money, he founded his own bank in Lisbon and bought enough shares in the Bank of Portugal to become a leading shareholder. A duplication of serial numbers led to his arrest in 1925 and fifteen years in prison. He died penniless.

Five great political forgeries

1. PROTOCOLS OF THE ELDERS OF ZION

This vicious forgery first appeared in a St. Petersburg newspaper in 1903. It was a document that purported to reveal a Jewish conspiracy to take over the world. In reality, the document was most probably put together by Tsar Nicholas II's police and succeeded because it reflected what the anti-Semitic Russian people wanted to believe. It was also translated abroad—especially in Nazi Germany—on the same basis. The sad fact is that even now, fifty years after the Holocaust, there are still evil racists who believe that there is a Jewish conspiracy extending from New York to Moscow—and that is entirely based on the original *Protocols of the Elders of Zion.* Which goes to prove that a lie can be halfway around the world before the truth has put its boots on . . .

2. RICHARD PIGOTT

In 1866, Pigott, the proprietor and editor of *The Irishman,* founded two new magazines, *Shamrock* and *Flag of Ireland* which reflected his nationalist political views. However, poor circulation obliged him (reluctantly) to sell his three periodicals to fellow nationalist, Charles Stewart Parnell. This displeased Pigott and he took his revenge on Parnell by forging papers which alleged that

Parnell and his supporters had taken part in crimes and condoned the Phoenix Park tragedy in which Lord Cavendish, the new Chief Secretary for Ireland, was hacked to death by extreme Irish nationalists. Pigott's forgery was discovered when he was cross-examined by Parnell's lawyer at an inquiry held after *The Times* had used him as a source for articles critical of Parnell. Pigott fled to Spain where he shot himself before he could be arrested.

3. THE HITLER DIARIES
Gerd Heidemann, a journalist with the German photoweekly *Stern,* claimed to have obtained Hitler's diaries which had been miraculously saved from an air crash near Dresden on April 21, 1945. These would be serialized by *Stern* on April 22, 1983. *Paris-Match,* Italy's *Panorama* and *The Sunday Times* all agreed serialization deals with *Stern.* Heidemann's biggest break came when the respected historian Lord Dacre (Hugh Trevor-Roper)—brought in by *The Sunday Times*—authenticated the diaries. Other experts were not so easily fooled. In the subsequent trial, it transpired that Heidemann, a man apparently obsessed with the Third Reich, had conspired with Konrad Kujau, a former nightclub owner and dealer in Nazi memorabilia who had actually written the forgeries.

4. THE ZINOVIEV LETTER
Just before the 1924 General Election in Britain, the Conservatives published a copy of a letter—supporting a British revolution—supposedly sent from Grigori Zinoviev of the Communist International to British Communists. Irrespective of the provenance of the letter, the Conservatives won the election with a huge majority.

5. THE NAZI BANK NOTE FORGERY
During the Second World War, the Nazis forged millions of near-perfect five-pound notes in order to undermine the British economy. The forgery was going to

continue after the war (in an Alpine hideaway) until the perpetrators were caught *in flagrante* in 1945 with notes worth £21 million. Interestingly, the British had tried the same trick themselves with the French in the early nineteenth century in order to undermine post-Revolutionary France.

Ten notable frauds

1. JACK DICKIE
In 1982 Craig Young was found shot dead. He was president and sole shareholder of a Montana finance company that was, in reality, just a shell controlled by Dickie who had persuaded Young to buy mining claims for $2.5 million from another shell company and take out insurance to cover this liability—the idea being that Dickie would get his hands on the insurance money after murdering Young. In 1987 Dickie was found guilty of doing just that.

2. JOHN KEELY
At the turn of the century, Keely, from Philadelphia, persuaded some businessmen that his scheme to produce power from water without the expense of converting it to steam was a good investment. The Keely Motor Co. was set up and was soon trading on stock markets around the world—raising huge amounts of money from several investors. However, in the twenty-four years that the company was in existence, all Keely's "experimental" machines were actually powered by air compressors. Fortunately for Keely, he had already died of natural causes when the truth emerged.

"How many crimes were committed merely because their authors could not endure being wrong!"

ALBERT CAMUS

3. REVEREND JIM BAKKER

In 1988, Bakker, the American televangelist, was exposed as having an affair with church secretary Jessica Hahn, whose silence he bought for $265,000. However, this led to his being exposed as a major fraudster. He was convicted of twenty-two counts of fraud and sentenced to forty-five years in jail.

4. HORATIO BOTTOMLEY

In 1908, Bottomley, the founder of *The Hackney Hansard* (1884), *The Financial Times* (1888) and *John Bull* (1906) and Hackney's Liberal MP, was prosecuted for manipulating the crash of his Joint Stock Institute. He defended himself brilliantly and was acquitted. However, when he stole over £150,000 from the Government's Victory Loan Scheme—set up to help finance the First World War—he was found guilty of fraud and sentenced to seven years of penal servitude in 1922. He died penniless in 1933.

5. JABEZ SPENCER BALFOUR

Balfour's companies were successful but were founded on the "snowball" principle by which shares in one company are floated and the money raised is used to finance another company. Eventually, one of his companies collapsed with debts of £8 million and this led to the whole edifice crumbling. Balfour fled from Britain to Argentina but was arrested and, in November 1895, was sentenced to fourteen years of penal servitude.

6. J. DAVID DOMINELLI

The American firm of J. David & Co. promised investors up to a massive forty percent annual return on their money, tax free, and with complete confidentiality. Needless to say, most of the money was spent by Dominelli on his personal life. When the balloon went up in 1984, it was discovered that Dominelli had only $600,000 in liquid assets to cover over $150 million in liabilities.

7. ALEXANDRE SERGE STAVISKY

In France, pawnbrokers were allowed to issue bonds to the value of the goods that they were holding. Stavisky (1888–1934) took advantage of this by having his accomplice, Gustave Tissier, appointed as the director of a pawnshop in Bayenne. He then put out fake jewelry for which he issued inexpensive bonds and, in this way, made about £2 million. The fraud was discovered in 1933 but Stavisky escaped to the ski resort of Chamonix where he was eventually tracked down. However, he shot himself before he could be arrested.

8. ROBERT MAXWELL

The egomaniacal Labor-MP-turned-newspaper-proprietor-and-publisher had an incredibly complex business empire which came to light after his death in 1991. Although much is still shrouded in mystery, what is not in doubt is that he defrauded thousands of his employees of their pensions to subsidize his businesses and incredibly lavish lifestyle, which included a private helicopter and yacht, the *Lady Ghislaine,* from which he fell to his death while sailing off the Canary Islands.

9. DR. CECIL JACOBSON

In 1992, Jacobson, the principal of a fertility clinic in Virginia, was offering childless couples artificial insemination. However, despite his assurances to his clients that the sperm on offer was from carefully selected male donors, the truth was that every woman was being inseminated with sperm from Jacobson himself. This fraud came to light after babies were born which all bore a strong resemblance to Jacobson. In total, he impregnated seventy-five women. He was sentenced to five years in jail.

10. WALLACE SMITH

Wallace Smith, a London businessman, perpetrated a fraud which netted £90 million. In 1994, he was convicted at the Old Bailey of fraudulent trading and obtaining property by deception and was jailed for six years.

Seven famous cons

1. PILTDOWN MAN
In 1912, in a gravel pit near Piltdown Common in East Sussex, England, Charles Dawson unearthed what was called the "missing link" between man and ape. As time went by, its authenticity was doubted. In 1953, tests proved that the teeth of the skeleton had been filed down and stained to make it look older and so it was conclusively proved to be a fake.

2. CORN CIRCLES
Although corn circles have been around for more than 300 years, there was a whole spate of them in Britain a few years ago when circular patterns in Wiltshire cornfields began appearing during the summer of 1990. Explanations put forward for the circles included wind patterns and UFOs. However, many—though not by any means all—of the recent crop of corn circles were in fact discovered to have been made by hoaxers using, among other implements, ropes and wooden stakes.

3. THE GIANT MAN FOSSIL
In 1868, New Yorker William Newell and his cousin, George Hull, exhibited what they said was the fossil of a giant man and fooled many scientists of the day into believing that it provided proof that such a creature once existed. In fact, Newell and Hull had hired a Chicago stonemason to make the "fossil" from gypsum and had it stained with sulphuric acid and ink to age it artificially.

4. HITLER—THE RETURN
In 1946, with rumors abounding everywhere that Adolf Hitler was still alive, William H. Johnson, a semi-literate miner from Middlesboro, Kentucky, pretended

to be Hitler—but only by post. He wrote to many people all over the USA, pretending to be Hitler and telling them of his plan to take over the USA and asking them to please send him some money. Amazingly—and frighteningly—he managed to collect $15,000 before he was exposed.

5. THE TURIN SHROUD
In 1988, the Turin Shroud, which had been believed to have come from the tomb of Christ and to contain his imprint, was finally and irrefutably exposed as a fraud. The shroud is now believed to date from between 1260 to 1390.

6. THE BANK THAT NEVER WAS
In 1908, Joseph "Yellow Kid" Weil went into partnership with a plainclothes policeman called Fred Buckminster who had earlier arrested him. Together, they ran many cons but perhaps their finest moment came when they rented an abandoned bank in Indiana and filled it with conmen who pretended to be wealthy investors—thereby fooling people into depositing their money in the bank.

7. SOUVENIRS FOR SALE
In 1925, Scotsman Arthur Ferguson persuaded American tourists to buy some of the world's great national monuments. He talked several Americans into paying £6,000 for Trafalgar Square and £1,000 for Big Ben. He then went to Washington where he managed to sell a ninety-nine-year lease on the White House. Eventually, he was arrested and sent to prison for five years.

"Crime is a logical extension of the sort of behavior that is often considered perfectly respectable in legitimate business."

ROBERT RICE

The areas of the UK with most fraud and forgery offenses

1. Greater London 6.15 (per 1,000 people in a year)
2. Scotland 5.18
3. South East (excluding Greater London) 4.32
4. South West 4.03
5. North West 3.54
6. Northern Ireland 3.02
7. North 2.80
8. Yorkshire and Humberside 2.75
9. East Anglia 2.73
10. East Midlands 2.65
11. Wales 2.51
12. West Midlands 2.32

England 3.02

The best clear-up rates for fraud and forgery in the UK

1. North West 74%
2. Scotland 71%
3. South West 69%
4. Northern Ireland 67%
5. Wales 62%
6. East Anglia 61%
7. Yorkshire and Humberside 58%
8. North 56%
9. East Midlands 52%
10. South East (excluding Greater London) 47%
11. West Midlands 46%
12. Greater London 44%

England 55%

We have to accept this list for what it is—while bearing in mind that so many frauds/forgeries are unreported.

Percentage increases in fraud and forgery offenses in the UK in the last decade

1. North West 19%
2. Scotland 25%
3. East Midlands 38%
4. Wales 40%
5. Greater London 43%
6. South East (excluding Greater London) 64%
7. West Midlands 69%
8. Northern Ireland 78%
9. North 80%
10. East Anglia 91%
11. Yorkshire and Humberside 97%
12. South West 103%

England 61%

THE POLICE

Bad apples . . . Nine cases of policemen who broke the law

I start from the premise that the police forces in Western countries are, by and large, honest. There are some policemen who become intoxicated with power to the extent that they believe themselves to be the law, rather than its servants but I suppose that is always going to happen to some extent. What has changed is that policemen themselves will no longer tolerate policemen on the take. It hasn't always been so: one is reminded of the Louisiana police chief of the 1930s who boasted— *boasted* mind—that his police force was "honeycombed with honesty."

1. JACOBUS COETZEE (South Africa)
In one of those bizarre, coincidental cases which the world of crime seems to throw up regularly, Jacobus Coetzee, a South African detective sergeant, was sent to investigate the murder of Gertrina Petrusina Opperman—a murder which he himself had committed on January 31, 1935. He was arrested after his victim's employer recalled seeing the two of them in bed together and he was found guilty of murder in May 1935. Coetzee was sentenced to imprisonment with labor for life but was released in 1947.

2. JAMES ROLAND ROBERTSON (UK)
On the night of July 27, 1950, P.C. Robertson, a serving police officer, ran over Mrs. McCluskey—who was the

mother of his child. The police decided it was deliberate and Robertson was tried for murder in Glasgow and was hanged on December 16, 1950.

3. MOHAMMED MUSTAPHA TABET (Morocco)
In 1993, Mohammed Mustapha Tabet, Morocco's chief police commissioner, was sentenced to death after being found guilty of more than 1,500 sex crimes.

4. HOWARD WILSON (UK)
On December 30, 1969, Wilson and two other armed men robbed the Clydesdale Bank in Bridge Street, Linwood, Scotland, and escaped with over £14,000 before driving to Wilson's flat which was close to the Southern Police Division's HQ. As they were unloading they were observed by Inspector Andrew Hyslop, who recognized Wilson as a former policeman. As the police began a search of the flat, Wilson fired at Hyslop and shot two other officers—killing one instantly. In February 1970, Wilson was convicted of murder and sentenced to life imprisonment.

5. STEPHEN WEBSTER and TYRONE PICKENS (USA)
On August 17, 1981, two men broke into Terry Johnson's Chicago flat. She took down the number on the police badge that one of them was wearing and the identity number on the fender of their police car. The officers were arrested and sent to jail.

6. WILLIAM NICHOLSON (South Africa)
Nicholson, a South African former policeman, killed his wife on September 1, 1956, by smashing her head with a hammer. He then made up a story that a colored intruder had forced his way into their house and killed his wife but that he had grabbed the hammer and rushed at the intruder who managed to escape. His story was not believed and he was hanged on August 12, 1957.

7. THE OBSCENE PUBLICATIONS SQUAD (UK)

In the 1970s, the Metropolitan Police's Obscene Publications Squad, which had been set up to police Soho's sex shops, was actually taking money from the pornographers on a systematic basis. The corruption spread all the way to the top and, in 1976, twelve officers (and former officers) were arrested and charged—including ex-Detective Superintendent William Moody, the former head of the Obscene Publications Squad, who was sent to jail for twelve years.

8. THE McDUFFIE RIOTS (USA)

In May 1980, Arthur McDuffie, a black man, was stopped for speeding on his motorcycle and beaten to death by four white Miami policemen. Though three officers testified under immunity that their colleagues had beaten McDuffie over the head, the policemen were acquitted. Violence broke out in Miami, and three white men were pulled from a passing car and killed. The riots claimed fourteen deaths and 300 people were injured.

9. THE KING RIOTS (USA)

In March 1992, four white Los Angeles police officers went on trial for the beating of black motorist Rodney King, aged twenty-five. This had occurred on March 3, 1991, and was videotaped, which allowed the whole world to see what looked to be an appalling case of police brutality. However, the four police officers were released and this sparked off a wave of violence and looting in Los Angeles. At least ten people were killed in the riots. In a subsequent civil action, Rodney King was awarded $3 million damages against the L.A. Police Department.

The murder of police officers

In 1830, P.C. Long became the first policeman to be murdered. The last person in London to be hanged for the murder of a police officer was Gunther Fritz Podola in November 1959 for the killing of Detective Sergeant Raymond Purdy.

Fortunately, the murder of police officers in London is still relatively rare (certainly compared to US cities). As proof, here is the list of Metropolitan police officers killed by criminals since 1900:

1900	P.C. Thompson
1909	P.C. Tyler
1915	P.C. Young
1919	P.C. Green
1920	P.C. Kelly
1929	P.C. Self
1930	P.C. Lawes
1942	P.C. Fuller
1948	P.C. Edgar
1952	P.C. Miles
1958	P.C. Summers
1959	D.S. Purdy
1960	P.C. Meeham
1961	Insp. Pawzey
1961	P.C. Hutchings
1966	P.C. Fox
1966	P.C. Wombell
1966	D.S. Head
1969	P.C. Davies
1973	P.C. Whiting
1975	P.C. Tibble
1980	P.C. O'Neil
1983	P.S. Lane
1983	W.P.C. Arbuthnot
1983	Insp. Dodd
1984	W.P.C. Fletcher
1985	P.C. Blakelock
1987	P.C. McCloskey
1990	P.C. Brown
1991	P.S. King
1991	D.C. Morrison
1993	P.C. Dunne
1994	P.S. Robertson

Fact: The British police force is the only one in the E.U. that does not automatically carry guns.

'Allo, 'allo, 'allo . . . Ten former policemen

1. Errol Flynn (legendary Hollywood star)
2. Jeffrey Archer (British politician and author)
3. John Arlott (the doyen of cricket commentators)
4. Aldo Ray (film star)
5. Geoff Capes (formerly the World's Strongest Man)
6. Christopher Dean (gold-medal-winning ice-skater—with Jayne Torvill)
7. Dennis Nilsen (British serial killer)
8. George Orwell (the author of *Animal Farm* and *1984*)
9. Ray Reardon (former World Snooker Champion)
10. Josef Locke (Irish tenor and the subject of the film *Hear My Song*)

The ten European countries where crime victims are least likely to go to the police

1. Spain
2. Finland
3. Norway
4. Northern Ireland
5. Germany
6. Belgium
7. Holland
8. Switzerland
9. England and Wales
10. France

The ten countries which spend the most on their police

1. Greece £334,032 (spent on the police per 1,000 people)
2. Singapore £316,272
3. Bermuda £193,460

4. Sweden £117,406
5. Trinidad and Tobago £94,722
6. Switzerland £90,546
7. Saudi Arabia £87,426
8. The Virgin Islands £84,648
9. Brunei £84,068
10. Greenland £72,732

Just outside this top ten list are the USA in eleventh place (£58,626) and the UK in twelfth (£52,854).

The ten countries which spend the least on their police

1. The Faeroe Islands £33 (spent on the police per 1,000 people)
2. Bangladesh £302
3. Nepal £331
4. Indonesia £511
5. Benin £759
6. Uganda £782
7. South Yemen £1,270
8. Tanzania £1,302
9. Pakistan £1,303
10. The Maldives £1,335

The ten countries with the highest ratio of people to police officers

1. The Maldives 35,710 (people per police officer)
2. Rwanda 4,650
3. The Ivory Coast 4,640
4. Gambia 3,310
5. Benin 3,250
6. Madagascar 2,900
7. Central African Republic 2,740
8. Bangladesh 2,560
9. Niger 2,350
10. Cambodia 1,980

Togo and Syria share eleventh position with a figure of
1,970.

The nine countries with the lowest ratio of people to police officers

1= The Cayman Islands 110 (people per police officer)
1= Montserrat 110
3= Mongolia 120
3= The Seychelles 120
3= Antigua 120
6= Iraq 140
6= United Arab Emirates 140
8= The Bahamas 160
8= Mali 160

The USA has 350 people for every police officer. The
UK has 400 people for every police officer [except when
you actually need one and then the figure goes up to four
million].

The areas of the UK with most police officers

1. South East 49,871 (Metropolitan Police 28,412;
   City of London 826; other forces in South East
   20,633)
2. North West 16,942
3. Scotland 13,923
4. West Midlands 12,335
5. Yorkshire and Humberside 11,704
6. South West 9,810
7. East Midlands 8,348
8. Northern Ireland 8,217
9. North 7,649
10. Wales 6,539
11. East Anglia 3,929

England 120,588

The areas of the UK with the highest percentages of ethnic minorities in the police force

1. West Midlands 1.9%
2. East Midlands 1.8%
3. South East 1.5% (Metropolitan Police 1.9%; City of London 1%; other forces in the South East 0.9%)
4. North West 1.3%
5. Yorkshire and Humberside 1%
6. East Anglia 0.8%
7. South West 0.5%
8= North 0.4%
8= Wales 0.4%
10. Scotland 0.2%
11. Northern Ireland 0%

England 1.3%

The areas of the UK with the highest percentages of women officers in the police force

1. West Midlands 13.5%
2. South East 12.7% (Metropolitan Police 13.1%; City of London 12%; other forces in the South East 12.3%)
3. North West 12.2%
4. Yorkshire and Humberside 10.9%
5. South West 10.7%
6= East Anglia 10.2%
6= East Midlands 10.2%
8. North 10.1%
9. Scotland 9.7%
10. Wales 9.6%
11. Northern Ireland 8.6%

England 12%

The areas of the UK with the greatest number of operations in which firearms were issued to the police

1. South East (including Greater London) 2,162
2. North 395
3. Yorkshire and Humberside 269
4= East Anglia 186
4= North West 186
6. South West 157
7. West Midlands 156
8. East Midlands 108
9. Wales 103
10. Scotland 61

England 3,619

For obvious reasons, there are no figures available for Northern Ireland.

The ten police forces with the best clear-up rates in England and Wales

1. Dyfed–Powys 50%
2. Gwent 47%
3. Lincolnshire 46%
4. Merseyside 45%
5= Cheshire 41%
5= Dorset 41%
7= Cumbria 40%
7= Lancashire 40%
7= Wiltshire 40%
10= Staffordshire 37%
10= Suffolk 37%

The ten police forces with the worst clear-up rates in England and Wales

1. Metropolitan Police 17%
2. Bedfordshire 19%

3: City of London 20%
4. Thames Valley 22%
5= Kent 23%
5= Surrey 23%
5= Sussex 23%
8= Avon and Somerset 24%
8= Warwickshire 24%
10. Nottinghamshire 27%

Percentage of people reporting crimes to the police in the USA

Type of crime	Reported to the police		Unknown/Not ascertained
	Yes	No	
Aggravated assault	62	37	1
Robbery	62	37	1
Crimes of violence	54	45	1
Rape	53	46	1
Simple assault	46	53	1
Crimes of theft	32	67	1

Police response time in the USA

	Crimes of violence	Aggravated assault
Within five minutes	28%	31%
Within ten minutes	31%	32%
Within an hour	32%	29%
Within a day	4.8%	4.4%
Longer than a day	0.7%	0.2%
Length of time not known	4.1%	3.9%

"A broad definition of crime in England is that it is any lower-class activity which is displeasing to the upper class. Crime is committed by the lower class and punished by the upper class."

DAVID FROST AND ANTONY JAY

	Burglary	Car theft
Within five minutes	13%	14%
Within ten minutes	19%	21%
Within an hour	48%	50%
Within a day	12%	9%
Longer than a day	1.5%	0.8%
Length of time not known	7%	6%

If these figures are accurate (and you always have to employ that caveat) then they really are very impressive. Eighty percent or more of all these crimes are responded to by police within an hour.

6
CAPITAL PUNISHMENT

A brief chronology of capital punishment in Britain

1671: The Coventry Act made it a capital offense to lie in wait with intent to disfigure by putting out an eye, disabling the tongue or slitting the nose.

1699: The Shoplifting Act made it a capital crime to steal from a shop goods valued at more than five shillings.

1723: The Waltham Blacks Act was passed to deal with the increasing amount of poaching and damage to forests and parks owned by the nobility. This Act increased the number of capital crimes from about thirty to 150. The last man to be executed under the Act was one William Potter who was executed for cutting down his neighbor's orchard.

1810: There were 222 capital crimes which included rape, sodomy, robbery, burglary, shoplifting, horse-stealing, forgery, adopting a disguise and sacrilege.

1818–33: Many offenses removed from the list of capital crimes, including horse-stealing, cattle-stealing, shoplifting and housebreaking.

1835: Sacrilege, letter-stealing and returning from transportation before finishing sentence ceased to be capital crimes.

1836: Forgery and coining removed from the list of capital crimes.

1841: Rape removed from capital crimes.

1861: The Criminal Law Consolidation Act reduced the number of capital crimes to four: treason, piracy, mutiny and murder.

1868: Parliament passed the Capital Punishment Within Prisons Bill to end public executions.

May 26, 1868: Last public execution—Michael Barrett at Old Bailey.

August 13, 1868: First execution behind walls—Thomas Wells at Maidstone.

***c.* 1875:** William Marwood introduced the "long drop."

1908: People under sixteen could no longer be executed.

1922: Infanticide Act: women who killed their newborn babies were no longer subject to capital punishment.

1931: Pregnant women no longer subject to capital punishment.

1948: The House of Commons approved the suspension of capital punishment for an experimental period of five years, but this was reversed by the House of Lords.

July 13, 1955: Execution of the last (and youngest) woman—Ruth Ellis for the murder of David Blakely.

March 1957: Parliament passed the 1957 Homicide Act limiting capital murder to five categories:

1. Murder in the course or furtherance of theft.
2. Murder by shooting or causing an explosion.

3.   Murder while resisting arrest or during an escape.
4.   Murder of a policeman or prison officer.
5.   Two murders committed on different occasions.

August 13, 1964: Last British hangings: Peter Anthony Allen and Gwynne Owen Evans for murder in the course of theft.

November 9, 1965: The Murder (Abolition of Death Penalty) Bill suspending capital punishment for murder for a trial period of five years was passed by Parliament.

December 1969: Parliament confirmed the abolition of capital punishment for murder.

May 29, 1992: Christie's auction the execution equipment of Albert Pierrepoint, Britain's last hangman (resigned 1956).

February 1994: In the most recent of a regular series of votes on the issue, Parliament voted by the largest-ever majority against restoring capital punishment.

Ten of the most used methods of execution in the world

1. Hanging (Last used in the USA in the execution of Westley Alan Dodd in Washington State on January 5, 1993. Formerly the sole means of execution in the USA, it is now rarely used there. Still in use in some countries, notably Malaysia and Iran.)

2. Beheading (By axe, sword or guillotine.)

3. Firing squad (Now widespread as a method of execution, in 1989 it was used by eighty-six countries. The weapons employed range from pistols to rifles, even sub-machine guns.)

4. Electrocution (Electrodes are attached to the victim's head and calf. A current of 1,800–2,000 volts is sent through the body for about five minutes. The electric chair first appeared in New York on June 4, 1888. The first person to die by this method was wife-murderer William Kemmler, in Auburn State Prison on August 6, 1890.)

5. The gas chamber (An American innovation first used in the state of Nevada on February 7, 1924 to execute Gee Jon, who died six minutes after the introduction of hydrocyanic gas into the chamber.)

6. Lethal injection (Introduced in 1980 and first used in 1982, this method of execution sparked off intense debate over the ethics of using medical procedures and medically trained people to take life.)

7. Hanging, drawing and quartering (The victim was hanged and cut down while still alive. Then his stomach was cut open and his bowels were taken out and burned in front of him. Finally, he was decapitated and cut into quarters.)

8. Burning (A sentence imposed on heretics: the fire was supposed to prepare them for the fires of hell that awaited them.)

9. The garrotte (A collar was put around the victim's neck and a post. A mechanism at the back of the collar was then tightened, driving a screw into the nape of the neck thereby cutting the spinal cord.)

10. Boiling (In water or oil which was either boiling already or heated after the victim had been placed in the cauldron.)

Methods popular in specific countries include: Trampling to death by elephants (India); The Death of Twenty-one Cuts (Japan) (the executioner would slice away pieces of the victim's body, killing him with the twenty-first and last cut); and The Cave of Roses (Sweden) (seventeenth-century punishment in which prisoners were put into a cave full of poisonous snakes).

Thirteen extraordinary hangings — and non-hangings

1. GREEN, BERRY and HILL (UK)
In 1679, Messrs. Green, Berry and Hill were hanged at Tyburn for a murder they committed . . . on Greenberry Hill.

2. THOMAS REYNOLDS (UK)
On July 26, 1736, Thomas Reynolds was hanged for robbery at Tyburn Hill. Having been cut down he was then placed in a coffin. However, as the hangman's assistant was nailing down the coffin lid Reynolds pushed the lid away and grabbed the assistant's arm. He was taken to a nearby house where he vomited three pints of blood and died.

3. WILLIAM JOHN GRAY (UK)
Sentenced to hang for the murder of his wife, Gray was reprieved on April 3, 1948, after medical examiners ruled that hanging would cause him too much pain. This was based on the extent of injuries to his jaw, and it was explained that if he were hanged the noose would not dislocate his neck and that he would either die of strangulation or he would be decapitated altogether as his injured jawbone was too weak to hold the rope around his neck.

4. ELIZABETH WILSON (USA)
She was hanged at Chester, Pennsylvania, in 1786, for the murder of her ten-week-old twin children. Elizabeth Wilson was reprieved but the news arrived twenty-three minutes too late for her. This has now become a Pennsylvanian folk-tale.

5. ROBERT ALEXANDER BURTON (UK)

In 1863, Robert Alexander Burton was hanged outside Maidstone Prison for the murder of Thomas Frederick Houghton. Burton's motive for murder was that he wished to be hanged. He was therefore successful in his mission—but so much for the deterrent effect of capital punishment . . .

6. WILLIAM KOGUT (USA)

When found guilty of murdering a woman in 1930, Kogut vowed that no one would execute him. He removed the red spots—containing nitrate and cellulose—from the hearts and diamonds of a deck of cards and out of these ingredients he made a bomb by which he blew himself to death.

7. JOHN ASHTON (UK)

In 1814, John Ashton ran up the ladder to the Old Bailey scaffold in London shouting, "I'm Lord Wellington! Look at me, I'm Lord Wellington!" When the trapdoor opened, Ashton bounced back, shouting, "What do you think of me now? Am I not Lord Wellington now?" However, after a struggle he died.

8. WILL PURVIS (USA)

Purvis, allegedly a member of the Ku Klux Klan, was due to be hanged in February 1894 at Columbia in Marion County, Mississippi for murdering his black neighbor, Will Buckley. Purvis repeatedly claimed his innocence and as he was about to be hanged the noose-knot came undone. So Reverend Sibley asked the crowd: "All who want to see this boy hanged a second time hold up their hands." No one did and he was released and later pardoned.

9. INETTA DE BALSHAM (UK)

De Balsham was hanged at precisely 9 a.m. on August 16, 1264. The king's messenger arrived a few seconds later with a reprieve. The hangman ran up the stairs and cut the rope with a sword. The victim's face had already turned blue but she managed to survive. (However, it was not only in the thirteenth century that death by hanging was not always instantaneous. Herbert Leonard Mills was hanged for murder on December 11, 1951, at Lincoln Prison but there is some doubt about the time of death. The medical officer reported at the inquest that Mills' heart had continued to beat for twenty minutes after the drop.)

10. ANN GREEN (UK)
Charged with the murder of her newborn baby, Ann Green was hanged at Oxford Gaol in 1650. After an hour, she was cut down but was seen to be twitching. One person jumped on her stomach and a soldier struck her on the head with his musket. Her body was then passed on to a professor of anatomy who was preparing to cut her open when he heard a noise from her throat. She was put into a warm bed and her breathing restarted. The next day she was almost fully recovered and she was eventually pardoned.

11. JOHN "HALF-HANGED" SMITH (UK)
In 1705, John Smith was hanged for burglary at Tyburn Tree. After he had been hanging for fifteen minutes a reprieve arrived and he was cut down. Amazingly, he was revived and managed to recover.

12. PATRICK REDMOND (Ireland)
In 1767, Patrick Redmond was hanged for robbery in Cork, Ireland. After hanging for twenty-eight minutes he was cut down by a surgeon who was waiting to conduct an experiment in tracheotomy (the corpses of hanged men were often used in medical experiments). Incredibly, Redmond was not dead and was revived by the surgeon. In fact, it is even alleged that the man was well enough to go to the theater the same evening.

13. JOHN LEE (aka "THE MAN THEY COULDN'T HANG") (UK)
On February 23, 1885, John Lee was due to be hanged at Exeter Gaol for the murder of his employer (on thin

circumstantial evidence). However, when the hangman put the noose around his neck, the scaffold's drop wouldn't respond to the lever. Lee was returned to his cell while the hangman tested the drop with weights until it worked perfectly. A second attempt was made, but once again the drop didn't work. When Lee stood on the scaffold for the third time again it proved impossible. Lee was returned to his cell while the Governor contacted the Home Office requesting a reprieve which was granted.

The man who short-circuited the electric chair

ALBERT HOWARD FISH (USA)

This was possibly the most grisly execution in the electric chair. In 1936, the sixty-six-year-old Fish was sentenced to death for being a child molester/murderer and cannibal. Fish was a masochist and, over the years, used to insert small needles under his skin. He went (willingly—indeed, he was looking forward to "the supreme thrill") to the electric chair and 3,000 volts were sent through him, causing blue smoke to come out of his head. However, all his needles short-circuited the electric chair so the executioner had to give him another prolonged charge of electricity. The fact that Fish didn't mind—in fact, enjoyed—the experience doesn't render it any less grisly.

Two Britons who have been executed since 1969

1. **KEVIN BARLOW** and the Australian Brian Chambers became the first foreigners to be executed in Malaysia for drug-trafficking when they were hanged on July 7, 1986, at Pudu Prison in Kuala Lumpur.

2. **DERRICK GREGORY** was caught in possession of drugs in Malaysia and was hanged on July 21, 1989.

On the other hand, the two British girls Patricia Cahill and Karen Smith were a lot luckier. On July 19, 1990, Cahill (aged seventeen) and Smith (aged nineteen) were arrested at Bangkok airport trying to smuggle heroin worth £4 million out of Thailand. They weren't executed but sent to jail and, in 1993, given a pardon and sent back to Britain.

Eleven British hangings for offenses other than murder

1. 1722: James Appleton at Tyburn Tree for the theft of three wigs
2= 1739: Henry Johnson at Tyburn Tree for stealing roof-lead
2= 1739: Thomas Beckwith at Tyburn Tree for robbery (his first offense)
4. 1741: Robert Legrose at Tyburn Tree for stealing clothes
5= 1750: Richard Butler at Tyburn Tree for forgery
5= 1750: Benjamin Beckonfield at Tyburn Tree for the theft of a hat
7. 1785: John Evans at Old Bailey for stealing books
8. 1817: Benjamin and Andrew Savage (twins) at Old Bailey for issuing forged notes
9. 1819: Thomas Wildish and John Booth at Old Bailey for letter-stealing
10. 1825: Henry Denham at Old Bailey for burglary
11. 1831: John Broach at Old Bailey for stealing from a dwelling house

Many children were also hanged for offenses which to us seem exceedingly trivial. In 1782, a fourteen-year-old girl was hanged for being found in the company of gypsies; in 1816, four boys aged between nine and thirteen were hanged in the City of London for begging and stealing; and in 1833 a nine-year-old boy was hanged for stealing a pennyworth of paint from a shop. It was not until 1908 that juveniles (under sixteen) could no longer be hanged in Britain.

He who lives by the rope . . . Four English hangmen who were themselves hanged

1. Cratwell (hangman 1534–8): hanged at Clerkenwell, London, in 1538 for robbing a booth at St. Bartholomew's Fair.
2. Stump-leg (hangman 1553–6): hanged at Tyburn Tree in 1558 for thieving. Machyn, a contemporary diarist, wrote of him: "He himself had hangyd many a man, and quartered many, and had beheaded many a nobulman."
3. Pascha Rose (hangman in 1686): hanged at Tyburn Tree in 1686 for housebreaking and theft.
4. John Price (hangman 1714–15): hanged in 1718 at Bunhill Fields, London, on the spot where he murdered an old woman. He was then hung in a suit of iron on the gibbet at Holloway Fields.

Albert Pierrepoint was also "sentenced to death" by the IRA for his execution of a terrorist in Dublin. Pierrepoint was the principal British executioner for twenty-five years and hanged more than 400 people—his record being seventeen in one day ("Was my arm stiff!"). In 1946 he ran a "school for executioners" in Vienna. Interestingly, he later campaigned for the abolition of the death penalty saying, "It did not deter them then, and it had not deterred them when they committed what they were convicted for." Albert Pierrepoint died in a nursing home in July 1992, aged eighty-seven.

Gallows humor . . . Three famous "last words" of men about to be executed in the electric chair

1. GEORGE APPEL (1952)
He was in the chair when he said, "Well, folks, you'll soon see a baked Appel."

2. FREDERICK CHARLES WOOD (1963)

When he was in the chair, he said to the assembled company, "Gentlemen, you are about to see the effects of electricity upon wood."

3. JAMES DONALD FRENCH (1966)

On his way to the chair, he said to a newspaper reporter, "I have a terrific headline for you in the morning: 'French Fries.'"

James "Hangman" Berry's thirteen drops for the hangman

The drop system was used in order to cause instant death by dislocation (rather than strangulation) and also to prevent any visible mutilation of the criminal.

	Victim's weight	Drop
1.	14 stone (196 lb.)	8ft.
2.	13½ stone (189 lb.)	8ft. 2in.
3.	13 stone (182 lb.)	8ft. 4in.
4.	12½ stone (175 lb.)	8ft. 6in.
5.	12 stone (168 lb.)	8ft. 8in.
6.	11½ stone (161 lb.)	8ft. 10in.
7.	11 stone (154 lb.)	9ft.
8.	10½ stone (147 lb.)	9ft. 2in.
9.	10 stone (140 lb.)	9ft. 4in.
10.	9½ stone (133 lb.)	9ft. 6in.
11.	9 stone (126 lb.)	9ft. 8in.
12.	8½ stone (119 lb.)	9ft. 10in.
13.	8 stone (112 lb.)	10ft.

"Capital punishment is as fundamentally wrong as a cure for crime as charity is wrong as a cure for poverty."

HENRY FORD

The number of executions in the USA by type of crime

Not surprisingly, nearly all executions have been for murder—as the following list illustrates—but the death sentence has also been passed for other crimes.

MURDER

Year(s)	Total
1930–39	1,514
1940–49	1,064
1950–59	601
1960–67	155
1968–76	–
1977–80	3
1981	1
1982	2
1983	5
1984	21
1985	18
1986	18
1987	25
1988	11
1989	16
1990	23
1991	14
1992	31

RAPE

Year(s)	Total
1930–39	125
1940–49	200
1950–59	102
1960–67	28

OTHER OFFENSES

Year(s)	Total
1930–39	28
1940–49	20
1950–59	14
1960–67	8

"Fear succeeds punishment: it is its punishment."

VOLTAIRE

The twelve US States with the lowest minimum age for the death penalty

	State	Minimum age
1.	South Dakota	10
2.	Montana	12
3.	Mississippi	13
4.	Utah	14
5=	Arkansas	15
5=	Virginia	15
7=	Indiana	16
7=	Kentucky	16
7=	Missouri	16
7=	Oklahoma	16
7=	Wyoming	16
12=	Georgia	17
12=	Texas	17

The ten US States with the most prisoners under sentence of death

1. Texas 349
2. California 323
3. Florida 315
4. Illinois 145
5. Pennsylvania 140
6. Oklahoma 125
7. Alabama 115
8. Georgia 110
9. North Carolina 105
10. Ohio 104

Total (spring 1992): 2,588

The fifteen US States that have executed the most prisoners 1930–90

1. Georgia 380
2. Texas 334
3. New York 329
4. California 292

5. North Carolina 266
6. Florida 195
7. Ohio 172
8. South Carolina 165
9. Mississippi 158
10= Louisiana 152
10= Pennsylvania 152
12. Alabama 143
13. Arkansas 120
14= Kentucky 103
14= Virginia 103

U.S. total: 4,002

The fifteen US States that have executed the fewest prisoners 1930–90

1= Alaska 0
1= Hawaii 0
1= Maine 0
1= Michigan 0
1= Minnesota 0
1= North Dakota 0
1= Rhode Island 0
1= Wisconsin 0
9= New Hampshire 1
9= South Dakota 1
11. Idaho 3
12= Nebraska 4
12= Vermont 4
14. Montana 6
15. Wyoming 7

Seven US States that have the death penalty for crimes other than murder

	State	Capital offense
1.	Alabama	Aircraft piracy
2.	California	Treason; aggravated assault by a prisoner serving a life term; train-wrecking

State (Cont'd)	Capital offense (Cont'd)
3. Georgia	Aircraft hijacking; treason
4. Idaho	Aggravated kidnapping
5. Mississippi	Aircraft piracy
6. Montana	Aggravated assault, or aggravated kidnapping by a State prison inmate with a prison conviction for deliberat homicide or by a State prison inmate who has been previously declared a persistent offender
7. Utah	Aggravated assault by prisoners involving serious bodily injury

The methods of execution in U.S. States which have the death penalty

Lethal injection	Electrocution	Lethal gas
Alabama	Arkansas	Arizona
Arkansas	Connecticut	California
Colorado	Florida	Maryland
Delaware	Georgia	Missouri
Idaho	Indiana	North Carolina
Illinois	Kentucky	
Louisiana	Nebraska	
Mississippi	Ohio	
Montana	South Carolina	
Nevada	Tennessee	
New Hampshire	Virginia	
New Jersey		
New Mexico		
North Carolina		
Oklahoma		
Oregon		
Pennsylvania		

"I'm all for bringing back the birch—but only between consenting adults."

GORE VIDAL

Lethal injection (Cont'd)	Hanging	Firing squad
South Dakota	Montana	Idaho
Texas	New Hampshire	Utah
Utah	Washington	
Washington		
Wyoming		

Twelve instruments of torture and punishment

1. FETTERS
These were leg-irons which resembled handcuffs and were locked around each of the prisoner's ankles and connected by a chain. When worn for any length of time, the unfiled edges of the fetters would cut into the prisoner's skin and many men (and women, for they were not exempt from this punishment) had to have their legs amputated as a result of gangrene caused by the fetters. There were regional variations: in Ely Gaol, prisoners were pinned to the floor by iron bars linked to a chain; in Worcester Castle, the prisoners were chained at night. The prison at York Castle even charged for leg-irons—thereby adding insult to injury: "At their first committing and entry, every Catholic yeoman shall pay ten shillings, every gentleman twenty shillings and every esquire forty shillings."

2. IRON COLLAR
The Iron Collar (aka "The Spanish Collar," a name which originated in the contraptions found in ships captured from the Armada) was some three inches deep and one inch thick. Its weight was usually about ten pounds but could be increased. There was also a spike at the top of the collar to stop the prisoner from resting his head on his chest.

3. THE SPOT
This was a relatively modern torture. In 1937, the chief warder of San Quentin Jail, California, devised the Spot which was a gray circle, two feet in diameter, in which the prisoner had to stand for up to four hours at a time.

4. THE TREADMILL

An early nineteenth-century British invention which solved the prison authorities' problem of finding something to occupy their prisoners. The Treadmill was a huge wheel—sixteen feet in circumference—which was able to hold twenty-four men standing shoulder to shoulder. The wheel—which was turned by prisoners climbing its steps—revolved every thirty seconds and some wheels had a mechanism by which a bell would ring at the end of each thirtieth revolution, thereby signalling a change of shift. The Treadmill was abolished in Britain by the Prisons' Act of 1898. It sounds ghastly but probably was no worse than the tortures otherwise sane people subject themselves to in health clubs all over the Western world.

5. THE LASH

Even into the 1930s, punishment by the whip was dealt out to British prisoners. The whip used was a cat-o'-nine-tails, consisting of a wooden handle nearly twenty inches long, with nine tails of whipcord, each about an eighth of an inch thick and thirty-three inches long. Corporal punishment was last used in Britain in 1962 (later in prisons for attacking a prison officer) and was abolished in 1967.

6. THE PILLORY

Stopped in 1816 (though not until 1832 for perjury), this wasn't just a question of a few rotten tomatoes or a couple of wet sponges. People could—and did—throw stones, bottles and oyster shells, and offenders were often blinded and sometimes killed in the pillory.

7. GAUNTLETS

A sixteenth-century punishment in which iron manacles were used to suspend the prisoner by the wrists with his feet off the ground. Squassation is a variation on this punishment whereby the victim was suspended with his wrists behind instead of in front.

8. THUMB SCREWS
A seventeenth-century torture in which the prisoner's thumbs were put into a metal contraption and then squeezed until squashed—or the prisoner confessed.

9. BRANDING
A burning iron was pressed against the base of the thumb. This continued into the nineteenth century.

10. THE GRIDIRON
A series of parallel metal bars held above a fire. The prisoner would then be placed on top and literally broiled to death unless he confessed.

11. THE DRINKING TORTURE
The prisoner was tied down and water was then slowly poured into his mouth until he confessed or choked.

12. THE SCOLD'S BRIDLE
As used on nagging wives, this was a metal contraption which fitted over a woman's head with a small flat plate at the front which was put into her mouth to stop her from talking.

● 7
PRISONS

WITHIN THOSE WALLS . . . PRISON FACTS

The four longest sentences

1. The longest non-murder sentence handed out in a British court was forty-five years in 1986 to Nezar Hindawi who attempted to blow up an El Al plane by giving his unwitting "girlfriend" a bomb to carry on board.
2. The longest non-murder sentence given to a woman in a British court was twenty years in 1961 to Lorna Teresa Cohen for conspiring to commit a breach of the Officials Secrets Act.
3. The longest sentence served by a British prisoner was forty years, eleven months by the murderer John Watson Laurie, before being reprieved in 1889.
4. The longest sentence served by an American prisoner was sixty-eight years, eight months by the murderer Paul Geidel before being released in 1980.

Four unfeasibly long sentences

1. 141,078 years: To Chamoy Thipyaso, a crooked businessman, in Bangkok, Thailand, in 1989 for cheating the public in a multi-million-dollar deposit-taking swindle. Assuming he gets a third

knocked off his sentence in remission for good conduct, I estimate that he will be released in the year 96041.

2. Twenty-one *consecutive* life sentences (and twelve death sentences): To John Gacy, a mass murderer, in Chicago, Illinois, in 1980 (he was executed in May 1994).
3. Life imprisonment + 963 years (to run concurrently): To Kevin Mulgrew, for murder, conspiracy to murder and attempted murder, in Belfast, in 1983.
4. Twenty-five years + 455 years (to run concurrently): To Ciaran Morrison, a brother of former Sinn Fein vice-president Danny Morrison, for terrorist crimes, in Belfast, in 1994.

The ten largest prisons in England and Wales

	Prison	Inmates
1.	Liverpool	1,204
2.	Wandsworth	1,027
3.	Birmingham	887
4.	Leeds	846
5.	Belmarch	727
6.	Pentonville	721
7.	Brixton	713
8.	Wormwood Scrubs	667
9.	Durham	626
10.	Moorland	604

The total prison population in England and Wales is 48,688 (March 1994).

Wandsworth Prison in South London has the largest

"People who go to prison are not just criminals but, by definition, unsuccessful criminals."

THE TIMES

capacity of any British prison. It has a certified capacity of 965 but has held as many as 1,556 prisoners. Barlinnie Prison in Glasgow has 750 single cells, while Mountjoy Prison in Dublin is the largest Irish jail with 808 cells. In terms of physical size, the Maze Prison in Northern Ireland is the largest in the British Isles. It covers 133 acres and has eight 100-cell blocks. However, there is no doubt which is the largest jail ever used for just one prisoner. That honor goes to Spandau Prison in Berlin, Germany, which was built for 600 prisoners but was used to imprison just one man—the Nazi war criminal, Rudolf Hess—for the last twenty years of his life. What's more, it took 105 staff to look after him—and they still couldn't stop him from killing himself . . .

Five well-known men who escaped from incarceration

1. GEORGE BLAKE
The Russian spy escaped from London's Wormwood Scrubs jail in 1966.

2. AIREY NEAVE
He was the first Briton to escape from Colditz in Germany during the Second World War. He later became an MP but was assassinated by Irish terrorists.

3. HENRI CHARRIÈRE (aka "PAPILLON")
A Frenchman who always wore a bow tie and had a butterfly tattoo. He and another prisoner used bags of coconuts to make a raft and escape from Devil's Island in 1941. In 1945, he was given a pardon and went on to become a best-selling writer.

4. WINSTON CHURCHILL
The man who would later become Britain's most famous Prime Minister escaped from a POW camp during the Boer War.

5. JOHN McVICAR
British criminal-turned-sociologist/journalist, McVicar
escaped during the course of one of his many prison
sentences.

Five amazing prison escapes

1. Ross Perot, the billionaire American businessman
   and ex-Presidential candidate, financed an operation led by Arthur "Bull" Simons, a retired Army
   colonel, to free two Americans from Gasre prison
   in Tehran, Iran, in February 1979. Eleven thousand other prisoners took the opportunity to leave
   at the same time.
2. In 1983, thirty-eight IRA prisoners escaped from
   the Maze Prison, in Northern Ireland.
3. In 1971, Raul Sendic and 105 other Tupamaro
   guerrillas got out of a prison in Uruguay.
4. James Kelly holds the record of thirty-nine years
   for the longest British escape. He broke out of
   Broadmoor in 1888 and went to live abroad before
   voluntarily returning to Broadmoor in 1927 and
   asking to be readmitted.
5. Leonard T. Fristoe holds the record of forty-six
   years for the longest American escape. He escaped
   from Nevada State Prison in 1923 but was handed
   over to the authorities by his son in 1969.

The fifteen US States that have a mandatory prison sentence for drunk drivers on their first offense

State	Minimum sentence
1= Montana	24 hours
1= Washington	24 hours
1= West Virginia	24 hours
4= Connecticut	48 hours
4= Kansas	48 hours
4= Kentucky	48 hours
4= Louisiana	48 hours

4=	Maine	48 hours
4=	Nevada	48 hours
4=	Oregon	48 hours
4=	South Carolina	48 hours
4=	Tennessee	48 hours
4=	Utah	48 hours
14.	Alabama	72 hours
15.	Colorado	5 days

The number of inmates in US jails (Federal and State)

Year	Number	Rate (per million)
1975	240,593	1,133
1980	315,974	1,392
1985	480,568	2,165
1986	522,084	2,304
1987	560,812	2,290
1988	603,732	2,440
1989	680,907	2,743
1990	739,980	2,950
1991	786,347	3,096

US jail inmates and their upbringing

People who raised them	All jail inmates (%)
Both parents	47.7
Mother only	35.5
Father only	3.6
Grandparents	7
Other relatives	3.1
Friends	0.4
Foster home	1.4
Agency or institution	0.6
Other	0.7

"If England treats her criminals the way she has treated me, she doesn't deserve to have any."

Oscar Wilde

The average daily population of US jails

Year	Males	Females	Juveniles	Total
1983	210,451	15,330	1,760	227,541
1984	212,749	16,195	1,697	230,641
1985	244,711	18,832	1,467	265,010
1986	243,143	20,970	1,404	265,517
1987	264,929	23,796	1,575	290,300
1988	306,379	28,187	1,451	336,017
1989	349,180	35,774	1,891	386,845
1990	368,091	37,844	2,140	408,075
1991	381,458	38,818	2,333	422,609

The ten US States with the highest average daily jail population

	State	Number of jails	Total inmates
1.	California	149	63,359
2.	Texas	275	29,124
3.	Florida	102	27,029
4.	New York	75	25,484
5.	Georgia	196	16,172
6.	Pennsylvania	75	13,563
7.	Louisiana	90	11,092
8.	New Jersey	28	10,978
9.	Tennessee	108	10,082
10.	Michigan	85	9,444

The ten US States with the lowest average daily jail population

	State	Number of jails	Total inmates
1=	Alaska	5	2,800
1=	North Dakota	26	2,800
3.	Wyoming	22	4,870
4.	South Dakota	29	5,140
5.	Montana	46	5,960
6.	Maine	15	6,510
7.	New Hampshire	11	7,850
8.	Idaho	37	8,200

State (Cont'd)	Number of jails (Cont'd)	Total inmates (Cont'd)
9. Iowa	90	10,620
10. Nebraska	66	11,100

It's interesting that New York, which has the fourth highest average daily prison population has fifteen fewer jails than Iowa, which has the ninth lowest.

The ten US States with the most deaths in jail (excluding executions)

1. California 99
2. Texas 51
3. Florida 40
4. New York 37
5. Georgia 34
6. Pennsylvania 31
7. New Jersey 27
8. Tennessee 22
9. Louisiana 19
10. Ohio 18

The number of sentenced prisoners in US State and Federal institutions

Year	Total prisoners
1925	916,690
1930	1,294,530
1935	1,441,800
1940	1,737,060
1945	1,336,490
1950	1,661,230
1955	1,857,800
1960	2,129,530
1965	2,108,950
1970	1,964,290
1975	2,405,930
1980	3,159,740
1985	4,805,680
1990	7,388,940

The ten US States with the most prisoners serving life sentences

	State	Male	Female	Total
1.	New York	7,882	510	8,392
2.	California	8,117	65	8,182
3.	Florida	4,132	136	4,268
4.	Texas	3,439	65	3,504
5.	Georgia	2,771	118	2,889
6.	Ohio	2,473	136	2,609
7.	Michigan	2,473	90	2,563
8.	Alabama	2,117	47	2,164
9.	Louisiana	2,009	64	2,073
10.	North Carolina	1,944	59	2,003

The ten US States with the fewest prisoners serving life sentences

	State	Male	Female	Total
1=	North Dakota	10	0	10
1=	Vermont	10	0	10
3.	New Hampshire	23	1	24
4.	Montana	27	0	27
5.	Maine	38	0	38
6.	Rhode Island	76	1	77
7.	South Dakota	87	3	90
8.	Wyoming	91	0	91
9.	Alaska	119	5	124
10.	Connecticut	125	2	127

Jail breaks . . . The ten US States with the highest number of escapes from correctional facilities

	State	Total escapes (1990)	Number of escapees returned
1.	California	1,405	1,260
2.	Michigan	1,073	763
3.	Florida	1,064	1,146
4.	Missouri	557	544

State (Cont'd)	Total escapes (1990) (Cont'd)	Number of escapees returned (Cont'd)
5. Oregon	478	138
6. North Carolina	382	406
7. Iowa	198	187
8. Illinois	193	171
9. Massachusetts	160	149
10. Washington	145	122

Some states (Florida, North Carolina)—and in the next table, Alaska, District of Columbia, Maine and South Dakota—had more escaped prisoners returned than escaped in the first place. This is due to escapees from a previous year being returned to custody.

The ten US States with the fewest escapes from correctional facilities

State	Total escapes (1990)	Number of escapees returned
1= Delaware	0	0
1= Mississippi	0	0
1= Oklahoma	0	0
4= Alaska	2	7
4= North Dakota	2	2
6. Idaho	3	1
7. District of Columbia	4	9
8. Hawaii	6	5
9. Maine	8	7
10= New Mexico	9	9
10= South Dakota	9	10

How male and female offenders were sentenced in England and Wales for all offenses in 1991

	All offenses (in thousands)	
	Male	Female
Absolute/conditional discharge	97.1	26.4
Probation order	39.3	8.2

| | *All offenses (in thousands)* | |
| | *Male* | *Female* |
	(Cont'd)	*(Cont'd)*
Supervision order	5.7	0.6
Fine	975.5	191.0
Community service order	40.3	2.2
Attendance center order	8	0.2
Care order	0.2	0.1
Young offenders institution	16.5	0.4
Imprisonment		
Fully suspended	25.4	2.7
Partly suspended	1.0	0.1
Unsuspended	41.4	1.8
Otherwise dealt with	17.4	2.2
Total immediate custody	58.9	2.0
Total number of offenders sentenced	**1,268**	**235.9**

● 8
MISCELLANEOUS

Fifteen notable miscarriages of justice

1. TIMOTHY EVANS
In 1949, Evans, who was educationally backward, walked into a police station in Wales and said he had "disposed" of his wife. Police discovered Beryl, his wife, and their daughter strangled to death in a small washhouse at 10 Rillington Place in London. Evans made a confession which he withdrew at his trial—stating that his landlord, Mr. John Christie, had killed Beryl while performing an abortion. Evans was hanged in 1950. Later Christie was revealed to be a serial murderer who, almost undoubtedly, committed the murders for which Evans was executed—although it should be noted that despite confessing to the murder of Beryl Evans, Christie denied murdering her daughter. Timothy Evans was posthumously pardoned in 1966.

2. CAPTAIN ALFRED DREYFUS
A Jewish officer in the French army—sentenced to Devil's Island for treason in 1894 (for supposedly selling military secrets to the German military attaché)—was a victim of anti-Semitism. He had served four years on Devil's Island before a second court-martial—convened as a result of public opinion rallied by Emile Zola's *J'Accuse*—pardoned him (although he was again found guilty). The affair wasn't properly settled until 1906 when Dreyfus was awarded the Legion d'Honneur.

3. JAMES MONTGOMERY
In 1923, in Waukegan, Illinois, Montgomery was accused—on the testimony of the sixty-two-year-old mentally ill "victim"—of rape. He was found guilty and sent to jail because the racist prosecutor suppressed the vital evidence that the "victim" was still a virgin and therefore couldn't have been raped. Montgomery was acquitted after a retrial—twenty-six years later.

4. LEONARD HANKINS
In 1933, Hankins was convicted of murdering three people in Minneapolis and was sent to jail for life. Three years later, the FBI arrested the real murderer, Jess Doyle, who freely confessed. However, the authorities in Minneapolis would not release Hankins because the FBI refused to give them the file on Doyle. Hankins remained in prison until 1951 before being pardoned.

5. MARINUS VAN DER LUBBE
This was the Dutchman who was wrongly convicted of setting fire to the Reichstag in Germany in 1933. This was clearly done by the Nazis as a pretext for banning rival parties.

6. ALGER HISS
In 1950, Hiss, a State Department official, was accused of having passed secret government papers to a former Soviet spy. The truth was that he was innocent but, in the anti-Communist McCarthyite atmosphere of the late 1940s—and with a zealous junior congressman named Richard Nixon snapping at his heels—Hiss didn't stand a chance. He was sent to prison for five years for "perjury" and served forty-four months. After Nixon, his tormentor, was disgraced, Hiss was pardoned.

7. ALBERT PARSONS
In 1886, at an open-air meeting at the Haymarket, Chicago, seven policemen died when an unknown per-

son threw a bomb. The authorities put out a warrant for one of the meeting's organizers, Albert Parsons, who gave himself up. The prosecution inflamed passions by quoting from subversive pamphlets written by the accused, though they had no bearing on the Haymarket bombing. Along with six other organizers, Parsons was—wrongly—executed.

8. JULIUS KRAUSE
In 1931, Krause and another man were convicted of murder in Ohio. Four years later, his "partner" made a death-bed confession that one Curtis Kuermerle—not Krause—was his partner. Krause was not released but he escaped from prison, found Kuermerle and persuaded him to confess. Kuermerle was found guilty but Krause was sent back to prison and not pardoned till 1951.

9. ROBERT HUBERT
The Great Fire of London, which started in the shop at 25 Pudding Lane in 1666, was popularly believed to have been started by "Papists and foreigners." A suspect was needed and Robert Hubert, a watchmaker from Rouen, France, was arrested. He made some strange confession (under who knows what sort of duress) and was hanged. Yet the truth was, *pace* the sworn testimony of Captain Peterson, the Master of the ship that had brought him to London, that Hubert did not leave the ship until two days *after* the fire had started.

10. DR. BENJAMIN KNOWLES
In Ghana, on the evening of October 20, 1928, Mrs. Knowles was getting ready for bed when she accidentally sat on a revolver which went off when she stood up, shooting her in the left buttock. In hospital, Mrs. Knowles realized that her husband was under suspicion and explained to the police that it had been an accident. Dr. Knowles was, however, tried (without a jury) and sentenced to die, though this was commuted to life

imprisonment. He was then transported to London where his sentence was quashed but he died three years later.

11. JUDITH WARD
Sentenced to life imprisonment by a British court for the 1974 M62 coach bombing (in which twelve people died), she was freed in 1992 after the Court of Appeal ruled that the forensic evidence was unsound and that her confession to the police was due to a mental disorder which led her to "fantasize."

12. LEO FRANK
In 1913, in Atlanta, Georgia, Leo Frank, the manager of a pencil factory, was arrested for the rape and murder of a thirteen-year-old girl who worked at the factory. He was found guilty and sentenced to death even though all the evidence pointed to the janitor as the true culprit. Although his sentence was commuted to life imprisonment, he was taken from the state penitentiary by a lynch mob and hanged. NB In 1983, an eighty-seven-year-old man who had witnessed the janitor committing the murder came forward finally to clear Leo Frank's name.

13. THE SCOTTSBORO CASE
In 1931, nine young black men were arrested for allegedly raping two white girls on a train traveling through Scottsboro, Alabama. Though medical reports proved that the girls hadn't been raped the men were sentenced to death (except the youngest who was only thirteen). None of them was executed but they were kept in jail for years before either being found innocent, given parole or dying. One of the two "victims" later admitted that she had been lying. This case is also famous because it was the first time that a defense lawyer (Samuel Leibowitz—later a distinguished judge) asked the question, "Why aren't black people allowed to serve on juries?"

14. LINDY CHAMBERLAIN
A dingo entered a camp site at Ayers Rock in Australia and "stole" baby Azaria Chamberlain leaving behind just her bloodstained clothes. However, in 1981, rumors started to the effect that Azaria had been murdered by her mother. The British pathologist, Professor James Cameron, stated that no traces of dingo saliva could be found on Azaria's clothes—even though her matinée jacket, which was the item of clothing she had been wearing on top, wasn't recovered. In 1982, Lindy Chamberlain was convicted of the killing of her baby. However, the matinée jacket was subsequently found and, after further extensive pathology tests, in 1986, Lindy was given a free pardon—as was her husband Michael for his conviction as an accessory.

15. STEFAN KISZKO
In February 1992, Stefan Kiszko was released from a British jail after serving sixteen years for the murder of schoolgirl Lesley Molseed. The forensic evidence that proved that he could not have been the killer was not shown during the trial. He died not long after his release.

A number of British miscarriages of justice

1. THE CARDIFF THREE
In December 1992, the Court of Appeal overturned life sentences on the Cardiff Three for the murder of prostitute Lynette White in 1988.

2. THE TOTTENHAM THREE
In November 1991, they were cleared of the murder of P.C. Blakelock in the Broadwater Farm riots in Tottenham, London, in 1985.

3. THE GUILDFORD FOUR
In October 1989, they were cleared of the 1975 Guildford pub bombings. Their convictions had been based

on "confessions" which they had only signed under duress.

4. THE BIRMINGHAM SIX
In March 1991, they were released—having spent seventeen years in prison after being wrongly convicted for the 1974 Birmingham pub bombings.

5. THE MAGUIRE SEVEN
In June 1991, they were released from prison where they had been sent on bomb-making charges. The forensic evidence which had helped convict them was discredited.

Six convicted people who may have been innocent

1. JAMES HANRATTY
Hanratty was one of the last men ever to hang in Britain (for the 1961 A6 murder). There is considerable doubt as to Hanratty's guilt.

2. FLORENCE MAYBRICK
In July 1889, Florence Maybrick was sentenced to death in Liverpool for poisoning her husband. The evidence was the fact that quantities of arsenic were found in the house but it was well-known to his friends that Mr. Maybrick took arsenic (and other poisons) as aphrodisiacs. What really convinced the jury of Mrs. Maybrick's guilt was the judge's hostile treatment of her—on account of her proven adultery. The doubt over the case eventually led to Mrs. Maybrick's death sentence being commuted to life imprisonment.

3. BRUNO HAUPTMANN
In 1936, in Trenton State Prison in New Jersey, Hauptmann was executed for kidnapping and murdering the baby son of the great aviator Charles Lindbergh. There are many people who believe Hauptmann to have been

innocent and some even think it is possible that Lindbergh himself murdered his child.

4. GEORGE FRATSON

Fratson was sentenced to die at Manchester Assizes, England, in July 1929 for the murder of George Armstrong, the manager of a men's clothing store. Fratson's lawyer won him a retrial on the basis of new evidence (a cardboard collar-box stained with blood and marked with a fingerprint that matched neither victim nor accused) which saved him from hanging but not from jail and he was given a life sentence. Years later, a man named Walter Prince was found guilty of murder and, faced with the death penalty, confessed to the killing of George Armstrong. Unfortunately, this didn't help Fratson as Prince was found to be insane and he remained in jail.

5. GEORGE RILEY

After sixty-two-year-old widow Adeline Smith was battered to death in Shrewsbury in 1961, George Riley was arrested and, under interrogation, confessed to the killing. He later retracted this confession but was still hanged.

6. ROBERT HOOLHOUSE

Mrs. Margaret Dobson was found stabbed to death on a cart track in January 1938 near Wolviston, Durham. Suspicion fell on Robert Hoolhouse, who fitted a vague description of a man seen in the area, as his face and hands were scratched, and his coat had blood and hair on it. His defense counsel called no witnesses and Hoolhouse was hanged—in spite of a petition.

In the case of William Sheward, the verdict was not in doubt but it is still possible to sympathize with the defendant. Sheward's marriage suffered when his Norwich tailoring business ran into trouble and he started to drink heavily. He murdered his wife Martha in 1851 and scattered her remains around Norwich. Eighteen years, one marriage and two sons later, Sheward could no longer bear the guilt of his crime and confessed to the police. He was tried for murder, found guilty and hanged.

The twelve most famous kidnappings of all time

1. CHARLES LINDBERGH Jr.

In 1932, the baby son of the solo transatlantic aviator Charles Lindbergh was kidnapped in New Jersey and then murdered. A man with a German accent had been paid $50,000 in marked notes and $20,000 in gold bonds. Bruno Hauptmann, a German-born immigrant who worked as a carpenter, was arrested. He was tried in 1935, convicted and was sent to the electric chair. There is now considerable doubt over this verdict.

2. ALDO MORO

In 1978, Aldo Moro, a former Italian Prime Minister, was kidnapped in Rome and murdered by members of the Red Brigade.

3. MARIAN PARKER

The daughter of successful American lawyer Perry Parker was kidnapped in a wealthy Los Angeles suburb in December 1927 by Edward Hickman who demanded a ransom of $7,500. Parker met Hickman and handed over the money. Hickman then gave Parker his daughter wrapped up in a blanket. However, Marian had been strangled and her legs had been cut off. Hickman was hanged at San Quentin in 1928.

"When I was kidnapped, my parents snapped into action: they rented out my room."

WOODY ALLEN

4. JOHN PAUL GETTY III
In 1973, John Paul Getty III was kidnapped by Italian gangsters in Rome in 1973 and held captive for six months. To help persuade his family to pay the ransom, his captors cut off one of his ears and sent it to them. His father paid $2.5 million and he was released. Giuseppe la Manna and Antonio Manpuso were found guilty of kidnap and were sentenced to sixteen and eight years in prison respectively.

5. BARBARA MACKLE
Barbara Mackle, the daughter of a wealthy Florida building contractor, was taken from her University (Emory in Atlanta) in December 1968. She was buried alive, but given food and water and enough air to breathe. Three days later, after a ransom demand which was raised but not handed over (because the kidnappers fled when they realized that the men making the payment were law officers), the FBI in Atlanta got a call telling them where the girl was buried. After eighty-three hours buried alive, Barbara Mackle's first words to her rescuers were: "You're the handsomest men I've ever seen." Her two kidnappers were caught and imprisoned.

6. PATRICIA HEARST
In 1974, Patti Hearst, the nineteen-year-old daughter of the millionaire publisher Randolph Hearst, was kidnapped by the Symbionese Liberation Army from her apartment in Berkeley, California. During her captivity, she was persuaded to join her captors (under the *nom de guerre* "Tania") and participated in a bank robbery for which she was sentenced to seven years' imprisonment.

7. VICTOR SAMUELSEN
In 1973, Victor Samuelsen, an executive with the oil company Exxon, was kidnapped in Argentina in 1973 but was released after his company paid the ransom.

8. CHARLIE ROSS
In 1874 in what has come to be regarded as the first

modern case of kidnapping, William Mosher and Joey Douglas kidnapped four-year-old Charlie Ross from his Philadelphia home and demanded $20,000 for the child's safe return. New York detectives identified the handwriting on the ransom notes as that of Mosher, a notorious burglar. Five months later, after three planned ransom pick-ups had been aborted, Mosher and Douglas were shot during a Brooklyn burglary and before dying Mosher admitted kidnapping the child. However, he didn't reveal the whereabouts of the boy who was never found.

9. MRS. MURIEL McKAY
In 1969, Mrs. McKay, wife of the deputy chairman of the *News of the World,* was kidnapped in London by Arthur and Nizamodeen Hosein who, mistaking their victim for the wife of Australian publishing millionaire Rupert Murdoch, made a ransom demand of £1 million. However, their attempts to collect the money were botched and Mrs. McKay ended up dead and the Hosein brothers were sent to jail for life in 1970.

10. GEOFFREY JACKSON
In 1971, Geoffrey Jackson, the British Ambassador to Uruguay, was kidnapped in Montevideo by left-wing guerrillas and held captive for eight months. He was released unharmed.

11. JAMES CROSS
In 1970, James Cross, a British diplomat, was kidnapped by members of the Quebec Liberation Front in Quebec, Canada but was released unharmed after two months in exchange for his kidnappers being allowed to fly to Cuba (as all kidnappers seemed to want to do in the 1970s).

12. JORGE and JUAN BORN
In 1975, the sum of 1,500,000,000 pesos was paid to the guerrilla group, Montoneros, in Buenos Aires,

Argentina, for the release of the brothers Jorge and Juan Born. This is the highest recorded kidnapping ransom (paid—as opposed to demanded) in modern times. The highest hijack ransom paid was the $6 million demanded from the Japanese government by the hijackers of a Japanese Airlines DC-8 aircraft at Dacca Airport in 1977.

Incidentally, when it comes to ransom demands, hostage-taking puts kidnapping in the shade. We saw an example of this in May 1993 when Eric Schmitt ("The Human Bomb") demanded 100 million francs in exchange for releasing the children he'd taken hostage in a Paris school. French police commandos burst into the school and shot him dead. Fortunately, none of the children was harmed—but it shows that hostage-taking is not exactly a foolproof way to make money.

Ten memorable criminal soubriquets

1. KENNETH BIANCHI (aka "THE HILLSIDE STRANGLER")
An American who, with his cousin Angelo Buono, carried out a series of murders in Los Angeles in the late 1970s.

2. CONRAD DONOVAN (aka "ROTTEN CONRAD")
British murderer at the turn of the century.

3. MARY ELIZABETH WILSON (aka "THE WIDOW OF WINDY NOOK")
British multiple murderess of the 1950s who was sentenced to death but was reprieved because she was in her late sixties.

4. NIKOLAI DZHUMAGALIEV (aka "METAL FANG")
Serial killer in the Soviet republic of Kazakhstan during 1980; so called because of his white-metal false teeth.

5. HENRI DESIRE LANDRU (aka "BLUEBEARD")
French serial killer during and after the Great War.

6. EDWARD LEONSKI (aka "THE SINGING STRANGLER")
Texan GI Leonski strangled three women in Melbourne, Australia "to get their voices." Despite pleas of insanity he was hanged on November 9, 1942.

7. KLAUS GOSMAN (aka "THE MIDDAY MURDERER")
German serial killer of the 1960s who shot his victims as Nuremberg's church bells rang at noon.

8. DAVID BERKOWITZ (aka "SON OF SAM")
An American who terrorized New York in 1976 and 1977 as "Son of Sam"—a name he invented after shooting his neighbor Sam Carr's noisy dog. Berkowitz reckoned that the dog spoke to him and was one of the voices that told him to go out and murder.

9. WERNER BOOST (aka "THE DÜSSELDORF DOUBLES KILLER")
A German who, with his partner Franz Lorbach, specialized in murdering couples in the 1950s.

10. LUCIAN STANIAK (aka "THE RED SPIDER")
A sort of Polish Jack the Ripper, Staniak raped, murdered and mutilated more than twenty women between 1964 and 1967.

And let us not forget the charming alias chosen by Jean Pierre Vaquier (aka "J. Wanker"), the French murderer (living in Britain) who, in 1924, bought two grains of strychnine—signing the register "J. Wanker"—and killed the husband of the woman with whom he had had a brief affair.

Thirteen US gangsters and their nicknames

1. Charles Floyd: Pretty Boy
2. George Nelson: Babyface
3. Al Capone: Scarface
4. Jack Diamond: Legs
5. George Kelly: Machine-gun
6. Charles Luciano: Lucky
7. Benjamin Siegel: Bugsy
8. Louis Amberg: Pretty
9. Louis Buchalter: Lepke
10. Johnny Torrio: The Brain
11. Vincent McColl: Mad Dog
12. George Moran: Bugs
13. Tony Accardo: Joe Batters

Art attacks! Ten violations of works of art

1. **1964:** As a "protest against the decapitation of buildings in Denmark," *The Little Mermaid* in Copenhagen was decapitated with a hacksaw.
2. **1977:** A Jo Baer painting was covered in lipstick kisses to "cheer it up" when it was on loan to the Oxford Museum of Modern Art.
3. **1978:** A Vincent Van Gogh self-portrait in Amsterdam was cut diagonally by a Dutch artist.
4. **1980:** The statue of Lady Godiva in Coventry was defaced with the words "Women are angry, they will fight back."
5. **1981:** Bryan Organ's picture of the Princess of Wales in the National Portrait Gallery, London was slashed.
6. **1985:** A portrait of King Philip IV of Spain by Rubens was set on fire by a German protesting about the "pollution of the environment."
7. **1986:** To mark International Women's Day, acid was thrown over a glass fiber woman in black underwear by the pop artist Allen Jones.
8. **1987:** A former soldier fired several shots at *The*

Virgin and Child with St. Anne and St. John, a
cartoon by Leonardo da Vinci in the National
Gallery, London.

9. **1987:** In Glasgow, eight statues of Greek gods had
their genitals cut off.

10. **1989:** Ten seventeenth-century Dutch master-
pieces in Amsterdam were slashed by a man
protesting against losing his job.

Six expressions that have entered the language through crime

1. SWEET FANNY ADAMS
A seven-year-old British girl named Fanny Adams was
horrifically battered to death by Frederick Baker in 1867
in Hampshire. Her body was so hacked to pieces that
the expression "Sweet Fanny Adams" started to be used
as a synonym for "nothing."

2. BOBBITT
On June 23, 1993, John Bobbitt initiated sexual inter-
course with his wife Lorena which she later claimed was
a rape attack. Once he had fallen asleep, she cut off his
penis and threw it away. It was later found and sewn
back on. Lorena Bobbitt was found not guilty due to
diminished responsibility but her surname has entered
the English language as a noun ("to do a bobbitt") and
as a verb ("to bobbitt someone").

3. BLOODY MARY
Mary (1516–58) was Queen of England and Ireland
from 1553 until her death. During this time, some 300
people were put to death as heretics—hence the nickname "Bloody Mary" . . . and the cocktail of vodka and
tomato juice known as "Bloody Mary."

4. GUY
Guy Fawkes (1570–1606) tried to blow up the Houses of
Parliament on November 5, 1605. Nowadays on that

date Guy Fawkes Day is celebrated in England by lighting fireworks and burning the "guy."

5. BURKE
William Burke (1792–1829) and his accomplice William Hare suffocated their victims and then sold them to an anatomist. Hare turned King's evidence and Burke was hanged but his name entered the English language as a transitive verb: "to burke"—i.e. to smother something to death or to hush something up.

6. RACHMANISM
Peter Rachman (1920–62) was a Polish immigrant landlord who became (in)famous for the illegal and ruthless treatment of his tenants in London. The word "Rachmanism" is now used to describe any such similar treatment.

Seven scientific advances which have helped capture criminals

1. FINGERPRINTING
The first murder conviction on fingerprint evidence was in Argentina in 1892 and it was the work of fingerprint expert Juan Vucetich. Two children, aged four and six, were found bludgeoned to death in their home in Necoshea, outside Buenos Aires, and their mother, Francesca Rojas, was also injured. Suspicion fell on a man friend of Francesca Rojas named Velasquez. Fingerprints in blood were, however, found on the shanty door, which matched those of Francesca Rojas herself. She was so astounded by this that she broke down and confessed.

In England in March 1905, Mr. and Mrs. Farrow were found battered at their paint shop in Deptford and their cashbox was empty. Thomas Farrow was dead and his wife died of her injuries three days later. Suspicion fell on Albert and Alfred Stratto, brothers with records of burglary. Yet the evidence was flimsy. However, using a new technique, a thumbmark was discovered on the cashbox which was photographed and enlarged. The thumbprints of the two brothers were taken and also enlarged. The mark on the cashbox was identical to Alfred's right thumb. The Stratto brothers were both hanged.

In the USA, the first fingerprint evidence admitted in a criminal case was in 1911. Detectives found perfect impressions of four fingers of a left hand on a newly painted window frame at the house in Chicago where Clarence Hiller had been shot dead. These prints matched those of Thomas Jennings's prison records. Jennings was sentenced to death for Hiller's murder.

2. THE WIRELESS TELEGRAPH
(*see* Crippen case—Murdering Doctors)

3. PSYCHOLOGICAL PROFILING
Using this technique, in 1957, American psychiatrist Dr. James A. Brussel identified New Yorker George Metsky as the man who had placed a bomb in Pennsylvania station in January 1953 injuring several people. In 1964 Dr. Brussel was absolutely spot on in his description of Albert DeSalvo, "The Boston Strangler," who sexually assaulted and killed thirteen women in 1962–4. Dr. Brussel said that the murders were all carried out by the same man and that he was about thirty years old, of average height, with thick black hair, unmarried and of Spanish or Italian origin.

In Britain, in 1986, mass murderer John Duffy ("The Railway Killer") was the first British man to be identified by a procedure known as psychological offender profiling (POP). Professor David Canter was able to deduce that the killer lived in the Kilburn–Cricklewood area of northwest London, was unhappily married and childless. Duffy was caught, found guilty on February 26, 1988 and given seven life sentences. However, as the recent case of Colin Stagg showed, psychological profiling does have its drawbacks.

4. IDENTIKIT
Edwin Albert Bush was the first murderer in Britain to be caught as a result of Identikit. On March 3, 1961, Elsie Batten was stabbed to death in a shop off the Charing Cross Road in London. Mr. Roberts, who owned a shop nearby, had seen a man and gave a description of him to a police artist. The Identikit portrait was circulated and on March 8, Edwin Bush was arrested and charged with the murder of Elsie Batten, for which he was later found guilty and hanged.

5. EARLY BIRD SATELLITE
In 1961, Georges LeMay robbed the Bank of Nova Scotia in Montreal, Canada, of over $4 million in cash, jewelry, bonds and rare stamps. Two years later he was captured with the help of the Early Bird satellite, which relayed his photo to TV screens all over the world. A man in Fort Lauderdale, Florida recognized LeMay's photo and contacted the police. The technology was bang up to date but, alas, the rest was a bit of a farce. LeMay was taken to Dade County jail but escaped before his trial. He hasn't been recaptured and the money is still missing.

6. FORENSIC ODONTOLOGY
This is a comparatively recent development which was introduced in the late 1960s. The Scanning Electron Microscope enables investigators to compare—with absolute precision—bite-mark evidence with a suspect's dentition.

7. DNA PROFILING
Professor Alec Jeffreys, a Research Fellow at the Lister Institute, Leicester University, achieved the breakthrough in 1984 that made DNA, the basic unique unit of a person's physical makeup, a practical way of positively identifying an individual. Many rapists and murderers have been caught through DNA samples taken from hair and semen. In 1994, Professor Bernard Knight extended the technique during his investigation

of the many skeletons found beneath Frederick West's house at 25 Cromwell Street, Gloucester. Professor Knight was able to establish the sex, age and height of the bodies, and, by using DNA bone marrow, built up a genetic "fingerprint" of the person.

Thirteen examples of criminal injury awards in the UK

1. Undisplaced nasal fracture £750
2. Displaced nasal fracture £1,000
3= Loss of two front upper teeth (plate or bridge) £1,750
3= Elevated zygoma (following injury to cheekbone) £1,750
5. Simple fracture of the tibia, fibula, ulna or radius with complete recovery £2,500
6. Fractured jaw (wired) £2,750
7. Laparotomy (exploratory stomach operation and scar) £3,500
8. Scar (young man) from join of lobe of left ear and his face across his cheek to within an inch of the left corner of his mouth £6,000
9. Scar (young woman) running from left corner of her mouth backward and downward ending just beneath the jawbone £9,000
10. Total loss of hearing in one ear £11,500
11. Total loss of taste and smell as a result of a fractured skull £12,000
12. Total loss of vision in one eye £17,500
13. Loss of one eye £20,000

Meanwhile, if a newspaper calls an actress "an old slag," then that can be worth half a million.

The cast of characters at Madame Tussaud's Chamber of Horrors

1. Adolf Hitler
2. Revolutionary Soldier

3. Guillotine Executioner
4. Guillotine Assistant
5. Guillotine Victim
6. Gary Gilmore
7. Bruno Hauptmann
8. American Prison Warder
9. Garrotte Executioner
10. Garrotte Victim
11. Hanging Victim (Percy Mapleton)
12. Hanging Executioner (William Marwood)
13. Hanging Warder 1
14. Hanging Warder 2

Happiness is a warm gun . . . Percentage of Americans who keep a firearm in the home

1973	47%
1974	46%
1976	47%
1977	51%
1980	48%
1982	45%
1984	45%
1985	44%
1987	46%
1988	40%
1989	46%
1990	43%
1991	40%

9
CRIMINAL TRIVIA

Fifteen actors who have been sent inside

1. Stacy Keach: nine months in 1984 for cocaine smuggling.
2. Zsa Zsa Gabor: three days in 1990 for assaulting a police officer.
3. Sophia Loren: eighteen days in 1982 for tax irregularities.
4. Phil Silvers: one year in reform school in 1923 for assaulting a teacher.
5. Ivor Novello: one month in 1944 for breaking wartime laws by driving his Rolls Royce.
6. Jane Russell: four days in 1978 for drunk driving.
7. Errol Flynn: two weeks in 1920 for assault.
8. Sean Penn: thirty-three days in 1987 for assaulting a film extra.
9. Ryan O'Neal: sixty days in 1960 for assault.
10. Judy Carne: three months in 1986 for drug offenses.
11. Steve McQueen: eighteen months in reform school in 1944 for unruly behavior.
12. Mae West: eight days in 1927 for performing in an "immoral show."
13. Robert Mitchum: seven days in 1933 for vagrancy, sixty days in 1948 for using marijuana.
14. Rory Calhoun: three years for stealing a car.
15. Stephen Fry: spent time in a young offenders' institution for credit card fraud.

Ten rock stars who have been inside

1. James Brown: sentenced to six years in South Carolina in 1988 for carrying a gun and aggravated assault—released in 1991.
2. Chuck Berry: two years in Indiana in 1962 for contravening the Mann Act and 100 days in California in 1979 for tax evasion.
3. David Crosby: eight months in Texas in 1985 for possession of drugs and carrying a gun.
4. Hugh Cornwell: two months in London in 1980 for possession of drugs and seven days in 1980 for inciting a riot.
5. Sid Vicious: two months in New York in 1978 charged with the murder of Nancy Spungen just before his death.
6. John Phillips (of The Mamas and the Papas): thirty days in Los Angeles in 1981 for possession of cocaine.
7. Paul McCartney: nine days in Tokyo in 1980 for possessing marijuana.
8. Grace Jones: four days in Jamaica in 1989 on drugs charges.
9= Mick Jagger and Keith Richards: one night in London in 1967 on drugs charges before being bailed; then, after a tidal wave of protest—especially a leader in *The Times* entitled "Who Breaks A Butterfly on a Wheel"—they were freed.

In addition, Jim Morrison (for being drunk and disorderly on an airplane), Joe Strummer and Mick Jones of The Clash (for stealing hotel towels), members of The Who (for trashing a hotel room) have been held in prison for one night or less.

Ten unexpected drug-users

1. Sigmund Freud (cocaine)
2. John F. Kennedy (marijuana)
3. Hermann Goering (morphine)

4. Victor Hugo (marijuana)
5. Robert Louis Stevenson (cocaine)
6. Queen Victoria (marijuana)
7. Otto Preminger (LSD)
8. Friedrich Nietzsche (marijuana)
9. Sir Arthur Conan Doyle (cocaine)
10. Cary Grant (LSD)

Nine sportsmen who have been inside

1. Muhammad Ali: sent to jail in 1967 for refusing to be drafted into the US Army—and stripped of his boxing titles. "No Vietcong ever called me 'nigger,'" pointed out Ali, not unreasonably.
2. David Jenkins: British 400-meter runner sentenced to seven years in jail in 1988 for conspiring to smuggle steroids into the US.
3. Eric Ramelet: French cycling champion jailed for two months in 1987 for drug abuse.
4. Norman "Kid McCoy" Selby: American Middleweight Boxing Champion in 1895 and 1897 before serving eight years in jail for murder, robbery and assault.
5. Robert Hayes: American athlete who won a Gold Medal for the 100 meters at the 1964 Olympics spent ten months in jail in 1978 for smuggling drugs.
6. Sonny Liston: later to become World Heavyweight Boxing Champion, spent five years in jail for robbery with violence.
7. Lester Piggott: British champion jockey sent to jail in 1987 for three years for tax evasion.
8. James Scott: American Light-Heavyweight Boxing Champion sentenced to thirty to forty years in 1976 for murder and armed robbery.
9. Mike Tyson: American World Heavyweight Boxing Champion sentenced to six years in 1991 for rape.

In June 1994, as the USA played host to the soccer World Cup finals, the entire nation was distracted from the world's greatest sporting spectacle, gripped by a televised car chase in Los Angeles. Police were attempting to apprehend O.J. Simpson—one of American football's best-loved heroes who then became an actor, playing the character Nordberg in the *Naked Gun* films. Stunned TV audiences watched live as police tracked Simpson's car down the freeway. He was wanted on suspicion of murder following the discovery of the bodies of his ex-wife Nicole and a male friend. Simpson, forty-seven, was subsequently charged with two counts of first-degree murder.

A soccer XI which has been incarcerated

1. Bert Trautmann: former German POW.
2. Peter Storey: jailed for smuggling pornographic videos.
3. Peter Swan: jailed for taking bribes.
4. Tony Kay: jailed for taking bribes.
5. Tony Adams: jailed for drunk driving.
6. Bobby Moore: held in a Colombian jail for allegedly stealing a bracelet.
7. Diego Maradona: held in custody for thirty-five hours on drugs charges.
8. Jan Molby: jailed for drunk driving.
9. Mick Quinn: jailed for driving while disqualified.
10. Bob Newton: jailed for reckless driving.
11. George Best: jailed for disreputable behavior.

Seven well-known men who were arrested or imprisoned for being gay

1. Oscar Wilde (Playwright)
2. Jean Genet (Playwright)
3. Leonardo da Vinci (Artist)
4. Montgomery Clift (Actor)
5. Pier Paolo Pasolini (Film director)
6. Bill Tilden (Tennis player)
7. Sandro Botticelli (Artist)

Six celebrities who were charged with sex offenses or offending public morals

1. ERROL FLYNN
Accused of raping two girls: a seventeen-year-old at a dinner party and a night-club singer on his yacht. He was found not guilty but there is no doubt that he frequently indulged in statutory rape—hence the expression "In like Flynn" . . .

2. ROSCOE "FATTY" ARBUCKLE
In 1920, Arbuckle was found not guilty of the rape and murder of Virginia Rappe (whose last words were: "I'm dying. Roscoe did it") but his career was over. A Merchant–Ivory film of the incident (with names changed), *The Wild Party,* was made in 1974.

3. LENNY BRUCE
The brilliant American comedian, was busted—and jailed—several times for using drugs and "for offending public morals." Interestingly, he was born on precisely the same day of the same month of the same year as former British Prime Minister, Margaret Thatcher. Makes you think about astrology . . .

4. CYNTHIA PAYNE
Prosecuted for running a brothel in Streatham. Her life was later dramatized in the movie *Personal Services.*

5. CHRISTINE KEELER
Sent to jail in 1963 for perjury and trying to pervert the course of justice, but the truth was that she was being punished for embarrassing the British establishment by going to bed with British Cabinet Minister John Profumo.

6. MAE WEST
Sent to jail for eight days in 1926 because her show *Sex* (which she also wrote) was "corrupting the morals of youth."

Ten celebrities who were shot dead

1. Marvin Gaye: by his father in 1984.
2. Peter Tosh (of The Wailers): by burglars in his house in 1987.
3. Sam Cooke: by the manageress of a Los Angeles motel in 1964.
4. Freddie Mills (British former World Light-Heavyweight Boxing Champion): by person(s) unknown in 1965.
5. James Jordan (father of basketball star Michael Jordan): in 1993 by Larry Demery and Andre Green who threw his body in a swamp.
6. John Lennon: outside his New York home by Mark David Chapman in 1980.
7. Dr. Herman "Hi" Tarnower (the author of the best-selling "Scarsdale Diet"): by his lover Jean Harris in 1980.
8. Sharon Tate (American film actress married to Roman Polanski): murdered—along with four other people—by members of Charles Manson's "Family" in 1969.
9. Stanley Ketchel (American former world heavyweight boxing contender): by Walter Kurtz, his rival for a girl's affections, in 1910.
10. Felix Pappalardi (manager/pianist with Cream): by his wife in 1983.

One celebrity to survive a stabbing is Monica Seles. She was stabbed in the neck on April 30, 1993 in Hamburg by Gunther Parche who later explained that he had wanted to injure Seles because she was the top-ranking tennis player in the world, ahead of his idol, Steffi Graf.

Three famous people who were tried after their deaths

1. THOMAS BECKET
More than three centuries after his death, King Henry VIII decided to put him on trial. So his skeleton was

brought before the notorious Star Chamber and, after a trial of sorts, convicted of treason. The skeleton was then publicly burned.

2. JOAN OF ARC
Twenty-four years after her death in 1431, Joan of Arc was retried by Charles VII, who felt guilty about not having stood by her in her hour of need. After hearing the case—including new evidence from Joan's family—the court reversed the earlier verdict.

3. MARTIN BORMANN
New evidence now proves—reasonably conclusively—that Bormann died in 1945. This means that his trial in 1946—at which he was found guilty of war crimes and crimes against humanity and sentenced to death—took place after his death.

Six people who lost their honors after committing offenses

1. Lester Piggott: OBE, in 1988 after being sent to jail for tax evasion.
2. Anthony Blunt: Knight Commander of the Royal Victorian Order, in 1979 after being publicly revealed as a spy.
3. Sir Roger Casement: Knighthood, in 1916 for treason.
4. Kim Philby: MBE, in 1965 after being revealed as a spy.
5. Benito Mussolini: The Order of the Bath, in 1940 after Italy joined the Axis.
6. King Victor Emmanuel of Italy: The Order of the Garter, in 1940 for the same reason—indeed, all Italians and Germans were removed from the Honors List that year.

Ten actors who have played real-life gangsters

1. Warren Beatty: "Bugsy" Siegel in *Bugsy* (1991)
2. Tony Curtis: Louis Lepke in *Lepke* (1975)

3. Dustin Hoffman: "Dutch" Schultz in *Billy Bathgate* (1991)
4. Warren Oates: John Dillinger in *Dillinger* (1973)
5. John Ericson: Charles "Pretty Boy" Floyd in *Pretty Boy Floyd* (1959)
6. Joe Dallesandro: Charles "Lucky" Luciano in *The Cotton Club* (1984)
7. Gary and Martin Kemp: Ronnie and Reggie Kray in *The Krays* (1990)
8. Ralph Meeker: "Bugs" Moran in *The St. Valentine's Day Massacre* (1967)
9. Mickey Rooney: George "Baby Face" Nelson in *Baby Face Nelson* (1958)
10. Rod Steiger: Al Capone in *Al Capone* (1958)

Fifteen actors who have portrayed real-life criminals

1. Tony Curtis: Albert DeSalvo in *The Boston Strangler* (1968)
2. Alan Bates: Guy Burgess in *An Englishman Abroad* (1983)
3. Alan Alda: Caryl Chessman in *Kill Me If You Can* (1977)
4. Chris Eccleston: Derek Bentley in *Let Him Have It* (1991)
5. Miranda Richardson: Ruth Ellis in *Dance with a Stranger* (1985)
6. Phil Collins: Buster Edwards in *Buster* (1988)
7. Burt Lancaster: Robert Stroud in *Birdman of Alcatraz* (1962)
8. Richard Attenborough: John Reginald Christie in *10 Rillington Place* (1971)
9. Donald Pleasence: Dr. Hawley Harvey Crippen in *Dr. Crippen* (1962)
10. Faye Dunaway: Bonnie Parker in *Bonnie and Clyde* (1967)
11. Warren Beatty: Clyde Barrow in *Bonnie and Clyde* (1967)

12. Tommy Lee Jones: Gary Gilmore in *The Executioner's Song* (1982)
13. Michael Rooker: Henry Lee Lucas in *Henry: Portrait of a Serial Killer* (1990)
14. Mick Jagger: Ned Kelly in *Ned Kelly* (1970)
15. Julie Walters: Cynthia Payne in *Personal Services* (1987)

The twelve greatest movie cops of all time

1. Clint Eastwood as Harry Callahan in *Dirty Harry* (1971)
2. Clint Eastwood as Harry Callahan in *Magnum Force* (1973)
3. Clint Eastwood as Harry Callahan in *The Enforcer* (1976)
4. Clint Eastwood as Harry Callahan in *Sudden Impact* (1983)
5. Clint Eastwood as Harry Callahan in *The Dead Pool* (1988)
6. Clint Eastwood as Sheriff Coogan in *Coogan's Bluff* (1968)
7. Gene Hackman as Popeye Doyle in *The French Connection* (1971)
8. Gene Hackman as Agent Anderson in *Mississippi Burning* (1988)
9. Richard Roundtree as John Shaft in *Shaft* (1971)
10. Kevin Costner as Eliot Ness in *The Untouchables* (1987)
11. Al Pacino as Frank Serpico in *Serpico* (1973)
12. Sidney Poitier as Virgil Tibbs in *In the Heat of the Night* (1967)

DIRTY HARRY

If there is any doubt that Harry Callahan is the greatest movie cop of all time, then just check out the following dialogue:

Dirty Harry (The Mayor tells Harry that his policy is "no trouble.")

HARRY: "Well, when an adult man is chasing a female with intent to commit rape, I shoot the bastard. That's *my* policy."

MAYOR: "Intent? How did you establish that?"

HARRY: "When a naked man is chasing a woman through an alley with a butcher's knife and a hard-on, I figure he isn't out collecting for the Red Cross."

Magnum Force

BEAUTIFUL GIRL: "What does a girl have to do to go to bed with you?"

HARRY: "Try knocking on the door."

The Enforcer (The Police Captain reproaches Harry for being violent to criminals.)

HARRY: "What do you want me to do, yell trick or treat at 'em?" (This goes down badly with the Police Captain who tells Harry that he's transferring him to Personnel.)

HARRY: "To Personnel? That's for assholes."

POLICE CAPTAIN: "I was in Personnel for ten years."

HARRY: "Yup."

Sudden Impact (Four hoodlums hold up Harry's favorite coffee bar. Harry tells them to put down their guns.)

HARRY: "We're not going to let you just walk out of here."

(One of the hoodlums asks—not too respectfully— who "we" is.)

HARRY: "Smith and Wesson and me."

And then, if more conclusive proof of Harry's supremacy is required, there is the greatest soliloquy in movie cop history: "I know what you're thinking. Did he fire six shots or only five? Well to tell you the truth, in all this excitement, I've kinda lost track myself. But being this is a .44 Magnum, the most powerful handgun in the world and would blow your head clean off, you've got to ask yourself one question: 'Do I feel lucky?' Well, do you, punk?"

Fifteen great detectives in fiction

1. Sherlock Holmes (Sir Arthur Conan Doyle)
2. Hercule Poirot (Agatha Christie)
3. Jane Marple (Agatha Christie)
4. Inspector Maigret (Georges Simenon)
5. Sam Spade (Dashiell Hammett)
6. Nero Wolfe (Rex Stout)
7. Philip Marlowe (Raymond Chandler)
8. Cordelia Gray (P.D. James)
9. Lord Peter Wimsey (Dorothy L. Sayers)
10. Inspector Wexford (Ruth Rendell)
11. Simon Templar (Leslie Charteris)
12. Father Brown (G.K. Chesterton)
13. Adam Dalgleish (P.D. James)
14. Gervase Fen (Edmund Crispin)
15. Albert Campion (Margery Allingham)

The biggest selling male crime writer is Erle Stanley Gardner; the biggest selling female crime writer is Agatha Christie.

The Crime Writers' Association's top ten crime novels of all time

1. *The Daughter of Time* (Josephine Tey, 1951)
2. *The Big Sleep* (Raymond Chandler, 1939)
3. *The Spy Who Came in from the Cold* (John le Carré, 1963)
4. *Gaudy Night* (Dorothy L. Sayers, 1935)
5. *The Murder of Roger Ackroyd* (Agatha Christie, 1926)
6. *Rebecca* (Daphne du Maurier, 1938)
7. *Farewell My Lovely* (Raymond Chandler, 1940)
8. *The Moonstone* (Wilkie Collins, 1868)
9. *The Ipcress File* (Len Deighton, 1962)
10. *The Maltese Falcon* (Dashiell Hammett, 1930)

Twenty great US TV detectives and cops

1= *Starsky and Hutch*
3. *Remington Steele*
4= *Cagney and Lacey*
6. *Cannon*
7. *Columbo*
8. *Kojak*
9. Steve McGarrett (in *Hawaii Five-0*)
10= Crockett and Tubbs (in *Miami Vice*)
12. Captain Furillo (in *Hill Street Blues*)
13. *Magnum PI*
14. Jim Rockford (in *The Rockford Files*)
15. Michael Knight (in *Knightrider*)
16. *A Man Called Ironside*
17. Sergeant Pepper Anderson (in *Police Woman*)
18. Mike Stone (in *The Streets of San Francisco*)
19= Maddie Hayes and David Addison (in *Moonlighting*)

Twenty great UK TV detectives and cops

1. Inspector Jack Regan (in *The Sweeney*)
2. *Inspector Morse*
3. John Steed (and sundry assistants in *The Avengers*)
4. *Dixon of Dock Green*
5. Inspector Burnside (in *The Bill*)
6. Inspector Frost (in *A Touch of Frost*)
7. Inspector Barlow (in *Z Cars*)
8. Johnny Ho (in *The Chinese Detective*)
9. Jane Tennison (in *Prime Suspect*)
10. Superintendent Lockhart (in *No Hiding Place*)
11= *Randall and Hopkirk (Deceased)*
13. *Paul Temple*

"I think crime pays. The hours are good, you travel a lot."

WOODY ALLEN

14. *Spender*
15. *Taggart*
16. *Jason King*
17. Commander George Gideon (in *Gideon's Way*)
18. *Shoestring*
19. *Bergerac*
20. *Anna Lee*

There is no doubt that Jack "put your trousers on—you're nicked" Regan in *The Sweeney* is the absolute number one British (world?) TV cop of all time. It is therefore also imperative to mention his sidekick—and restrainer, "Don't, guv, he's not worth it"—Sergeant George Carter.

Ten movies featuring serial killers

1. *No Way To Treat a Lady* (1968)
2. *Henry: Portrait of a Serial Killer* (1990)
3. *The Silence of the Lambs* (1990)
4. *Kind Hearts and Coronets* (1949)
5. *Dirty Harry* (1971)
6. *Psycho* (1960)
7. *Manhunter* (1986)
8. *Frenzy* (1972)
9. *Arsenic and Old Lace* (1942)
10. *Sea of Love* (1989)

Ten actors who have played Philip Marlowe

1. Robert Mitchum in *The Big Sleep*
2. Dick Powell in *Murder My Sweet*
3. Elliott Gould in *The Long Goodbye*
4. Lloyd Nolan in *Time To Kill*
5. Robert Montgomery in *The Lady in the Lake*
6. George Montgomery in *The Brasher Doubloon*
7. Michael Arlen in *The Falcon Takes Over*
8. Humphrey Bogart in *The Big Sleep*
9. James Garner in *Marlowe*
10. Powers Boothe in *Marlowe—Private Eye*

Ten actors who have played Sherlock Holmes

1. Basil Rathbone in *The House of Fear*
2. Roger Moore in *Sherlock Holmes in New York*
3. Nicol Williamson in *The Seven-per-cent Solution*
4. Stewart Granger in *The Hound of the Baskervilles*
5. Michael Caine in *Sherlock and Me*
6. Peter Cushing in *The Hound of the Baskervilles*
7. Christopher Lee in *Sherlock Holmes and the Deadly Necklace*
8. Ian Richardson in *The Sign of Four*
9. Christopher Plummer in *Murder by Degree*
10. Peter Cook in *The Hound of the Baskervilles*

A criminal top ten

1. *I'm Gonna Get Me a Gun* (Cat Stevens, 1967)
2. *Killer on the Loose* (Thin Lizzy, 1980)
3. *Back Stabbers* (The O'Jays, 1972)
4. *Jailhouse Rock* (Elvis Presley, 1958)
5. *Breaking the Law* (Judas Priest, 1980)
6. *Street Fighting Man* (The Rolling Stones, 1971)
7. *I Fought the Law* (The Clash, 1988)
8. *Guilty* (Barbra Streisand and Barry Gibb, 1980)
9. *Rubber Bullets* (10CC, 1973)
10. *I Shot the Sheriff* (Eric Clapton, 1974)

Eight criminals who have had songs written about them

1. Joe Hill (*The Ballad of Joe Hill*—traditional—made famous by Joan Baez)
2= Bonnie Parker and Clyde Barrow (*Ballad of Bonnie and Clyde* by Georgie Fame)
4. Christine Keeler (*Christine Keeler* by The Glaxo Babies)
5. George "Machine-Gun" Kelly (*Machine-Gun Kelly* by James Taylor)
6. Ronnie Biggs (*Ronnie Biggs Was Only the Tea Boy* by The Train Robbers)

7. Janie Jones (*Janie Jones* by The Clash)
8. Charles Manson (*Song for Convict Charlie* by The Birdmen of Alcatraz)

In addition, Ronnie Biggs was featured as a singer (of a "punk prayer") on The Sex Pistols' highly idiosyncratic cover version of *My Way*.

10

THE LIGHTER SIDE OF CRIME

Twenty incompetent criminals

1. In 1994, six British robbers attacked a security van in a secluded spot in Crawley, West Sussex. They had spent months researching the raid and sliced through the side of the ten-ton truck with blow torches. However, in doing so they set light to the notes (worth £1 million) and so lost all the cash.

2. In 1976, two British car thieves stole a car but were caught when they tried selling it . . . to its real owner.

3. In 1980 a man robbed a store in Albuquerque, New Mexico, but his trousers fell down as he made his escape and he dropped his gun and some of his haul. The police arrested him and while he was protesting his innocence, his trousers fell down again.

4. In July 1978, two British robbers took £4,500 in bags from a post office and then attempted a getaway. However, the driver turned the ignition key the wrong way and jammed the lock. They then got into another car where they did precisely the same thing.

5. In 1971, in Billericay, Essex, armed robbers broke into a post office—only to find that it had been closed for twelve years.

6. In 1978, a man named Charles A. Meriweather broke into a house in Baltimore and raped a woman. He then demanded her money but she

had hardly any so he told her to write him a check. The woman asked him who she should make the check out to and the man replied, "Charles A. Meriweather." He was caught a few hours later.

7. In 1979, a man tried shoplifting from British Home Stores in Barnsley. He wasn't to know, of course, but there was a store detectives' convention going on there at the time.

8. In 1933, a man tried robbing a Paris antique shop . . . in fifteenth-century armor (as a disguise) which, needless to say, woke up everyone.

9. In 1972, a British man stole a Thames barge but was caught because he was the only man out on the river that day. There was a dock strike.

10. In 1967, a Nigerian laborer changed his pay check from £9-4s-0d to £697,000,009-4s. Sounds good, but he couldn't find a bank to cash it for him.

11. In 1969, a man tried to rob a bank in Portland, Oregon. To avoid attracting attention, he decided to write down all his instructions rather than talk. He wrote "Put all the money in a paper bag" and gave the message to the cashier who read it and then wrote back "I don't have a paper bag." The would-be robber did precisely what you and I would have done: he ran off empty-handed.

12. In 1968, an American burglar took his dog with him when he went to burgle a home in Detroit. Unfortunately (for the burglar) he left his dog at the scene of the crime. When the police arrived, the dog led them home to his master. Clearly, burglars should follow the same rule as actors: never work with children or animals.

13. In 1975, an American robber accidentally shot himself dead while carrying out an armed robbery of a restaurant in Newport, Rhode Island.

14. And then there were the three British bank robbers who got stuck in the revolving doors . . .

15. And the unknown American mugger who ran off with a lady's carrier bag—ignorant of the fact that

all it contained was doggy poo which the dog's conscientious owner had earlier scooped up to dispose of later.

16. Once a British gang tried to break into a safe with what they thought were cutting tools but which were, in fact, welding tools. They had merely made the safe even safer.

17. A British lad stole from a store and made his getaway on a motorbike, cleverly wearing a crash helmet as a disguise. Not so cleverly, the thief had put his name in big letters across the top of his helmet. He was arrested soon after.

18. An American gang got caught in a club they were trying to burgle when one of their number—a seventy-two-year-old—had to take a rest.

19. Perhaps the most incompetent British criminal was the man who gave a Southampton cashier £10 to open her till and then fled with the proceeds . . . £4.37.

20. And the "best" American is the guy from Tulsa, Oklahoma, who was put on trial for attempting to snatch a woman's purse. He pleaded not guilty and decided to conduct his own defense but was undoubtedly ill-advised to ask the victim in cross-examination: "Did you get a good look at my face when I took your purse?" Not surprisingly, he was found guilty.

Ten curious American State laws

1. In South Carolina it is illegal to drink water in a bar.
2. In Wisconsin pet elephants being taken for a walk on public streets must be kept on a lead.
3. In Oregon a girl under the age of twelve can't buy a coffee after 6 p.m.
4. In Idaho it is illegal to eat snake on a Sunday.
5. In Nebraska barbers can't eat onions between 7 a.m. and 7 p.m.

6. In Indiana you can't ride on a bus within four hours of eating garlic.
7. In Kentucky you can't carry an ice-cream cone in your pocket.
8. In California there is a fine of up to $500 for "killing, disturbing or threatening" a Monarch butterfly.
9. In Alabama you can't beat your doormat against a wall after 8 a.m.
10. In Oklahoma it is illegal to intoxicate a fish.

Eleven British laws which are still in existence

1. To place any line, cord or pole across a street "or hang or place any clothes thereon" is illegal.
2. Tethering an animal so that it stands across or upon a footway is illegal.
3. Slaughtering or dressing any cattle in the street is a crime (unless the animal has just been run over).
4. No person is allowed to wilfully disturb any animal grazing in the Victoria Embankment Gardens, Shepherds Bush Common or any other open space in London.
5. It is illegal to cleanse, hoop, fire, wash or scald any cask or tub in the street.
6. Going from door to door to collect money for the Guy or carol-singing without the permission of the local Chief Constable is against the law.
7. Keeping a pigsty which opens on to the street without a sufficient wall or fence to prevent the pig from escaping is against the law.
8. It is illegal to play or watch football.
9. It is against the law to hew, saw, bore or cut any timber, stone or slack, or sift lime in the street.
10. It is unlawful to beat or shake any carpet, rug or mat in the streets of provincial towns after 8 a.m.
11. It is illegal to fly a kite in the street.

Eleven strange laws which have been repealed

1. Philip the Fair of France (reigned 1285–1314) banned single women from owning more than one dress.
2. The people of Minnesota were not allowed to hang underwear of different sexes on the same washing line.
3. Books on geography and astrology were banned in England in the 1550s because they were supposedly infected with magic.
4. Pigs were banned from the streets of France after one caused an accident involving a member of the royal family.
5. In France in the 1630s the growing of potatoes was made illegal because it was thought that they caused leprosy.
6. In Central America in the eighteenth century people risked excommunication if they consumed drinking chocolate.
7. Between 1642 and 1652, Christmas in England was abolished.
8. Turks caught drinking coffee in the sixteenth century risked execution.
9. Women with waists measuring more than thirteen inches were barred from the sixteenth-century court of Catherine de Medici.
10. In sixteenth-century England, husbands were banned by law from beating their wives after 10 p.m.
11. Elizabeth I of Russia (reigned 1741–62) banned everyone apart from herself from wearing pink.

Never mind income tax . . . Nine repealed taxes which the British tried to evade

1. Chimney Tax
2. Bread Tax
3. Servants Tax

4. Hearth Tax
5. Clock Tax
6. Beard Tax
7. Window Tax
8. Dog Tax
9. Hair-powder Tax

Ten politically correct ways to describe criminals and their crimes

1. Morally different: crooked
2. Ethically disoriented: dishonest
3. Sobriety-deprived driving: drunk driving
4. Femicide: homicide
5. Humanslaughter: manslaughter
6. Alternatively sexually gratified: pervert
7. Sex-care providers: prostitutes
8. Managers of sex-care providers: pimps
9. Socially misaligned: psychotic
10. Non-traditional shopping: shoplifting

Nine cases of animals that were put on trial

As the 1994 film *The Hour of the Pig* demonstrates, in past centuries animals used to be put on trial with all the formality normally associated with human trials. Given that they couldn't put up much of a defense, they usually ended up being found guilty and then executed.

1. In 1685 in Ansbach, Germany, a wolf had been killing people and animals. The word went around that the town's late mayor had turned into a werewolf, so that when the animal was eventually caught and killed, it was dressed up as the mayor

---

"The history of the great events of this world is scarcely more than the history of crimes."

VOLTAIRE

and put on trial. The dead animal was found guilty and hanged from a windmill.

2. In 1474 in Basle, Switzerland, a hen was put on trial for laying an egg which had no yolk (apparently, yolk-less eggs were believed to come from Satan). Anyway, the hen and the egg were put on trial, found guilty and burned at the stake.

3. In 1606 in France, Guillaume Guyart was sentenced to be hanged and burned for having sex with a dog. The dog was also sentenced to death.

4. In 1924, Pep, a black labrador, was sent to jail in Pike County, Pennsylvania, for killing a cat. Pep was given a prison number (C2559) and spent the rest of his life (another six years) in prison where, needless to say, he was spoiled rotten by his fellow inmates—and doubtless loved every moment of it.

5. In 1519 in Stelvio, Italy, burrowing field mice were damaging crops. There was a hearing at which the mice were represented by defense counsel who argued that, on balance, the mice did more good than harm. The judge disagreed but ordered that the mice should not be slaughtered but exiled— even giving an extra fourteen days' grace to "all those which are with young, and to such as are yet in their infancy."

6. In 1905 in South Bend, Indiana, there was a law against smoking in public. A fairground chimp puffed some smoke in front of an audience and was brought up before the court where it was convicted and fined.

7. In seventeenth-century America there was a man named Potter who used to "relax" with animals. He was eventually sentenced to be hanged—along with three sheep, a cow, two heifers and two pigs [or, rather, sows since, to paraphrase the old joke, there was nothing queer about Potter].

8. It is common for animals to be put down when they kill, but it is rare for them to be judicially tried first. In 1933 in McGraw, New York, four

dogs were put on trial for biting a six-year-old girl. The dogs were represented by a lawyer who argued their case in all seriousness but he was unable to save them from being put down or, rather, executed.

9. Similarly, in 1913 in Kingsport, Tennessee, a circus elephant named Mary killed her trainer. The next day, the circus moved to the town of Erwin where the authorities ordered that Mary should be hanged—which she was in the railroad yard from a 100-ton derrick with a huge chain around her neck.

● 11
OTHER CRIME STATS

The twelve countries with the highest crime rates

Given that the crime rate in any country depends on the number of *recorded* crimes, it is obvious that in backward or totalitarian countries there will be a lower crime rate than in sophisticated democracies where even minor infringements of the law are noted in triplicate. Still, with that caveat, here is the running order:

1. Dominica 183,280 (crimes reported per million people)
2. Finland 133,809
3. New Zealand 125,091
4. Sweden 117,852
5. Canada 108,024
6. Denmark 88,235
7. Netherlands 74,250
8. Bermuda 74,130
9. Australia 68,974
10. Germany 67,550
11. France 67,141
12. UK 65,455

The twelve countries with the lowest crime rates

1. Zaire 103 (crimes reported per million people)
2. Togo 108

3. Niger 325
4. Indonesia 444
5. Syria 544
6. Tanzania 639
7. Burundi 821
8. Gabon 1,345
9. Turkey 1,786
10. Qatar 2,126
11. Senegal 2,353
12. Angola 2,401

US crime rates (offenses per million inhabitants)

	1960	1965	1970	1975
Total	18,872	24,490	39,845	52,817
Violent crime	1,609	2,002	3,635	4,815
Property crime	17,263	22,488	36,210	48,002
Murder	51	51	79	96
Forcible rape	96	121	187	263
Robbery	601	717	1,721	2,182
Burglary	5,086	6,627	10,849	15,259
Car theft	1,830	2,568	4,568	4,694

	1980	1985	1990
Total	59,500	52,065	58,203
Violent crime	5,966	5,560	7,318
Property crime	53,533	46,505	50,885
Murder	102	79	94
Forcible rape	368	366	412
Robbery	2,511	2,085	2,570
Burglary	16,841	12,873	12,359
Car theft	5,022	4,620	6,578

One would have thought that "Forcible Rape" was a tautology.

In thirty years, crime has tripled: it doesn't require an enormous brain to work out that, at this rate, in another thirty years it will triple again. The only glimmer of hope is that the rates for murder and rape haven't risen as fast as those for other crimes.

The areas of the UK with the best overall clear-up rates

1. North West 39%
2= East Anglia 36%
2= Northern Ireland 36%
4= North 35%
4= Wales 35%
6. West Midlands 32%
7= Scotland 31%
7= Yorkshire and Humberside 31%
9= East Midlands 30%
9= South West 30%
11. South East (excluding Greater London) 21%
12. Greater London 17%

England 29%

When you consider how many of these figures include the sort of minor offenses like policemen booking people for dropping litter they're even worse than at first glance.

The ten countries with the highest number of sex offenses (including rape)

1. The Maldives 1,613 (sex offenses per million people)
2. New Zealand 1,004
3. Bermuda 881
4. Australia 772

"Crime, like virtue, has its degrees."

RACINE

5.   Lesotho 722
6.   The Bahamas 664
7.   Germany 653
8.   Netherlands 622
9.   Kuwait 608
10. Canada 589

The UK, with 411, ranks below the likes of the Seychelles, Israel, Sweden, Austria and Denmark. I don't
have figures for sex offenses in the USA, only figures for
rape—358—which would, I reckon, place it well within
the world's top three for all sex offenses.

The ten countries with the lowest number of sex offenses (including rape)

1.   Egypt 4.1 (sex offenses per million people)
2.   Tanzania 4.6
3.   Gabon 4.8
4.   Burundi 12.6
5.   Niger 14.4
6.   Nigeria 17.9
7.   United Arab Emirates 26.5
8.   Portugal 29.8
9.   Lebanon 31.7
10. Indonesia 32.2

Obviously, in a lot of these countries, sexual offenses
carry an even greater taboo than they do in Western
countries. Perhaps the fact that in one or two of the
above countries, sexual offenders are dealt with in such
a way that they have no means of ever re-offending—
and, as we know, sexual offenders have the worst record
for re-offending of all offenders—explains such impressive figures.

The ten European countries where women are at the greatest risk of being sexually assaulted

1.   Germany

2. Scotland
3. Spain
4. Norway
5. Belgium
6. France
7. Holland
8. Northern Ireland
9. Finland
10. England and Wales

Percentage increases in sexual offenses in the UK in the last decade

1. Northern Ireland 162%
2. Greater London 104%
3. Wales 73%
4. South East (excluding Greater London) 67%
5. East Anglia 60%
6= South West 50%
6= Yorkshire and Humberside 50%
8. Scotland 49%
9. North 46%
10. East Midlands 34%
11. North West 24%
12. West Midlands 22%

England 47%

The figures in Northern Ireland are alarming but might reflect an increasing willingness on the part of victims to come forward.

The best clear-up rates for sexual offenses in the UK

1. Wales 93%
2. South West 88%
3. Northern Ireland 87%
4= East Anglia 83%
4= North 83%

6= East Midlands 80%
6= North West 80%
8= Scotland 77%
8= Yorkshire and Humberside 77%
10. West Midlands 76%
11. South East (excluding Greater London) 64%
12. Greater London 54%

England 74%

Drug use among young Americans (16-18)

	Mari-juana	*LSD*	*Cocaine*	*Tranquilizers (non-prescribed)*
Class of 1979	51%	7%	12%	7%
Class of 1980	49%	7%	12%	9%
Class of 1981	46%	7%	12%	8%
Class of 1982	44%	6%	11%	7%
Class of 1983	42%	5%	11%	7%
Class of 1984	40%	5%	12%	6%
Class of 1985	41%	4%	13%	6%
Class of 1986	39%	5%	13%	6%
Class of 1987	36%	5%	10%	6%
Class of 1988	33%	5%	8%	5%
Class of 1989	30%	5%	7%	4%
Class of 1990	27%	5%	5%	4%
Class of 1991	24%	5%	5%	4%

It isn't surprising to see that marijuana use has fallen—
after all, there are very few young hippies any more—
but it *is* surprising (and gratifying) to note the drop in
cocaine use.

Marijuana, cocaine and heroin use among high school seniors in the USA (1991)

	Never used	*Used*
	MARIJUANA	
All seniors	63%	37%
Male	60%	40%

	Never used	Used
	MARIJUANA (Cont'd)	
Female	67%	33%
	COCAINE	
All seniors	92%	8%
Male	92%	8%
Female	93%	7%
	HEROIN	
All seniors	99.1%	0.9%
Male	99%	1%
Female	99.4%	0.6%

US attitudes toward the legalization of the use of marijuana

1973	Should legalize	18%
	Should not legalize	80%
	Don't know	2%
1975	Should	20%
	Should not	75%
	Don't know	5%
1976	Should	28%
	Should not	69%
	Don't know	3%
1978	Should	30%
	Should not	67%
	Don't know	3%
1980	Should	25%
	Should not	72%
	Don't know	3%
1983	Should	20%
	Should not	76%
	Don't know	4%
1984	Should	23%
	Should not	73%
	Don't know	4%
1986	Should	18%
	Should not	80%
	Don't know	2%

1987	Should	16%
	Should not	81%
	Don't know	3%
1988	Should	17%
	Should not	79%
	Don't know	4%
1989	Should	16%
	Should not	81%
	Don't know	3%
1990	Should	16%
	Should not	81%
	Don't know	3%
1991	Should	18%
	Should not	78%
	Don't know	4%

Availability of drugs or alcohol at US schools (according to the students)

	Easy	Hard	Impossible	Not known
Alcohol	31%	31%	16%	22%
Marijuana	30%	27%	16%	27%
Cocaine	11%	33%	25%	31%
Crack	9%	29%	28%	34%
Uppers/Downers	20%	26%	17%	37%
Other drugs	14%	27%	19%	40%

Other drugs include illegal drugs such as heroin, LSD, PCP, and unspecified drugs that may be available at school. The "Not knowns" include those students who had never heard of the drugs in question.

This list obviously carries its very own health warning. Ask a school student if he or she (but especially he) can get hold of drugs and of course he's going to say "yeah, easy." By the same token, there will be quite a few teenage junkies who will innocently protest their ignorance of such matters or say "oh no, it's impossible." So I guess the figures will probably balance out.

The areas of the UK with the most people found guilty (or cautioned) for all drugs offenses (rates per 1,000 people)

		1981	1991
1.	South East (including Greater London)	0.57	1.24
2.	North West	0.27	0.95
3.	Scotland	0.17	0.83
4.	East Anglia	0.36	0.76
5.	South West	0.30	0.57
6.	Wales	0.28	0.56
7.	West Midlands	0.15	0.52
8.	Yorkshire and Humberside	0.18	0.49
9=	East Midlands	0.18	0.44
9=	North	0.19	0.44
11.	Northern Ireland	0.06	0.07
	England	*0.34*	*0.89*

Notwithstanding "The Troubles," the figures in Northern Ireland are substantially lower than elsewhere in the UK.

The areas of the UK with the most people found guilty (or cautioned) of drug trafficking offenses (other than cannabis) (rates per 1,000 people)

		1981	1991
1=	East Anglia	0.05	0.14
1=	North West	0.03	0.14
1=	Scotland	0.01	0.14
4.	Wales	0.02	0.09
5.	North	0.02	0.08
6=	East Midlands	0.02	0.07
6=	Yorkshire and Humberside	0.03	0.07
8=	South East (including Greater London)	0.12	0.06
8=	West Midlands	0.03	0.06

	1981 (Cont'd)	1991 (Cont'd)
10. South West	0.03	0.03
11. Northern Ireland	0.01	0.02
England	*0.06*	*0.11*

The best clear-up rates for trafficking in controlled drugs in the UK

1. East Midlands 107%
2. Scotland 100%
3= East Anglia 99%
3= North 99%
5. Wales 96%
6. North West 94%
7= South West 92%
7= West Midlands 92%
9. Northern Ireland 90%
10. Yorkshire and Humberside 89%
11. South East (excluding Greater London) 86%
12. Greater London 68%

England 93%

Obviously the East Midlands' figures (and I suspect Scotland's too) include cases cleared up from previous years.

The areas of the UK with most offenses of criminal damage

1. North 26.17 (per 1,000 people in a year)
2. Greater London 22.13
3. North West 18.68
4. Wales 17.64
5. Scotland 17.59
6. Yorkshire and Humberside 17.08
7. East Midlands 15.92
8. South East (excluding Greater London) 15.89

9. West Midlands 14.0
10. South West 10.96
11. East Anglia 9.86
12. Northern Ireland 1.5

England 16.1

The Northern Ireland statistics are extraordinary but this might be explained by different definitions of criminal damage.

The best clear-up rates for criminal damage offenses in the UK

1. Northern Ireland 32%
2. North 29%
3. North West 25%
4. Wales 24%
5= East Anglia 23%
5= South West 23%
7= West Midlands 20%
7= Yorkshire and Humberside 20%
9= East Midlands 19%
9= Scotland 19%
11. South East (excluding Greater London) 13%
12. Greater London 10%

England 19%

Percentage increases in criminal damage offenses in the UK in the last decade

1. Northern Ireland −56%
2. Scotland 48%
3. West Midlands 81%
4. East Anglia 93%
5. South East (excluding Greater London) 95%
6. Greater London 96%
7. Yorkshire and Humberside 100%
8. North West 110%

9.   East Midlands 113%
10. South West 116%
11. Wales 148%
12. North 193%

England 106%

The areas of the UK with most crimes of violence against the person

1.   Greater London 5.24 (per 1,000 people in a year)
2.   East Midlands 4.63
3.   Yorkshire and Humberside 4.43
4.   North 4.06
5.   West Midlands 3.91
6.   Wales 3.90
7.   South East (excluding Greater London) 3.68
8.   North West 3.25
9.   South West 3.10
10. Scotland 3.05
11. East Anglia 2.99
12. Northern Ireland 2.48

England 3.74

The best clear-up rates for crimes of violence against the person in the UK

1.   Wales 88%
2=   East Anglia 85%
2=   South West 85%
4.   Yorkshire and Humberside 82%
5=   East Midlands 81%
5=   Scotland 81%
5=   West Midlands 81%
8.   North 79%
9.   North West 76%
10. South East (excluding Greater London) 69%

11. Greater London 63%
12. Northern Ireland 62%

England 77%

I don't like clear-up rates because they give no idea of the degree of severity of the crimes which are cleared up.

Percentage increases in crimes of violence in the UK in the last decade

1. North West 50%
2. Northern Ireland 61%
3. West Midlands 69%
4. East Midlands 75%
5. North 78%
6. Yorkshire and Humberside 81%
7. East Anglia 93%
8. Scotland 98%
9= South East (excluding Greater London) 108%
9= Wales 108%
11. South West 109%
12. Greater London 140%

England 85%

Hold on to your wallet . . . The ten European nationalities which are least trusted by all other Europeans

1. Portuguese
2. Greeks
3. Spanish
4. Irish
5. Italians
6. French
7. Luxembourgeois
8. Danes
9. British
10. Belgians

This list is based on the results of a pan-European opinion poll in which people were asked: "Which other European people do you trust the least?" I don't know what everyone's got against the poor old Portuguese but it's extraordinary that more Europeans distrust the Luxembourgeois than they do the British.

The ten European countries where you are most likely to have your car vandalized

1. Germany
2. Holland
3. Scotland
4. Spain
5. England and Wales
6. Belgium
7. France
8. Northern Ireland
9. Norway
10. Finland

Keep your eyes on the road . . . The ten European countries with the most deaths on the road

1. France
2. Germany
3. Turkey
4. Italy
5. Spain
6. UK
7. Portugal
8. Belgium
9. Greece
10. Austria

I've included this list because a high proportion of deaths on the road are caused by drunk driving—which is, of course, a crime (even, I think, in France).

● AFTERWORD

Just you wait . . . Ten things they'll make illegal one day

1. Traveling in a car without a crash helmet
2. Being overweight
3. Standing two abreast on escalators
4. Smoking in a built-up area
5. Leaving your car door unlocked
6. Cash
7. Walking the wrong way down a one-way street
8. Not using the postcode
9. Swatting flies
10. Booking at a restaurant and not showing up

● BIBLIOGRAPHY

Abbot, Geoffrey, *Rack, Rope and Red-hot Pincers,* Headline, 1993
The Amnesty International Report 1993, Amnesty International Publications, 1993

Bailey, Brain, *The Assassination File,* W.H. Allen, 1991
Beeching, Cyril Leslie, *A Dictionary of Eponyms,* Oxford, 1988
Begg, Paul and Keith Skinner, *The Scotland Yard Files,* Headline, 1992
Begg, Paul, Keith Skinner and Martin Fido, *The Jack the Ripper A to Z,* Headline, 1992
Bland, James, *True Crime Diary,* Warner Books, 1993
The Book of Numbers, A & W Publishers, 1978
Brown, Craig and David, *The Book of Sports Lists,* Sphere, 1983
Brown, Craig and Lesley Cunliffe, *The Book of Royal Lists,* Sphere, 1983
Byrne, Richard, *The London Dungeon Book of Crime and Punishment,* Little, Brown & Co., 1993

Calvocoressi, *Who's Who in the Bible,* Penguin, 1988
Chronicle of America, Longman
Chronicle of Britain, Longman, 1992
Chronicle of the 20th Century, Longman, 1988
Chronicle of the Year 1988, Longman, 1988
Chronicle of the Year 1989, Longman, 1989
Chronicle of the Year 1990, Longman, 1990
Chronicle of the Year 1991, Longman, 1991
Chronicle of the Year 1992, Longman, 1992
Chronicle of the Year 1993, Longman, 1993

A Chronology of Crimes of the 20th Century, Crescent Books, 1991

Crime in the United States 1992, US Department of Justice, 1993

Criminal Justice, HMSO, 1992

Criminal Justice Magazine, Vol. 12, No. 1, Howard League, 1994

Criminal Statistics England and Wales 1991, HMSO, 1991

Crystal, David (ed.), *Nineties Knowledge*, Chambers, 1992

Dunkling, Leslie and Adrian Room, *The Guinness Book of Money*, Guinness, 1990

The Economist Book of Vital World Statistics, Hutchinson, 1990

Fido, Martin, *The Chronicle of Crime*, Little, Brown & Co., 1993
  Deadly Jealousy, Headline, 1993

Fitzhenry, Robert I. (compiler), *Book of Quotations*, Chambers, 1990

Flanagan, Timothy J. and Kathleen Maguire (eds.), *Sourcebook of Criminal Justice Statistics 1991*, US Department of Justice, 1992

Fothergill, Stephen and Jill Vincent, *The State of the Nation*, Pan, 1985

Gambaccini, Paul, Tim Rice and Jonathan Rice, *British Hit Singles*, Guinness, 1993

Gaute, J.H.H. and Robin Odell, *The New Murderers' Who's Who*, Headline, 1989

Gerber, Albert B., *The Book of Sex Lists*, Star, 1982

Goodman, Jonathan, *Murder Files*, Mandarin, 1993

The Guinness Book of Answers (9th edn), Guinness, 1993

The Guinness Book of Records 1994, Guinness, 1993

Halliwell, Leslie, *Halliwell's Film Guide*, Grafton, 1922

Hammer, Richard, *The Illustrated History of Organized Crime*, Courage, 1989

Hart, Michael, *The Ranking of the Most Influential Persons in History,* Simon & Schuster, 1993

Hartnell, David with Brian Williams, *I'm Not One to Gossip, But . . . ,* Futura, 1990

Hyman, Robin (compiler), *The Pan Dictionary of Famous Quotations,* Pan, 1989

Jones, Frank, *Murderous Women: True Tales of Women Who Killed,* Headline, 1991
White-collar Killers, Headline, 1993

Kingsley, Hilary and Geoff Tibballs, *Box of Delights,* Papermac, 1990

Kurian, George Thomas, *The Book of World Rankings,* Macmillan, 1979
The New Book of World Rankings (3rd edn), Facts on File, 1991

Lane, Brian, *The Butchers,* True Crime, 1992
The Murder Yearbook, Headline, 1993
The Encyclopedia of Forensic Science, Headline, 1993

Lane, Brian and Wilfred Gregg, *The Encyclopedia of Serial Killers,* Headline, 1992

Larkin, Colin (ed.), *The Guinness Encyclopedia of Popular Music* Vols. 1–4, Guinness, 1992

Lax, Roger and Frederick Smith, *The Great Song Thesaurus,* Oxford, 1989

Lee, Min (ed.), *Quick Facts,* Chambers, 1991

Longman Dictionary of 20th Century Biography, Longman, 1985

Lucas, Norman, *The Sex Killers,* True Crime, 1992

McAleer, Dave, *Chart Beats,* Guinness, 1991

Magnusson, Magnus (ed.), *Biographical Dictionary,* Chambers, 1990

Marriner, Brian, *Cannibalism: The Last Taboo,* Arrow, 1992

Masters, Gerald (compiler), *The Pan Book of Dates,* Pan, 1990

Metcalf, Fred (compiler), *The Penguin Dictionary of Modern Humorous Quotations,* Penguin, 1987

Monaco, Richard and William Burt, *The Dracula Syndrome,* Headline, 1993

Moody, Susan (ed.), *Hatchards Crime Companion,* Hatchards, 1990

Murray, Peter and Linda, *The Penguin Dictionary of Art and Artists,* Penguin, 1987

Nash, Jay Robert, *World Encyclopedia of 20th Century Murder,* Headline, 1993

Newnham, Richard, *Fakes, Frauds and Forgeries,* Guinness, 1991

Parsons, Nicholas, *The Book of Literary Lists,* Fontana, 1986

Pile, Stephen, *The Book of Heroic Failures,* Routledge and Kegan Paul, 1979

Rees, Dafydd and Luke Crampton, *Book of Rock Stars* (2nd edn), Guinness, 1991

Rees, Nigel (ed.), *A Dictionary of Twentieth Century Quotations,* Fontana/Collins, 1987

Regional Trends 1993, HMSO, 1993

Robertson, Patrick, *The Book of the Movies,* Guinness, 1987

    Movie Facts and Feats, Guinness, 1993

Robins, Joyce, *Lady Killer,* Chancellor Press, 1993

Rose, Simon, *One FM Essential Film Guide,* HarperCollins, 1993

Rutledge, Leigh W., *The Gay Book of Lists,* Alyson, 1987

Sifakis, Carl, *Encyclopedia of Assassinations,* Headline, 1993

Smith, Steve, *Bits and Pieces: The Penguin Book of Rock and Pop Facts and Trivia,* Penguin, 1988

Statistical Abstract of the United States 1993, US Department of Commerce, 1993

Stockman, Rocky, *The Hangman's Diary,* Headline, 1993

Thematic Dictionary of Quotations, Bloomsbury, 1989

UK Data Book, Guinness, 1992

Vandome, Nick, *Crimes and Criminals,* Chambers, 1992

Vernoff, Edward and Rima Shore, *The International Dictionary of 20th Century Biography,* Sidgwick & Jackson, 1987

Wallechinsky, David and Irving and Amy Wallace, *The Book of Lists,* Corgi, 1978
The Book of Lists 3, Corgi, 1984
Wallechinsky, David and Irving, Amy and Sylvia Wallace, *The Book of Lists 2,* Elm Tree Books, 1980
Ward, Bernie, *Families Who Kill,* Pinnacle Books, Windsor Publishing Corp., 1993
Wilson, Colin, *A Criminal History of Mankind,* Paragon, 1993
Wilson, Kirk, *Investigating Murder: The Top Ten Unsolved Murders of the 20th Century,* Robinson Publishing, 1993

● INDEX OF KILLERS

C

D

E

T

U

V